THE DEAD DETECTIVE

THE DEAD DETECTIVE

A Sam and Vera Sloan Mystery

Robert L. Wise

A JANET THOMA BOOK

THOMAS NELSON PUBLISHERS®
Nashville

A Division of Thomas Nelson, Inc.
www.ThomasNelson.com

Published in Nashville, Tennessee, by Thomas Nelson, Inc.

Library of Congress Cataloging-in-Publication Data

Wise, Robert L.
The dead detective : a Sam and Vera Sloan mystery / Robert L. Wise.
p. cm.
ISBN 0-7852-6696-8 (pbk.)
1. Aircraft accident victims' families—Fiction. 2. Private investigators—Fiction. 3. Missing persons—Fiction 4. Married people—Fiction. I. Title.
PS3573.1797 D43 2002
813'54—dc21 2002001356

Printed in the United States of America

02 03 04 05 06 PHX 5 4 3 2 1

For Gabriella Tatum Wise—
the latest in a long line of splendor

1

THE MORNING SUN HAD BARELY DAWNED. Gray clouds covered the Colorado sky, casting dark shadows across the white landscape. Crisp, freezing wind threatened another snowfall. Two days earlier Christmas had come and gone, not leaving many December days for George Alexander to finish his highly necessary task.

Few people on Alexander's block were up when he crawled into his Mercedes-Benz S-600 and drove the massive black car out of his three-car garage. The door automatically settled as he backed away from his two-story stone mansion, located off Colorado Springs's Lake Avenue. On this dreary Monday morning, Alexander left for the office at an especially early hour.

Driving faster than usual, he steered the S-600 onto Interstate 25, turning off onto Highway 87, which would take him to the downtown business area. Snow still lay piled up against the exit signs. Eight years earlier, the Alexander family had moved from Arlington, Virginia, where over a period of years Alexander had learned the ins and outs of the international banking market. He had also studied three languages and become proficient in Russian. George Alexander had never been a small-time boy.

Highway 87 went straight north. On Bijou Street, Alexander turned right. The Colorado branch of the International Investment Bank lay straight ahead. Situated at the corner of Corona Street, the austere, straight-lined building dominated the block, reaching six stories up into the sky. Snow began to float down and settle over the curbs.

At forty-five, George Alexander was beginning to show his age. His thinning, light brown hair began at the edge of an obviously receding hairline. In a couple of years, Alexander's topside would require a toupee or a thick stocking cap this time of the year. His full, rounded face and protruding belly reflected self-indulgence at every opportunity. Even though Alexander wore expensive pinstriped suits and silk ties, he didn't stand out. Bruno Magli shoes added nothing but opportunities for occasional comments about O. J. Simpson.

Apart from his investments, the most distinctive aspect of Alexander the man was the fact that he drove the largest and most expensive car Mercedes made and lived in a house that looked more like a fortress than a home. He surrounded himself with ornamentation worthy of a European head of state. Both his desk and office at home reflected luxury: pens and other tools plated in gold, a rich leather chair, an exquisite, gleaming mahogany desk. In the corner of the home office, a complete set of body armor hung on a rack as if waiting for a knight to walk in and suit up.

Alexander's office accoutrements reflected his singular success in a relatively small town. For years Colorado Springs had been a nice, quiet little community that pushed up against the even smaller burg of Manitou Springs. The two towns welcomed multitudes of tourists each summer as they passed through on their way up Pikes Peak. Shortly after the United States Air Force Academy built facilities north of town, the Springs started growing and spilling over its edges. The perimeters of the old gold-mining village, Colorado City, which had once laid claim to the title of state capital, disappeared within the continuing expansion of the Springs. Still, none of the Chamber of Commerce's public relations brochures explained why an international bank operated at the foothills of the Rocky Mountains.

Most of the local citizens used other places, such as the Bank of America or a Peak National Bank drive-in. Yet international currency from Europe and Asia had, for some time, found a clandestine home with International Bank. Alexander discovered that investment opportunities in Colorado, Utah, and Wyoming moved right along with little interruption from government agencies. The Springs had proved to be an excellent location for Alexander's professional and personal interests.

George pulled his S-600 around to the back of the International Bank, where he kept a coveted parking place marked *Reserved*—no one else dared to park in his sacred space!

Even though his impeccable work record had taken him to the top of the bank's promotion ladder and catapulted him into the presidency, George Alexander had a tendency that had gone unnoticed by the bank's other VIPs. His private tastes were exceeded only by his wife's fervent devotion to making the right appearances, which always cost a significant amount of money. Because the Alexanders periodically needed more than his affluent job paid, George had found a banking client who offered him the opportunity to skim off the top of a bulging account. Only occasional bookkeeping adjustments were required to cover his tracks.

But something had gone wrong, and today he had to attempt to straighten out his position in the illegal transaction of funds. Alexander was worried. When he grabbed his briefcase and stepped from the car, a .44 Magnum revolver clunked against the bottom of the case. The hollow thud made a disconcerting sound.

Cold, northern air sliding down off the mountains slapped Alexander in the face, and he braced himself for the short but quick walk across the parking lot. Snow lay piled up across the pavement in little heaps. Many of the bank's employees had taken Christmas week off, and Alexander knew there wouldn't be much business that day. He was starting early enough to have the time he needed to adjust the records and shore up his private transfer of stolen funds before customers demanded his time. Pulling his cashmere overcoat up around his neck, George hurried toward the back door.

When Alexander was only five feet from the bank, a figure stepped out of the shadows from behind a narrow concrete pillar. A green-and-brown-camouflage hunting mask covered the thug's face, and a dark brown trench coat concealed everything but gloved hands. Before Alexander could move, the figure aimed a short, narrow metal tube at him. The popping of an air gun sounded, and at that moment a vial of liquid exploded in Alexander's face.

Instantly, the frightening pain of blood vessels suddenly constricting caused George Alexander to drop his briefcase and grab his throat. He sucked in a deep gasp of air and felt his knees buckle beneath him. By the time Alexander had tumbled to the pavement, the masked figure had run past the Mercedes and was halfway across the parking lot, gracefully sidestepping each pile of snow. Alexander gasped again and gagged, falling on his face.

The trench-coated guerrilla came upon the bushes at the east end of the parking lot and broke through with barely a sound. The figure easily hurtled over a low brick fence and darted down the walkway behind the adjacent office building. In less than a minute, he was gone.

Alexander rolled back and forth on the ground. His entire body ached and his face stung. Kicking his feet, the bank president fought for air, but breathing was slowly becoming impossible. With a trembling hand, Alexander inched down the right side of his neck. A stinging swelling had begun to rise below his jaw, adding to his intense pain.

George touched the wound gently, realizing that the world around him was slipping out of focus. One last time he gasped for air.

The snow continued to fall silently, sprinkling the bank president who lay motionless in his crumpled black overcoat. In a few minutes he was covered in a cold blanket of white.

2

AT 7:30 ON MONDAY MORNING, SITTING AT their wooden kitchen table, Sam and Vera Sloan finished eating breakfast with their fifteen-year-old daughter, Cara. In the last couple of years, Cara had matured into a lovely young lady. With flashing blue eyes and flowing, curly blond hair, Cara was striking yet sullen looking. She ate silently, listening to her parents talk.

From the Sloans' kitchen windows, Pikes Peak towered over Colorado Springs and provided a stunning view. In the last year the Sloans' kitchen had virtually become the center of family life, since most of their extended conversations happened over a meal. Decorated with curios and ornaments purchased during many vacation trips, the kitchen always had a personal, warm, cozy feel.

"Since you're still on vacation, what's on your list of things to do today?" Sam asked as he smiled at his daughter.

Cara hedged and shrugged her shoulders. "I don't know."

"'Don't know'?" Sam frowned. "Come on. You've already got every minute of this day planned. Admit it."

Even though he was forty-two years old, Sam looked much younger. Thinning brown hair didn't change his youthful appearance. Almost identical with Cara's, Sam's blue eyes turned intense when scrutinizing a suspect or pondering a problem. "What's up for today?"

Cara rolled her eyes and shrugged.

"They're called 'the cave years,'" Vera interjected, pouring Sam another cup of coffee. "Cara comes out of the dark only for emergencies and unexpected interruptions." She kissed Sam on the cheek. "I love you," she whispered in his ear.

Cara shot her mother a negative glance and ate another spoonful of her Wheaties, saying nothing.

"Unfortunately, I've got to get back to the police station this morning," Sam said. "Santa Claus didn't leave any vacation passes for me."

"Sorry, dear," responded Vera in a bright tone. "I'm *so* glad to be graduated from college. Thank the Lord that I don't have to do one thing today." She shook her fist in the air. Vera's blue eyes highlighted a highly attractive face framed by a full head of red hair. Although small, Vera had an attractive figure usually concealed under her loose-fitting clothes. "Feels like freedom's returned." She sighed. "Finishing my last examination a couple of days ago, was . . . was beyond wonderful."

"Dear, it was no small accomplishment, completing that degree in criminology," Sam admitted. "You've really paid the price the last few years."

"Doesn't seem like three years ago since I first helped you with that strange murder case involving Ape, and that weird Jester character." Vera smiled. "That proved to be a genuine turning point in my journey. Then there were those two smaller cases. Can you believe I actually ended up still wanting to become a detective?"

Cara grimaced. "Mother, you still sound weird when you talk about all this cops-and-robbers stuff. Man!"

Vera smiled tolerantly. "My, my. Cara seems completely bored with her parents. Imagine that!"

Sam laughed. "Better watch out, Cara. Your mom's already passed the firearms test. She's qualified to hide a gun in her purse or under her arm. She might turn out to be worse than me."

"Yes, and I know that if I had to, I could pass a private investigator's exam as well." Vera shrugged. "Fortunately, Colorado doesn't require a test."

Sam rubbed his mouth and pulled at his chin. "You aren't still pursuing that thing, are you?"

"'Thing'?" Vera raised her eyebrows. "I don't think I heard you right."

"Come on," Sam groused. "We've been over this many times before. You need to get five years on the local police force before you even consider going off on your own."

"Really?" Vera bristled. "Listen, I studied enough in college to qualify me for anything I want to do—and the karate lessons I've been taking for the last year and a half are way ahead of those simple self-defense classes they teach your boys and girls down at the police training center. You've already taught me how to pick locks and do electronic surveillance. I don't need to take a state test or any other exam to begin working as a private investigator tomorrow morning. You're just prejudiced!"

Sam's eyes narrowed. "I've been in this business for nearly two decades, and I'm only trying to point you in the right direction. Show a little respect for my personal history."

Cara put her spoon down. "You two sound worse than the kids across the street. I've heard this argument a hundred times before."

Sam spoke more sharply than usual. "Hey, young lady, I don't need any more flak floating down at me from the balcony."

Cara smirked with the side of her mouth and started eating her cereal again.

"Please, Sam," Vera said in an uncompromising tone. "I've already had an initial conversation with Ace Newton down at the All-City Confidential Agency. He's definitely interested in my working with him."

"Well, I happen to have the inside track down at the Colorado Springs Police Department, and I can assure you that they'd welcome you with open arms."

"I think I'm going to my room." Cara got up and put her cereal bowl in the sink. "Things are quieter there."

"Careful, young lady." Vera looked her daughter straight in the eye.

Clara glanced back at her mother and then walked out of the room, looking down at the floor.

"Vera, what I'm trying to tell you is that police training is beyond anything you learned at the college." Sam started gesturing forcefully with his index finger. "Furthermore, you can make contacts, develop relationships that could have important consequences in the future."

Vera took a deep breath and looked up at the ceiling. "Sam, you've told me all of this before. I have a different point of view."

"'Point of view'!" Sam's voice rose to a high pitch. "You're talking to a trained—"

"Sam," Vera interrupted, "I know your history quite well. I live here. Remember?"

Sam stared at his wife, fuming but trying to hold his temper. "Obviously, I remember."

"Okay. Just give me a little room for my own opinions. All right?"

Sam started drumming on the table with his fingertips as Vera removed the rest of the dishes and carried them to the sink. Tension stalled the conversation. Sam stared at the wall.

"How's that new man working out?" Vera asked, more to break the silence than anything else.

"Who?"

"You said he was from Lebanon, Jordan, or someplace."

"Oh, you mean Basil Abbas." Sam's voice softened. "Fascinating guy. Probably the most extensively educated policeman I ever saw."

"Really?" Vera started rinsing the dishes, trying to appear as unruffled by their argument as possible. "How so?"

"The man is . . . well, different from anybody down at the station house. He's one of the best-read people I've ever met. Really a rather radical Christian. Studied for the priesthood in the Orthodox Church once."

"How exactly is he different?"

"He goes around quoting the early-church fathers all the time. The man thinks like a computer. He's brilliant, but he turns everything going on in the police force into a philosophical debate. And Abbas looks as strange as he talks."

Suddenly the phone rang. Sam picked it up and answered, "Sloan here."

Vera looked up, watching her husband's face.

"Yes . . . yes." Sam's voice dropped. "You're kidding," he whispered.

Vera noticed Sam's expression changing. His blue eyes grew dark and intense, and his face took on a hard look. The shift in the policeman's demeanor signaled that something was seriously wrong. Vera listened more intently.

"When did it happen?" Sam took a pad out of his pocket.

Vera watched as Sam wrote in the typical sprawling scribble he used when he was agitated. His face fell.

"He's been dead for a short while?" Sam took a deep breath. "I understand. I'll be there as quickly as I can. Have the lab people and the coroner been called?" He listened carefully. "I see. Good. Yes, I can be there in ten minutes." He hung up the telephone.

"What's happened?" Vera asked.

Sam looked out the window almost as if he hadn't heard her. "Yes," he murmured. "I've got to leave quickly."

"You don't look well."

Sam didn't answer. He walked to the closet, picked up a shoulder holster, and put a Smith and Wesson .38-caliber pistol under this arm. "I don't know when I'll be back," he said, obviously deep in thought.

"Sam . . . Sam." Vera reached out as he headed for the back door but didn't catch him. "Can I help?"

"No, no, thank you." Sam walked out quickly.

Vera heard the door slam and the car start. She hurried to the living room window to watch Sam back out. He turned quickly and shot down the street. Vera saw his car disappear and instantly felt bad that their conversation had turned into an argument.

Hope he's not gone long, she thought, and went back to the kitchen. Vera picked up the telephone and hesitantly dialed All-City Confidential.

3

ON MONDAY AT NOON VERA SLOAN WALKED into Pancho's Mexican restaurant on Nevada Street. Located a few blocks from the Colorado Springs Police Department, the warm little café run by Gomez and Maria Martinez was one of Vera's favorite meeting spots. The freezing temperatures had escalated her usual ravenous appetite for their border food today, and Ace Newton had said he'd be there shortly after noon.

"*¡Mi amiga!*" Maria opened her arms when Vera came in the front door. "*¿Que tal?*"

"*¡Muy bien!*" Vera hugged her friend. "*¡Yo tengo mucho hambre!*"

"*Siempre.*" Maria giggled.

"I'm expecting a business acquaintance," Vera explained. "We'll need a quiet table."

"Follow me." Maria pointed toward a booth in the back as she walked. "No one will bother you back there."

Vera sat down, glancing around the large room filled with colored tables and chairs. The bright reds and greens on the walls lent the restaurant a lively air, and the aroma of spicy food touched ancient needs within Vera's digestive system. She picked up a menu and quickly scanned the already familiar bill of fare.

Out of the corner of her eye, Vera saw the front door open and a large, paunchy man in his late forties walk in. Ace Newton always wore a brown leather pilot's coat and looked like somebody rolling in at a bus station. His black hair was parted on the left side and had a Vitalis plastered-down look. Even though he seemed casual, Ace was always working: his brown eyes constantly shifted back and forth across the room, assessing everything and everyone in sight. Newton saw Vera and immediately headed for the back.

Vera motioned for Newton to sit down. "I'm glad that it worked out for us to get together today."

Newton sat down and smiled. "Sure. Business is always slow over the holidays. Not a great time to be nailing the bad boys to the wall. Things will pick up by next Monday."

"My husband says that crime doesn't take holidays. You agree?"

Ace rolled his brown eyes and grinned. "Who am I to contradict anything that Sam Sloan says?" He laughed. "Sure, somebody could be getting shot at this very moment, but in my business, little usually happens during Christmas and New Year's. Most of the bad boys are trying to be good guys. It's the Santa Claus syndrome."

"You know Sam?"

"Sure. He's solved some of the toughest cases that ever dropped into this part of the world. Sloan's a legend in this town."

Vera smiled. "That's nice to hear." She glanced at the menu. "Maybe we should order before we talk. What would you like, Ace?"

Newton closed the menu. "I always have the same. Enchiladas are my favorite."

A waiter with coal-black hair walked up to the table. The young man, with an apron tied around his waist and a notepad in his hand, asked in accented English, "What can I get for you?"

"Give me the cheese enchiladas and a Diet Coke." Vera handed him the menu.

"Make that two and water," Ace added. "Supposed to be watching my waist, and it's getting out there where I can see it."

Vera smiled and cut to the chase. "Well, Ace, I'm definitely interested in talking about the possibility of working with you. A few days ago I finished my last exam, and even though I don't have the diploma in hand, I've officially graduated with a degree in criminology. I've got a permit to carry a gun, and I've had a year and a half of karate training."

"Wow!" Ace exclaimed. "And I'll bet living with Sam Sloan must have filled in a thousand other little details about how you catch murderers and thieves."

Vera smiled. "I have helped Sam solve a couple of cases." She lowered her voice. "Actually, I can pick locks better than the average crook, and I know how to do electronic surveillance as well as a few other assorted tricks that my husband taught me. I've made the rounds."

"I bet the downtown cops enjoyed having you looking in on their business matters." Ace raised an eyebrow. "You've got to remember that I worked for ten years with the local police. I know their operation like the back of my hand."

Vera kept smiling but she abruptly felt uncomfortable. Ace

had started his career by traveling the exact path that Sam described earlier that morning. Her lack of experience might be a problem.

"As I recall, the police aren't big on their officers' sharing confidential information." Ace stretched out his legs and folded his fingers together over his bulging stomach, looking at Vera expectantly.

"We keep those capers to ourselves." Vera kept smiling. "But I've had plenty of experience in watching murders get solved, and my academic studies filled in lots of gaps. During my college work, I studied forensic science and learned how to cover a crime scene. They taught me what sort of physical evidence to search for—I studied glass and soil collection and preservation . . ." Vera started talking faster; just mentioning the subjects excited her. "I studied organic analysis and the use of mass spectrometry. Hair, fibers, prints, drugs were part of the study. I can tell you about one that—"

"Sorry." Newton interrupted, shaking his head. "Private investigators don't get into those types of cases more than once in three decades. The fact of the matter is that most of what we do is rather boring."

"Boring?"

"Look, Vera. Most of the time I'm out doing surveillance work on fakers trying to beat their insurance companies. I actually make my living by running down relatively confidential information for employers, trying to find out the truth about their possible future employees. I check to see if people have a criminal record or a bag full of bad debts. The truth is, most of what I do is mundane. I even wear ordinary clothes so that no one pays attention to me."

The waiter returned and put steaming plates in front of Newton and Vera. He gave Vera her soda and placed a glass of water before Ace. Both dug into their enchiladas.

"I grew up down in the southern part of the state, near Pueblo," said Ace. "Used to eat Tex-Mex stuff about twice a week. Lots of Mexicans down there."

Vera nodded and kept eating. Her mind raced to identify what might impress Newton. She'd spent plenty of time checking him out before applying for a position. The word up and down the Colorado Springs streets was that Ace Newton was a straight shooter, a family man who had two children, with the oldest in high school. People at Vera's church told her stories about Barbara Newton that always put the family in a solid position. They described her as a devoted mother and Ace as a dedicated, affectionate father. As Vera's thoughts spun, she could think of nothing that might really capture Newton's fancy. She kept eating.

Ace set his fork down for a moment and pressed his point. "Most of what I do would bore a teenage boy to death. The cops get all the big-time action, and the private investigators don't do anything but run around town, picking up all the leftovers. If you're looking for excitement, the police department offers a full plate."

Vera kept eating. She tried not to look depressed, but Ace Newton was sounding like Sam. She couldn't tell the detective that part of the reason for talking to him was a desire to make her own way.

"No, sirree." Newton shook his head. "Tenacity is the name of my game."

"That's why I'm talking to you, Ace. I want a predictable

job. I'm not interested in working with someone who will go bankrupt in six months. I'd like a steady, predictable income."

Ace eyed her more carefully. "Steady, huh?"

"I'll let Sam have the shoot-outs. I want a job I can count on, week after week." Vera watched Newton's eyes. For the first time since he'd come in, he seemed to be taking her seriously, so she continued, "I need to make a living. Obviously, I'm qualified. I learn fast and will quickly absorb anything you want to teach me."

"Teach you?" Ace frowned.

"Ace, I know how to pull a criminal's rap sheet and how to do computer work. If you're on the Avert program, I can download data as fast as anyone. I can pull driving records as well as run credit checks. I even know how to access the sex-offenders' registry. What more could you want?"

Ace scratched his head and looked at her out of the corner of his eye. "I run a first-class operation, Vera. No funny stuff. Everything's straight up. My specialty is the 'good ol' boy' style, but you'd need to have a professional look unless the assignment calls for casual. Get me? Unless the assignment calls for it, you don't need to look like a housewife."

Vera nodded, instantly realizing that she'd need new clothes. "Yes, I understand exactly."

"Wouldn't want any problems with Sam. We've been friends, and I'd want to stay on a good professional basis with him. That's how I relate to all the cops."

"Of course," she answered. Regardless of their argument a few hours before, Vera knew she wouldn't work with Newton or anyone else if Sam didn't say yes. "I'm prepared to meet all of those requirements."

Newton rubbed his chin. "Truth is that I've been way too busy lately and I do need some help. Biggest job is checking out the police and driving records for employers." He looked at Vera critically. "You willing to run down those tired old records?"

"Absolutely."

"Okay. I'll see you at my office next Monday morning. A week from today."

"Excellent!" Vera beamed. "I'll be there."

4

THIRTY MINUTES AFTER LUNCH WITH ACE Newton, Vera Sloan stopped at Von's to pick up groceries. Snow fell gently over the town, settling on the customers hurrying in and out of the large store. Walking down the long aisles crammed with canned goods, Vera quickly found the few items she needed to feed the family through New Year's Day. Holding her filled basket in hand, she got in line at the checkout counter.

"Hear about that tragic death down at the bank?" the woman in front of Vera hollered across the aisle to her friend on the other side. "Happened this morning."

"No kidding," a middle-aged lady in a black jogging suit called back. "Who kicked in?"

"I heard the man was president or something like that," the woman in front of Vera called back. "Some big dog downtown.

Died this morning before eight o'clock. They found him in the parking lot."

"Do tell," the jogger shouted back with sustained indifference. "That's wild."

Vera glanced at her watch. She wasn't interested in hearing the female version of Tweedledee and Tweedledum honking out gossip. Instead she kept thinking about her conversation with Ace. She was actually going to have a job of her own, making real money!

The idea of going to work hadn't been part of her life plan. Sam had agreed that raising Cara meant everything. Of course, they'd hoped for another baby, but one never came along. Cara grew up, went to school, and kept on growing taller, until one day Vera discovered that she had time on her hands. Only then did helping Sam discover clues become more than a pastime.

The woman pushed her cart away from the cashier, and Vera put her groceries on the conveyer belt. The loudmouthed woman and the jogger continued their noisy conversation, departing through separate doors.

"Don't have much," Vera told the smiling checker, who immediately started picking up groceries. "Won't take long."

Staring at the cash register blankly, Vera thought about a hitch in the Sloans' plans that had developed during her last year in college. While completing her degree in criminology, Vera had discovered a yen to become her own person—a professional detective on her own. She didn't want to stand in Sam's shadow any longer. Sure, everybody knew and respected Sam, but that was the crunch. Vera wanted to establish herself in her own right.

"Anything else, ma'am?"

"Uh, no. You can sack it in paper."

Of course, Vera wanted Sam's approval of a position with Newton, but she knew that even if Sam stonewalled this job, she would look elsewhere. She simply didn't want to start working at a police location with such strong connections to Sam.

"That'll be $35.24," the cashier said.

Vera scrawled quickly in her checkbook, handed the lady the check, and hurried out of the store. Fifteen minutes later she pulled up in the Sloans' driveway. Her wristwatch read 2:15. She slammed the door and hustled into the house as snow started falling in profusion.

A quick glance said that someone had been there. *Probably Sam,* Vera thought. She strolled through the kitchen, looking for a note. On the cabinet next to the stove, Vera found his memo stuck above the sink where she couldn't miss it.

12:10 P.M.

Dear Vera,
Can't tell you much. On an unusual secret assignment. Something terrible happened today. Looks bad. Have no alternative but to follow the lead. Hope to be able to call you tomorrow—or the next day. Picked up some clothes and will be leaving town. Will tell you more when I get back.

Love you—
Sam

Vera could tell from Sam's handwriting that he had been in a hurry. She studied the scribbling again as she sat down at the kitchen table. If Vera had been a police officer, Sam would have left her more detailed information. Outsiders simply didn't hear what employees heard—*Score five points for Sam's side of our argument,* she thought.

She stuck the note in her pocket. Sam wouldn't be home for supper tonight or probably the next night. If life with Sam had taught Vera anything, it was to keep on plowing, regardless of the circumstances. She began to put away the groceries.

Two hours later, the back door by the garage entrance slammed. Vera looked up from *Presumed Innocent,* the book she was reading, knowing that it must be Cara. She closed the cover slowly. Would her fifteen-year-old daughter show up with childlike affection, or would she act like the eighteen-year-old, vehemently opposed to all parental guidance?

"Mom, you here?" Cara shouted from the back door.

"I'm in the bedroom, reading."

Cara bounded through the door, red-faced from the freezing weather. "Wow! Did I have fun this afternoon!" She plopped down on the bed next to Vera. "I've been sliding down the hillside on Sandra's snowboard. What a terrific day!" She tossed her hair back and forth, fluffing out the back.

My eighth grader's here, Vera thought. *Thank the Lord for that blessing!*

"The snow got my hair sort of wet."

"Oh?" Vera raised an eyebrow. "Sounds like you've found your voice since this morning's breakfast."

Cara waved her hand as if brushing the comment aside. "We had lunch at McDonald's. A bunch of kids came over. What an awesome time."

"Any boys a part of lunchtime?" Vera studied her daughter's face.

"Mom!" Cara sounded bored. "Really! Of course, boys were there. Boys are always at McDonald's."

Vera rolled her eyes. "No kidding. Now, let's go back to breakfasttime, when you seemed to be living in another world. As I vaguely recall, your father couldn't get you to talk to him."

Cara squirmed. "Mom, I'm sorry. I know I didn't do very well this morning, but Dad really turned me off when he started trying to pry into my world." She shrugged. "I don't know why, but sometimes he hits all my off switches."

Vera squeezed her daughter's hand. "I understand, but your father was only attempting to express his interest in you."

"Dad always treats me like a suspect on the police lineup."

"But he doesn't intend to, Cara. Your father's only trying to be your friend."

"Doesn't sound like much of a friend to me," Cara insisted. "And I also thought Dad was cramming the Colorado Springs Police Department job down your throat."

Vera laughed. "Your father and I get into quick, heated arguments because we love each other. That's all."

"It makes me uncomfortable." Cara held her ground. "He always sounds like a know-it-all."

"Cara?" Vera raised her eyebrow again.

"Okay, okay." Cara held up her hands. "I'll apologize when Dad comes home tonight."

"Sorry." Vera reached into her pocket and pulled out a piece of paper. "Your father left a note. Looks like he won't be coming home tonight and might be gone for several days."

Cara's face fell. "He's out of town?"

Vera shook her finger teasingly in Cara's face. "See? You

need to treat Dad well because you never know what his schedule will demand."

Cara leaned back against the bedstead. A sulking look covered her face. "Mom, I don't know why I get into these squabbles. I don't mean to." She shook her head.

Vera reached over and hugged her daughter. "We love you, Cara." She kissed her on the cheek. "Growing up isn't easy, but I think you're doing fine."

Cara hugged her mother back. "I don't know." She ran her hands nervously through her dark hair. "I get so mixed up sometimes."

Vera watched Cara's face for a moment. *Sometimes Cara thinks like a twenty-year-old, and ten minutes later she acts like a first grader*, she thought. *Just part of adolescence.*

"I understand," Vera said, rubbing her daughter's arm. "By the way, did you bring anything home from school to work on? I know that you always have a considerable amount of reading for your advanced literature class."

Cara's frown shifted into a broad smile. "I've been reading the most fascinating book that I'm supposed to analyze during the holidays. The book's depressing but thought-provoking."

"What's it called?"

"*One Day in the Life of Ivan Denisovich*," Cara said. "Alexander Solzhenitsyn wrote it. Ever hear of him?"

"Absolutely," Vera enthused. "My goodness, but you've been assigned an amazingly difficult book for an eighth grader."

"Well," Cara said, pretending to boast, "it *is* an honors class, after all."

"Sure, but didn't Solzhenitsyn receive the Nobel prize for literature? That's heavy reading."

Cara nodded. "It's supposed to be hard. My job is to figure

out how I can relate my life to what the author writes. We have to think about the underlying themes."

Vera rubbed her chin. "How would a book about the brutality of Stalin's forced-labor camps ever touch an American teenager?"

Cara stretched out across the bed, frowning at the ceiling. "That's the jackpot question." She put her hands behind her head. "I've thought about it some, and I have a few ideas."

"Go ahead," Vera coaxed. "You can tell me."

"Promise you won't laugh?"

"Of course I won't."

Cara looked thoughtful for a moment. "Well, the characters live in a camp on the Pechora River, which flows into the Siberian Barents Sea. The men were arrested for no other reason than because they said something negative about the Stalinist regime. Apparently, the government feared they might hold ideas contrary to the party line. The prisoners ended up in jail for all the wrong reasons."

"And how does that fit you, Cara Sloan?"

"Honestly?" Cara bit her lip. "Sometimes I feel like I'm on trial because you're afraid that I have ideas that are different from yours and Dad's. Not that I actually do—but you seem to think so."

Vera squirmed. "Sometimes we are afraid, dear. But there are moments when we *all* seem to be on trial for heaven knows what. We can't identify anything that we've done, but we still appear to be guilty of some unexplained deed that sent us into our own exile. Know what I mean?"

Cara nodded her head. "Sure I do. Sometimes I feel exiled."

Vera stared at her daughter. Cara's thoughts seemed to be light-years ahead of those of her peers—but that could just be a proud mom's opinion, she mused. Literature seemed to bring out Cara's mature side. "Yes, dear. Sometimes I feel very adrift from where I want to be too."

Cara smiled slyly. "See? Solzhenitsyn ties into my life more than you thought."

5

DURING THE NIGHT, SNOWFLAKES KEPT falling rapidly. By Tuesday morning, more than a foot of snow covered the Sloans' driveway and ran into the street in one smooth stream of unbroken white. Sunlight bounced off the frozen surface like a million diamonds. Twenty-third Street looked like a Christmas card.

But Vera didn't appreciate the endless flow of white beauty. When Sam was gone, she had no alternative but to get out the snowblower and clean the driveway, or she wasn't going anywhere in the car. Actually, she wouldn't even be going down the street until a snowplow passed their house or the weather warmed up. The beauty of winter flurries disappeared quickly on days when she had to clear a path to the outside world.

"Cara," Vera called from the living-room window. "I've got a little something for you to do this morning!"

No answer meant Cara had already awakened, looked out the window, and come to the same conclusions that Vera had about the snow.

"Cara!"

A groan sounded from the bedroom.

"I need your help."

"I know," Cara mumbled. She clearly understood that she should get up and dress for clearing off the snow.

Morning unfolded like every vacation day did at the Sloans'. Somewhere around eleven o'clock, Cara started the snowblower. The sun appeared to be coming out from behind the clouds. *The streets should be passable by late afternoon,* Vera thought as she shuffled around the house, hoping to hear from Sam. No calls came. By noon she and Cara had had a hot lunch, and both returned to reading their books. They said little, as if they were avoiding talking about Sam's absence.

At three in the afternoon, Vera put her book down and began to feel concerned. Sam often took more time to call than she liked, but he usually checked in within twenty-four hours. They were now past that mark. Possibly she ought to check. Vera reached for the phone and dialed the police department. After the receptionist answered, Vera said, "Give me Dick Simmons."

Simmons had been a longtime friend of Sam's, and the Sloans occasionally saw him and his wife socially. Physically large and a tough-talking Southerner, Simmons always dressed like he ran a big-time local business. Sam thought Dick's attempts at being stylish were rather amusing. The man wore the most expensive suit on the police force; he even put the police captain in the shade. Vera knew that behind the huff and puff and enormous ego, Simmons had always proved to be a good friend and someone she could count on.

"Simmons here," Dick said in his usual gruff voice.

"My, my, sounds like I got the Bear Department."

"What?" Simmons said more roughly. "Who is this?"

"'Who is this?'" Vera laughed. "You don't recognize your old girlfriend?"

Simmons paused, then grumbled, "Good heavens. It's Vera Sloan."

"Just checking on you this afternoon, Dick."

"Well, I'm down here working hard."

"Better than I can say for my husband. Do you have any idea where Sam might be?"

"Sam?" Simmons's voice became softer. "Gosh, I haven't seen him all day. In fact, I don't remember seeing him yesterday."

Vera bit her lip. "He's out on some special assignment. That ring any bells?"

"Special assignment? Ain't heard about any of those in quite a while. No, that doesn't help me at all."

An icy finger of fear ran down Vera's spine. "Probably a unique situation. I was wondering if you'd help me get in touch with Sam. He hasn't called the way he usually does, and I'm a bit worried. Any possibility of making some inquiries around the station?"

"Sure. Of course. May take me a while."

"I understand. Would you please call me before you leave today? I'd like to talk with Sam soon, if it's possible."

"Give me a little time. I'm sure I can come up with something. Don't worry. Before long ol' Sam will come flying around the corner like Rudolph the Red-Nosed Reindeer. He'll probably call before I get back to you."

Vera hung up, feeling somewhat more confident but bothered that Simmons hadn't known *anything* about what Sam was up to. Usually Dick had his nose in everybody's business.

Forty-five minutes later, Cara wandered into Vera's room, carrying her copy of *One Day in the Life of Ivan Denisovich.* Vera looked up. "What's on Mr. Solzhenitsyn's mind this afternoon?"

Cara sat down and stared out the window thoughtfully. She opened the book and looked at a few pages. "It's interesting that Ivan is a sort of an everyman character. You don't find any great heroes in this story. They all appear to be common people."

"What do you make of that, Cara?"

Cara rubbed her mouth thoughtfully. "I think Solzhenitsyn wanted to expose how the Communist system degraded people we could identify with. The book trashes the entire Communist world and the way the system hurt people and put down average citizens like us."

Vera listened carefully, thinking about each word Cara said. "What kind of people do you think that system produced?"

"Well, I think that some of today's descendants of the Communist way of life—if they lived close to the work-camp situation—could be very vicious, frightening criminal-types. That system seriously destroyed the way people felt about themselves. They must have had a very hard time knowing right from wrong."

"Interesting. Yes, Cara, I believe that the extreme problems of what once was the Soviet Union must partially be due to the pain that people like Ivan felt as they struggled to survive."

Cara closed the book. "Have you heard from Daddy?"

"No, I haven't." Vera glanced at her watch, which said it was nearly five o'clock. "I thought that I'd hear something by now." For a moment she worried that even Dick Simmons hadn't called. "Sometimes emergencies come up unexpectedly and the police get distracted. I imagine we'll hear soon."

Cara pursed her lips thoughtfully. "Why don't we eat supper out tonight?" She smiled. "Helps pass the time."

Cara obviously knew that idea would interest Vera, and yet they might miss Sam's call. Vera hesitated to answer.

"Don't you need to buy anything at the mall?" Cara urged.

Vera remembered Ace Newton's comments about her looking smart at the office. She did need to do some shopping. On the other hand, she could do that tomorrow.

"I'd be glad to help you, Mom. Anything I can do?"

"*You* want to go to the mall, right, Cara?"

A large grin broke across Cara's face. "Actually, if it helped you do something that you need done, I'd be—"

"Glad to go!" Vera finished. "Yes, you'd be thrilled to steer me through the innumerable stores, especially the Old Navy outlet."

Cara kept smiling. "Just making suggestions."

"I bet you are." Vera looked at her watch again. "Okay. In thirty minutes we'll run over for a hamburger and a quick look around the mall."

"Great!" Cara bounded out of the room.

I may be sorry, Vera thought, *but then again I can call Dick Simmons when I get back if there's nothing on the phone recorder. Cara and I need to get a little fresh air anyway. Maybe a drive will be good for us.* She closed her book and walked into the kitchen to check the answering machine for what seemed like the hundredth time that day.

At 8:40, Vera and Cara returned home. They had visited a number of stores and Vera had picked up a few ideas about new clothes. Cara always pushed her mother to be a bit more daring fashionwise, but they had found a number of stylish dresses and suits that Vera thought looked particularly good.

Vera unlocked the back door and hurried over to the telephone recorder, expecting that she'd probably missed Sam. No messages. She bent down to look closer. Dick Simmons hadn't even called. Vera frowned.

"Anything on the recorder, Mother?"

"No," Vera said. "We didn't get one call."

"Really?" Cara grimaced. "I'd hoped we would."

"Me too." Vera turned away, keeping her thoughts to herself. She quickly went back to her bedroom.

Strange, she thought. *Very strange. Why wouldn't Simmons have called me back? He's never been unreliable in the past. And I honestly believed that Sam would have called by now.* She sat down in a chair, feeling uncomfortable. *Maybe I should call Dick at home.* She reached for the phone.

When Simmons recognized her voice, he immediately said, "I apologize for not calling earlier."

"No problem. I'm sure that something important came up and you—"

Simmons interrupted, "Actually, I didn't call because I wasn't sure of what to tell you, and I hoped to have something more develop."

"Oh?"

"Yeah, no one seemed to have anything to say about where your husband is."

"No one?"

"I . . . uh, couldn't get in to see the police chief. And everybody else appeared . . . um, preoccupied. You know we have quite a number of people still gone for the Christmas holidays."

Vera detected an unexpected quality in Simmons's voice. He

generally sounded like he ran the police station, but tonight she sensed an evasiveness, as if he knew more than he was saying.

"Some of our key people haven't come back yet and won't be back until after New Year's," Simmons continued. "I bet you'll hear from Sam before I run those folks down."

Vera wasn't sure how to answer. "What if I don't?" she finally said.

"Oh," Dick drawled, "I guess you could always talk to Chief Harrison yourself. That's about all I know."

That isn't all you know, Vera concluded. *That's all you're saying. If anybody has his eyes on all the machinery down on Nevada Street, it's you, Mr. Big Boy.*

"Probably you could find Harrison if you truly had an emergency." Simmons's voice changed so abruptly that he sounded more like a machine dispensing information. He wasn't an actor and she knew the man too well to be fooled. "I'm sure that the chief will be around during the next several days."

"Thank you, Dick. I appreciate your help."

"Any time." Simmons hung up immediately.

Vera slowly laid the receiver down as cold chills ran down the back of her neck. When Sam wrote "an unusual secret assignment," he wasn't kidding! Something *highly unusual* was unfolding down at the police station. Either Simmons knew all about it and was lying or he couldn't discover a thing. Vera wasn't sure which was true, but obviously something was wrong.

She began pacing back and forth across her bedroom, thinking, worrying, probing. This little caper wasn't fitting together right and she wasn't going to get any information from officers like Dick Simmons. Her stomach tightened and she felt shaky. Vera had to fight spinning off into a panic. Sam always warned her that she must keep her head, particularly when the circumstances got tight. She took a deep breath and walked out of the room.

Vera sat down at the kitchen table and stared out into the black night. If she didn't hear from Sam by nine o'clock Wednesday morning, she was going downtown to pull the police chief's chain.

6

FOR A LONG TIME AFTER CARA HAD GONE TO bed, Vera sat in a chair in the bedroom, brushing her hair and thinking. The quiet solitude of the night made her bedroom feel even emptier. She kept thinking about Sam and where he must be tonight. So many times he had gone off on some secret pursuit, but he'd always let her know where he was staying. It was strange and disconcerting—not knowing.

This life of chasing criminals had been so odd, with many unexpected dimensions. On some evenings, Vera had no idea how they'd ever gotten into it in the first place—but Sam had this "thing" about running down offenders. She remembered the evening they had talked about why he was a detective. They lived in a small apartment then, closer to the Nevada Street police station. He'd been doing that sort of police work for only a short time, but his enthusiasm for the job had become almost legendary.

"Why are you so passionate about these criminals?" Vera had asked. "Most of the bad guys are the scum of the earth. I find them to be a repulsive lot."

"You should have grown up in Chicago." Sam stretched out his legs under their small dining table. "You'd have learned that even the wicked have a story to tell. Sure, most of the sociopaths are repeaters in prison and many aren't very bright, but they're still God's creations." Sam grinned.

Vera ran her hands through her hair. "Most of the people I've seen down there being run through your police lineups," she said, "well . . . I wouldn't let them dig out there in my garden. Good heavens!"

"That's a nice Christian attitude," Sam chided.

"I know that's not the right way to look at some of those unfortunate people, but I'm just trying to be honest. Sam, many of those corrupt people can kill as easily as I fixed breakfast this morning."

Sam nodded. "Down at the police station we certainly get more than our share of the psychos, the nut cases. What can I say? We pick up murderers and druggies every day. Sometimes the good people get killed only because some addict was higher than a kite. You're right."

"Then I want to know why you keep working with these clowns," Vera pressed. "Why do you mess with these losers?"

Sam looked intently at his wife. "Would you believe that I have religious reasons?"

"You're kidding!" Vera's mouth dropped slightly. "Please explain."

Sam put his hands behind his head and massaged the back of his neck. "You must understand that some of this is only me and may be completely wrong. Of course, I got a bunch of my thoughts from the Scriptures and a good amount of what I think is the way that faith and my experiences come together in my head. I don't claim anything perfect or absolute."

Vera shook her head and looked up at the ceiling. "I'm prepared for anything, but I thought we were talking about why you keep chasing the outstanding losers in America."

"Yeah, I got the picture." Sam shifted in his chair. "Vera, I think that we are born into a world that is something like a big battlefield. Every day of the week we get up, put our clothes on, and go to war. Sometimes the shooting and bombing is big-time; sometimes it's small potatoes. But the war never stops."

"During the sixties the war must have been really escalating." Vera winked. "Remember all the crazies?"

"Yes," Sam agreed. "World War II, Vietnam—those were times when the issues were obvious. What I'm describing is like a physical aspect of spiritual warfare."

Vera raised her eyebrow. "Hmm. Interesting. Be a tad more specific."

Sam scratched his head. "Say it's like playing baseball. God has good people on His team and the evil one has another crew—unfortunately, they're bad. One side is committed to the right thing and the other to destruction. In between these two sides are many people who don't even know there's a battle going on. They just stand around and watch, like visitors floating through Disneyland. The area of conflict where the two teams hit head-on is the locality where people get hurt. That's when I show up."

"You're the referee?" Vera laughed. "Come on, I don't buy that scenario."

"No, I'm not a ref. I'm more like the cleanup guy after the game is over. I make sure that things turn out right as much as is humanly possible."

Vera took a deep breath. "What a strange thought."

"I've found that there are people in this world who make wrong decisions and get themselves in trouble. Then there are people who become so completely controlled by evil that everything they do is wrong. They may have good reasons for why they've slipped off base, but they're still captured by destructive tendencies. If left uncontained, these people end up possessed by calamity and will eventually hurt and damage the good folks. People like our daughter Cara."

"That one hit home, Sam. So you and the police downtown are actually in the business of beating back the devil every day that you go to work?"

"I feel a little uncomfortable putting it in those terms, but that's about what it amounts to."

"You're not saying that these criminals are possessed by some demon, are you? I mean, wouldn't that be on the far-out side?"

"*Possessed* is a strong word, Vera, but I do believe that many of the people that I lock up have had their motivations twisted and are generally occupied by evil. Sometimes as children they were gripped by fear, anger, guilt, whatever, and the end result became a way of life: compulsively stealing, doing drugs, extorting, and maybe even killing. Their only hope is getting out from under the control of this force by being caught and having to face the consequences of their behavior."

"And your catching crooks can actually set people free?"

"I can't guarantee that going to prison will liberate them, but criminals can become different people while serving their terms. Sometimes prisons just help them become professional criminals, but I've also seen men who came out completely redeemed."

Vera nodded. "That's a new twist on an old job."

"Dear, I attempt to prove to corrupt people that their behavior doesn't work. If they've got a brain left in their head, eventually they'll conclude that there has to be a better way than the one they've taken."

"I guess I always thought of a policeman as somewhat like Mom and Dad catching us when we've been naughty. Their system worked on the idea that they were the big rule enforcers."

"I don't see myself that way, Vera. I'm not running around trying to hang it on people who didn't follow the right directions."

"Good, Sam."

Sam shook his head. "The law isn't a bunch of rules that legislators wrote down in a book of jurisprudence to make people follow. Our legal system is based on the way God wants this world to be. Oh, I know that there are laws that have to be changed periodically, and sometimes they've been enacted for wrong reasons because society is incomplete and imperfect. Legislatures have to straighten out those messes, but the law that counts is nothing but a reflection of what we find in the Good Book."

"I like that angle, dear. You are God's agent to keep people on the right track."

"That also makes me feel a bit uncomfortable." Sam rubbed his chin. "What I'm trying to do is to make sure that evil doesn't obscure those guidelines until no one can remember right from wrong. Along the way I bring in the criminals and protect the streets so people like Vera Sloan don't have to worry when they go to the grocery store."

Vera studied his face for a moment. "I think that makes you an exceptionally good man, Sam Sloan. It certainly makes me proud to be your wife. I understand you better."

Sam grinned sheepishly. "That makes my heart sing." He winked at her.

Vera laid down her hairbrush and stared in the mirror. Wherever Sam was tonight, he still believed that his job helped to make the world a better place. What could she say? Maybe Sam was one of God's special outposts in this world, making sure that evil didn't win those periodic assaults on righteousness.

7

VERA AWOKE AFTER AN UNCOMFORTABLE night's sleep. She went through the usual habits of the morning: taking a shower, putting on makeup, getting Cara up, eating breakfast. Time dragged but she didn't say anything, trying to keep a smile in place. Her emotions were close to slipping out of control: Sam always called by this time and she couldn't see any reason for such a protracted delay.

Sure, she and Sam had tilted back and forth about her working with the All-City Confidential Agency, but their disagreements were far from a war. No reason there for Sam not to call. He'd probably not given the matter much thought since he left home.

After putting the dirty dishes in the washer, Vera straightened up the living room, made her bed, and checked to see if Cara had done the same. Each task was nothing more than marking time and Vera knew it. Finally, she sat down by the kitchen phone and stared out the window.

Pikes Peak had turned completely white, and their backyard was level with snow covering the grass, the flower beds, the brick walkway. All that she could see had turned into a pristine, shining brightness. If only life's worries could be masked so simply and completely.

Vera watched the kitchen wall clock. The moment it read nine o'clock, she grabbed her car keys and rushed for the door. Enough was enough. She was going to find out what was going on—regardless!

"I'm Vera Sloan," she told the police receptionist. "I need to see Chief Harrison."

"Oh?" The receptionist looked skeptical. "You have an appointment?"

"I'm Detective Sam Sloan's wife," Vera said determinedly. "The chief will see me."

The receptionist tilted her head and raised her eyebrows slightly as if to say, "Whatever." She dialed Harrison's office.

Vera had been in occasional meetings with Al Harrison. She couldn't say that she actually knew the chief, but he shouldn't have any trouble remembering who she was. Vera's memory served up a picture of an overweight man who looked like a lineman on a professional football team, but who spoke in a gentle voice. She couldn't imagine Harrison not being responsive.

"A Mrs. Sam Sloan here to speak with the chief," the receptionist said over the phone.

If Harrison wasn't available, Vera was ready to go charging through the entire police department, even if she had to plow over the receptionist. Nobody was going to stop her from finding out what was going on, even if she had to turn extremist.

"Sure. Okay. I understand." The receptionist hung up the phone. "Mr. Harrison will see you. You can find him—"

"I know where he is," Vera answered, already walking past the woman's desk and heading for the offices behind the entryway. A minute later she walked into the secretary's area in front of Harrison's office. "Excuse me," she said to the woman, whose back was turned.

The dark-haired woman shut a drawer and turned around. "Ah, you must be Mrs. Sloan."

"Yes, I am."

The secretary extended her hand and smiled. "I'm Dorothy Waltz. Glad to meet you."

"Thank you. My pleasure."

"Chief Harrison is in an important meeting at this moment, but he'll be free shortly. He said to make sure that you were comfortable. The chief is looking forward to speaking with you."

Vera relaxed. "I appreciate his concern." She took a deep breath. "Yes, very much so." She moved to the waiting area.

"Can I get you a cup of coffee?"

"No, I'm fine." Vera slipped into a chair but didn't touch the available magazines. For the first time she realized how keyed up she'd become. It wasn't like her to get so upset; usually Sam's trips didn't affect her. For some reason, this particular situation made her feel edgy, wary. Vera took another deep breath. She was probably blowing everything out of proportion.

"I believe you just finished college?" Dorothy asked.

"Why, yes I did—a week or so ago."

"Sam was in here the other day, talking to the chief about your progress. Sounded like he thought you might work down here."

"Really?" Vera smiled but didn't like her comment. *That* was exactly why she didn't want to work in the Colorado Springs Police Department.

The secretary went back to work and Vera looked around the room. The terrazzo tile floors were the same in Sam's end of the building. Somehow the sight of them depressed her. They looked like someone had put them in thirty years ago. Still, the walls had been painted recently and Chief Harrison kept a sharp-looking outer office. Yes, this part of the building suggested efficiency.

Vera stood and started pacing nervously, irritated that waiting for Chief Harrison was taking so long. At that moment, a tall, slender man walked through the door.

"Detective Abbas!" Dorothy said. "Do you know Sam Sloan's wife?"

"No," the dark-complexioned man answered. "I don't believe that I've had the pleasure."

Vera immediately recognized Basil Abbas, the man with all of the quirks that Sam had spoken of so often: a portion of thinning hair draped over his eyebrow with a slight twist upward at the end, the protruding ears, and reading glasses perched awkwardly on a bulbous nose. The man's large hands seemed out of proportion to the rest of his body, as did his loose-fitting clothes. Basil looked like he'd come from another world, one far beyond Colorado Springs.

"Mrs. Sloan," Dorothy said, "I'd like you to meet Basil Abbas. He's recently joined the force here for a short training visit."

"How do you do?" Vera offered her hand.

Abbas took her hand almost as if he were going to kiss it. "I have enjoyed very much working with your husband. Sam Sloan is a man of significant insight."

"I believe Sam told me that you originally came from Amman, Jordan, Mr. Abbas," Vera said. "Is that right?"

"Yes, yes." The detective waved his hand nervously, revealing that he also bit his fingernails. "I actually came directly to Colorado Springs from Atlanta, Georgia, but I am only here for training experiences. Please call me Basil."

"And Sam said that you are a Syrian Orthodox Christian, a member of the Orthodox Church. Have I got the information correct, Basil?"

Abbas smiled a sly grin and rolled his large, dark eyes. "My goodness, you already know a great deal about me."

"I'm going to let the two of you talk." Dorothy turned back to her work. "I've got some papers to file. Don't mind me. I'll disappear while you chat."

"I'm here to inquire about Sam," Vera explained. "We haven't heard from him for several days, and I am worried."

"Hmm," Basil said, rubbing his chin. "I haven't seen him myself for at least that long. I'm sure that he is only detained on some special assignment."

Vera nodded. "I trust so." She sat down awkwardly and changed the subject. "Sam is always quoting you. He says that you've read more books than anyone he knows."

Abbas smiled and shoved his hands into his pockets as if embarrassed. "I suppose that I do spend an enormous amount of time reading. Once I studied to become a priest in the Orthodox Church, but I came to believe that I was called to another kind of work. My theological studies certainly started me down the road to keeping my nose in books. It all helps me to be a thorough detective."

"Orthodox priest? What an unusual background for police

work. Just last Monday Sam was quoting something to our daughter, Cara, that you'd said about human dignity."

Abbas nodded, and the strand of hair hanging down over his eyes bobbed against his shaggy eyebrows. "My people have always been firm believers in the importance of human dignity. We believe that worth must be safeguarded at all cost."

"That's about what Sam was saying. As I recall, he was talking about your views on evil." Vera watched the Arab's slender face cupped by a broad double chin. Basil Abbas certainly couldn't be called a handsome man.

"The Orthodox have spent time thinking about the problem of evil in this world. I am always concerned for the intrusion of the evil influence into people's lives. One of the most important tasks that we have in police work is to combat this force." Basil raised his finger in the air like a lecturer making a point. "'Fiery darts,' Saint John Chrysostom warned us. We must forever be vigilant, lest evil hit us with an attack."

"Yes," Vera agreed. "That's certainly Sam's perspective."

Suddenly the chief's door opened and several policemen walked out.

"Good morning, Mrs. Sloan," the first man said with sober respect.

"Morning." The second officer took off his cap.

"Good to see you," Vera responded, nodding to both men. Their somber greetings chilled rather than warmed her. Even the secretary looked up in curiosity.

"Chief Harrison is waiting to see you," the first officer said. "Please go on in."

Vera walked past the officers into Al Harrison's office, feeling awkward and apprehensive. "See you later," she called to Basil Abbas.

He smiled.

"Vera!" Harrison immediately got to his feet and hurried around the desk with his hand out. "I'm glad you could come so quickly."

"Come quickly?" Vera blinked several times. "I don't understand."

"You got my phone call on your recorder?" Harrison looked confused. "I called shortly after nine o'clock."

"No. No, I didn't."

"My goodness. What brought you down here then?" The chief pointed at the chair behind Vera. "Please sit down."

"I called because my husband left town on Monday and I haven't heard from him since then. In fact, I can't find anybody in this department who will tell me anything about where Sam is, or at least if he can be reached."

Harrison tightened his jaw and sat down opposite Vera. His face looked strained, his eyes troubled. He nodded. "I understand. We've kept a firm lid on Sam's activities for some time now. In fact, I'm the only person in the entire department who knows . . ." Harrison turned uncomfortably in his chair. "And unfortunately, I don't know the entire matter."

Vera felt the energy drain from her body. "You're telling me that my husband, a regular detective, is on some assignment that you, the chief of the entire Colorado Springs Police Department, don't completely understand?" Vera could feel her voice rising. She stopped and took another deep breath. "Am I getting this right?"

Harrison looked pained. "Yes. Sort of. I mean, there are some aspects of this assignment that I haven't been fully apprised of—and probably won't be for some time." He rubbed his cheek nervously. "We're involved in a highly unusual problem."

Unusual? Vera wanted to scream.

Harrison swallowed hard. "Let me go back to the beginning. Nine months ago, the CIA came to me, asking for a special officer to help them investigate a local bank employee. They believed that someone at this bank was illegally harboring large sums of money received from abroad. Naturally, I turned to Sam and assigned him to work with the CIA, helping them maintain surveillance over the situation."

"Wait a minute." Vera held up her hand. "You're saying that one of our local banks was laundering money from the international scene. You mean drug money?"

Harrison shook his head. "I can't go into the details, but apparently a local bank got involved because it was less noticeable than some bank on either the East or West Coast. Yes, those are the facts."

Vera wrung her hands. "So, in effect, Sam became an agent for the CIA?"

"On loan from us." Harrison kept clenching his teeth and puffing out his lower lip nervously. "That's the idea."

Vera shook her head and looked out the window. "I had no idea that Sam was involved in anything of this order."

"Vera, the risks were too high to let people around the department know what Sam was doing. We were afraid that if word leaked out, Sam might even be killed. We're talking high security here."

"I see." Vera looked down at the floor, trying to grasp where this conversation might go.

"Monday morning, the case took a very unexpected turn."

"That's the day he left a note for me at home and left town."

Suddenly the door opened behind her. Vera turned to find an officer she hadn't seen before standing there. He had a kind face.

"Hello, Chaplain Owens." Harrison waved the man in. "I want you to meet Vera Sloan. She's Sam's wife."

"Glad to know you." The officer extended his hand and smiled.

"Thank you." Vera shook hands perfunctorily.

"Sit down, Bill." The chief pointed to a chair in the corner.

Vera looked back and forth between the chief and the chaplain. They seemed to understand clearly something about which she knew nothing. "Excuse me." She turned back to Harrison. "Isn't it irregular to have the chaplain in here during our confidential conversation?"

Harrison looked knowingly at Owens. "Generally, it is. Today I believe Chaplain Owens's presence is appropriate. He is already aware of what I'm about to tell you."

Vera looked carefully at the chief. Signs of strain lined his eyes. The big man almost looked like he might begin to cry. The chaplain leaned forward on the edge of his chair, almost to the point of falling off. At that moment Vera's mind slipped to another realm. It was as if the entire world had switched to slow motion. She seemed to be standing outside her body, listening to other people talk.

"The fact is that yesterday afternoon Sam flew to the Washington, D.C., Dulles Airport in an airplane provided by the CIA," the chief continued. "We thought he arrived there last night." Harrison took another deep breath. "This morning at 8:30 we received word that the airplane didn't land as was expected, and was reported missing. I tried to call you this morning, just after nine, to have you come down here."

Vera's heart thumped hard. She felt her face flushing. She wasn't sure she could still speak. "I'd already started down here by then," she whispered.

"Just before you came into Dorothy's office, I received a communiqué saying that the airplane had been found in a field north of Culpeper, Virginia, just north of Highway 29." He took a deep breath. "They crashed."

Vera's heart seemed to stop. The world froze in its spinning orbit. Her breathing seemed suspended. She stared at Al Harrison and realized tears were in the corners of his eyes.

"No one survived, Vera. Sam's gone."

For a moment all life on the planet stopped. Vera wanted to scream, but nothing would come out of her mouth. The office vanished in a sea of white as she tumbled out of her chair onto the floor.

8

PAIN SURGED THROUGH VERA SLOAN LIKE A subway train. Having married Sam at twenty, she could not imagine living without the man she passionately loved. Whatever desire she previously felt to be a separate entity from Sam was now a stake through her heart. Every ounce of her body screamed at the thought of going on without this man to whom she was devoted.

Police Chaplain Bill Owens and Police Chief Harrison had struggled to get Vera conscious again and sitting on a couch. Two other officers were needed to help her out of the station and back home again. Friends soon poured in, but both she and Cara remained inconsolable. By one o'clock, the news had spread through their church. More friends came over to the house, but Vera could barely talk.

At 2:30, Reverend Bill Dozier, the new pastor at the Sloans' church, arrived and ushered Vera to Sam's office where they wouldn't be disturbed. He shut the door and sat down across from the grieving woman.

"Vera, what can I say? My heart is broken. Sam was one of the finest men I've ever known." He reached over and hugged her. "God bless you."

Vera nodded, knowing that her red eyes must be nearly swollen shut from weeping and her face puffy. "Thank you." Her voice was barely audible.

"When will they release Sam's body for services?"

Vera shook her head. "I . . . I . . . don't have . . . any idea."

"I don't understand." The reverend frowned.

"The chief of police was vague . . . He didn't seem to know many of the details about anything." Vera shrugged. "I don't remember much of what was said. I may have missed something, but the impression that I was left with was . . . was . . . that everything is . . . up in the air."

Reverend Dozier leaned back in the chair. "Hmm, I see. Certainly makes planning somewhat difficult, doesn't it?"

Vera nodded her head.

The door opened behind her, and Cara came in to sit down next to her mother.

"I suppose that we'll have to wait for the police to tell us," Reverend Dozier said.

Vera took Cara's hands. "The entire matter is part of a secret assignment that Sam was working on. I'm sure that the police won't want publicity about what's happened. I don't see any option except to go along with their wishes at this time. I know that's what Sam would desire."

Dozier rubbed his mouth. "Well . . . it does make matters a little difficult. I suppose we'll simply have to let them tell us what the timetable will be."

Vera ran her hands nervously through her hair. "I feel like I've slipped into a tunnel and dropped into a crazy machine. Everything is out of sync, broken, bizarre, bewildering. Nothing fits together."

Cara put her arms around her mother's neck and sobbed.

"It doesn't seem right," Vera suddenly exclaimed. "One minute I'm sitting at my kitchen table waiting for my husband to call, and the next moment I learn that he'll never call me again. He's off on some secret assignment and then—*Boom! The airplane explodes!*"

Reverend Dozier's eyes widened. "An explosion?"

"I'm not sure that's what happened," Vera said stiffly and looked at Cara. "We're not sure about much of anything."

Dozier wiped his mouth nervously. "Does seem to be a complicated situation."

Vera took a couple of deep breaths and looked hard at the minister. "Reverend Dozier, you're fairly new to this community, but people will tell you that Sam and I have been faithful, churchgoing people. Always have been."

"Absolutely!" the minister affirmed strongly.

"We've tried to live our lives as the Bible directs," Vera continued, "and we've brought up our daughter in the same way." She looked at her weeping child.

The ministered smiled thinly and nodded his agreement.

Vera again took another deep breath and wiped the tears from her cheeks. Her face hardened, and her lips quivered. "We weren't perfect people, you understand, but we lived on a level that certainly didn't qualify for waking up one clear morning and discovering that our husband and father had been blown up."

Vera suddenly reached over and grabbed the minister's coat. "Now, I have a question for you, Reverend Dozier."

The minister blinked several times and nodded his head.

"I want to know why God let this tragedy happen. Why in the world would he let the horror of death fall on our house?" Vera pulled harder on the minister's coat. "Why has God dealt so severely with me?" Vera let go of his coat and sank back in her chair.

The minister rubbed his hands together and then folded them across his chest, looking almost like he was praying. For a few moments, he glanced out the small window, obviously trying to compose his response. Total silence settled over the room.

"I've been in the ministry for fifteen years," Reverend Dozier began. "Through those years there have been days when time hung heavy on my shoulders, especially when I had to stand by the casket of someone who died a tragic death. Vera, in every one of those situations, the family looked at me with the same question in their eyes. Oh, they might not have said it as directly as you just did, but they all wanted to know why."

Vera silently nodded her head.

"I must tell you a hard thing," Dozier continued. "I've found that God seldom tells us why. The question mark seems to hang in the sky, surrounded by a vast vacuum. Most of the time 'why' floats away unanswered like a formless cloud drifting by."

Vera squinted at the minister. "You can't tell me?"

"Oh, I could give you some perfunctory answers. An engine failed. A pipeline broke. The weather turned bad. Whatever. The problem is that I might be explaining a bona fide fact but it wouldn't begin to touch the emotion you're feeling. You want a good reason to explain why, in the scheme of daily living, your husband was suddenly yanked out of this world." Dozier took a deep breath. "I know that it doesn't sound like much of an answer, but I don't believe anyone in this whole world can give you a satisfactory explanation to answer your pain."

"But what should we do then?" Cara interjected. "How do we go on with our lives?"

Dozier nodded his head. "I believe that we have to turn whys into whats. I've found that God does give people extraordinary strength when they start asking, 'What can I do with this situation?' The issue before you and your mother is, how will you handle what's happened and make something good out of it?" He raised his eyebrows and looked compassionately at both Vera and Cara.

Vera wrapped her arms around Cara and stared at the floor. "I . . . I . . . don't know," she muttered.

"You can't know what to say, how to act right now," Reverend Dozier explained. "It's too early, but in time you'll begin to have a sense of what the two of you must do."

Vera rubbed her forehead and kept shaking her head. "I simply don't know," she said over and over again.

"You've told us to ask for more than an answer to our whys," Cara said, "but we hurt too much. I still can't see any purpose in what's happened."

Reverend Dozier kept rubbing his hands together and staring at his fingers. "God's purposes aren't as easy to fathom as we often think," he said slowly. "Most of the time it takes a long while to figure out what He has in mind." Dozier scratched his head. "But I have learned that omnipotence is not so much the ability to blow up the world in one big explosion as the ability to achieve a purpose, a special result that often requires great restraint. Maybe more discipline, control, waiting, is needed than we believed possible." He raised his eyebrows again. "I've learned that often what we can't fathom can still be redeemed . . . Vera, you can hang on to that promise."

Vera searched the minister's face. More than merely sounding understanding, Reverend Dozier was giving her the best answers that he had. Maybe, the best that anybody had. She swallowed hard but couldn't speak.

Once again, silence settled over the room. Cara hugged her mother. Gentle sobbing broke into the hush. For a long time, no one said anything.

Finally, Reverend Dozier said, "Vera, don't let the quietness in the room fool you. God is here with us right now. When He is dealing with us, silence doesn't equate with absence. Strange as it sounds, silence is one of the ways He speaks. The calm forces us to listen more attentively than we ever have before."

Vera began to nod her head slowly. "I'm going to have to spend a lot of time thinking about what you've said." She looked up at the minister. "At this moment, I only feel helpless."

The minister reached over and squeezed her hand. "Yes. I understand." He nodded his head. "I think that it's in the midst of our helplessness that we generally find the help of God."

Again, Vera ran her hands nervously through her hair. "So many questions have to be answered before I have any idea of what to do next. The police must clarify many details. I don't think I have any alternative but to put everything on hold and see what happens."

"Sounds like that to me," Dozier concluded.

Vera stood up. "We'll need to get their response later in the day and then I'll call you back. At this point, I suppose Sam's situation is more like a 'missing-in-action report.' Let me see what Chief Harrison tells me later this afternoon."

"Of course." Reverend Dozier reached over and put his arm on Vera's shoulder. With his other hand, he gripped Cara's palm. "Let me pray for you before I leave."

"Certainly," Vera said.

"Our heavenly Father," the minister began, "in our helplessness we need Your help. We can't even see beyond the sunset tonight, but You have the ability to lift our eyes above the mountains and see everything in light of tomorrow's dawn. Only You know where we're going, and we sure need Your sense of direction. Please help Vera and Cara to discover the assurance that if they should let go of Your hand, You won't let go of theirs. Please, Lord, help us get through this dark night. Amen."

Vera rubbed her eyes. "Amen," she feebly echoed.

9

As Pastor Dozier drove away, Vera stood at the living room window, dabbing a tissue at her wet eyes. A police car drove up the street and halted at the front curb. Detective Abbas got out and started up the front walk. Vera opened the front door before he had time to knock.

"Basil," she greeted him, "how gracious of you to come."

The Arab extended his big hand. "I was deeply grieved to hear the terrible report." He lowered his head respectfully. "I came to pay my respects."

"Thank you," Vera said, choking. "That is very kind. Please come in." She stood back from the doorway. "Come on back to the kitchen, where we can talk alone."

Basil nodded to the friends seated around the living room as they walked through the crowd toward the kitchen. He pulled a pair of half-glasses out of his inner coat pocket and perched them on the end of his large nose.

"Please sit down." Vera pointed to one of the chairs at the breakfast table. "We won't be bothered in here."

Abbas sat down at the opposite side of the table with rigid dignity. "I do not have the complete story, but I wanted you to know that I am available to help in any way. Do you need assistance? Suggestions? Money? Anything?"

Vera forced a smile. "It's thoughtful of you to offer, but right now we are just trying to understand what has happened. We have too many unanswered questions to know how to proceed." She sat down at the opposite side of the table. "At this point, I'm walking more in the darkness than the light."

Abbas nodded his head knowingly. "Darkness more than light." He rubbed his chin. "An excellent expression. I understand. It is a time in which you must guard your heart."

Vera blinked several times. "Guard my heart?"

"I have found that severe emotional trauma tends to toss us off balance. Thinking becomes affected and our sense of direction is distorted. At these moments we must be careful that nothing corrupts our emotions, the root system from which our energy flows."

"I'm not sure I'm following you," Vera admitted. "Of course, right now it's a little difficult for me to stay focused on what people say to me."

"Yes, yes." Basil kept nodding his head. "This is the exact phenomenon of which I speak. We tend to slip out of gear, so to speak, and this distraction offers opportunity to the evil one to attack us."

"The evil one?" Vera rubbed her forehead, thinking Basil

spoke about evil as he would some crook down at the police station.

"After we have suffered loss, our human dignity is diminished. We feel small and broken. We thrash around like a wounded animal, seeking to escape from a trap, a cage. Our guard is lowered and we unintentionally offer entry to the evil one in ways that we wouldn't have thought possible."

Vera tried to grasp Basil's words, but the ideas seemed to slip past her. "I'm not sure I understand."

"One of the primary goals of the evil one is to break down our human dignity and reduce us to creatures far below the stature of animals. We are left as nothing more than entities possessed by fear." Abbas's reading glasses bobbed up and down on his nose. His ears stuck straight out. "We must maintain our guard, lest we become deluded by this malevolent force."

Vera could hear his voice clearly, but Abbas didn't seem to be making any sense. She wasn't sure how to respond. The best she could do was nod her head.

"When tragedy falls, our minds are rattled." Abbas's eyes grew larger and seemed more intense. He folded his hands together. "If evil had its way, our distraught emotions would be turned loose. Our best intentions would be ground up like sausage. We would lose our way and become like children lost in a blizzard. Tragedy can tear us apart and break us into little pieces. Do you understand?"

Vera shivered. "I don't mean to offend you, but you sound rather frightening today. You make me want to hide under a rock."

Basil raised a shaggy eyebrow and the stray lock of hair hung down even farther in his eyes. "With all due respect, and nothing but intended kindness, my words are meant to give you concern. Your friends will come and tell you comforting things, but I dropped by to tell you the truth. This is a time to protect yourself, lest you stray and fall off in the ditch without knowing how you landed there."

"I'm sure you're right." Vera's words floated out of her mouth aimlessly. She wasn't actually sure of what to say. Nothing about Abbas had been predictable.

Taking her hand, Basil massaged Vera's palm as if trying to relieve the pain and make the tension disappear. "I am suggesting that human dignity decreases in the midst of such terrible onslaughts, and people have a habit of listening to things that they would have previously ignored. The half-truths, the exaggerations, the stories that have something wrong that we can't quite identify, slip together in our minds, causing us to listen and take seriously what, under other circumstances, we would have dispensed with." He suddenly let go and shook his finger like a teacher lecturing a schoolgirl. "We must, and I will say it again, *must* be ready to resist this onslaught."

Vera looked up into the huge brown eyes that gazed down at her with laser-beam intensity. "You seem to know a great deal about this."

"I grew up in a world where evil lived at our elbows. I have even seen people possessed by destruction set free through the prayers of the faithful. Here in the United States, you seldom acknowledge such facts that come tumbling out of the Bible, but believe me, Mrs. Sloan, I am telling you nothing but the facts."

Basil's words made Vera feel dizzy and uncertain. She pushed herself back firmly in the chair, barely nodding. "I see," she said hesitantly.

"Most of the stumbling Americans that I have met started

their downward journeys because they accepted so-called facts that were as tarnished as the truth." Basil frowned. "Often they listened to gossip and thrived on destructive stories. One thing led to another, until they accepted the lie as easily as they snapped their fingers." He suddenly clicked his thumb and middle finger together with a loud snap. "Without ever knowing what happened, they slid into the subterranean world that eventually empties into hell. Boom! Their dignity disappeared!"

Vera wanted to stand up and dash out of the room. Instead she stared at her lecturer.

"Many have taken this path," Basil warned. "Every day at the police station, I see multitudes who have done terrible deeds walk in like robots, talk mechanically, and whine like babies." He leaned closer to Vera. "They are actually dead people, breathing cadavers with arms swinging. These walking dead from whom all semblances of dignity have been stripped frighten me the most."

Vera was now beyond any capacity to respond. She said the only thing that came to mind: "Thank you for coming. I will do my best to remember what you have told me."

The detective's eyes searched Vera's. Vera could read skepticism in his face.

"I remain your servant in this difficult situation." Abbas rose and bowed. "Please know that I am always available."

Vera smiled faintly. "Thank you. I appreciate that."

Basil Abbas turned and marched out of the house like a knight returning to battle. Before entering the police car, he tucked his half-glasses in his pocket. Then he sped away.

Vera stared out the window, watching Abbas drive down the street. *My, my,* she thought. *What an extraordinary man! His advice is sound, if a bit fuzzy: Guard your heart.*

"I will," she whispered.

10

THROUGHOUT THE NIGHT, VERA KEPT WAKING up. Chief Harrison had promised to call with any new information that came to his office, and periodically she imagined she had heard the phone ring. Sleeping proved nearly impossible. The hours dragged by.

Vera tossed and turned until finally she ended up fully awake. She thought about Sam, their life together, and she wept constantly. How good everything had been so much of the time.

A thousand memories flooded her mind, but the most meaningful was remembering how their relationship had begun. Sam always filled her life with an expectation that made each event seem special. Remembering the tender times seemed almost to put his hand back in hers.

They had met in a crowded Subway restaurant where Vera had started eating lunch near her office. She was Vera Leestma then, a redheaded young woman from Shelton, Iowa, who liked sandwiches. The diet-conscious café helped keep her slim and friends usually joined her there. That day, though, she had come by herself.

"Excuse me," a handsome young man abruptly said to her. "Doesn't look like any other seats are left. Would you mind?"

Vera looked up, delighted that a man wanted to sit with her. The blue-eyed guy with brown hair had a kind, boyish look on top of a strong, muscular build, adding to the attraction. "Sure. Sit down."

"I'm Sam Sloan." He extended his hand. "You must work around here."

"Yes. I'm a secretary."

"Great." Sam unwrapped his sandwich and set a bag of potato chips in front of the tray. "I like these Subway places. They make a great sandwich."

"Me too." Vera studied his face. He had the wholesome look she liked, and he seemed like a nice guy. "Tell me about yourself."

Everything started with that simple request. Later Sam confessed that he'd seen her eating in the Subway a number of times, but that he never ate in those restaurants. That day he had followed her in, hoping for the opportunity to sit next to her and get acquainted. His comments about the great sandwiches were only a ploy.

Back in those days, Sam had been a computer specialist who still needed a couple of months to finish technical work at a local university. Vera had never seen anyone with the ability he had to make a computer dance. He could operate any type of machine and eventually helped her learn to use her IBM with skill and insight. In fact, that was how their relationship came to the big turning point.

"Why don't you come over to my place?" Sam had asked one morning over the phone. "I think I can help you learn to use your word processor better if we work on the big machine I have at the house. Some of my new software will help you."

"Okay," Vera said with slight hesitancy. "Why not?" After all, they had been going together for five months. "Sure. I can come over today."

"Why don't we have supper together first?" Sam suggested. "We can talk before we get down to business."

No reason to worry about time. It was Friday night and she wouldn't have to work the next day. "Where would you like to eat?" Vera asked.

"How about something different from fast food?" Sam responded. "Maybe—"

"Chi-Chi's!" Vera interjected.

Sam laughed. "I could have predicted that. Let's meet at 6:30."

Vera agreed. "See you this evening."

Supper had proved superb. The charming white-stucco-covered restaurant smelled wonderful and Sam had requested that the mariachi band come by their table and serenade them. Rather than his usual jeans and shirt, Sam wore a sport coat and tie. The evening felt especially romantic.

During supper, Sam told Vera more Chicago stories about his misspent adolescent days, when he cruised around a neighborhood that sounded frightening to Vera.

Vera studied Sam's face while they talked. Not only did he always treat her with thoughtfulness, Sam seemed to have a sixth sense about what made Vera happy. He bent over backward to keep a smile on her face. She didn't want to admit the fact out loud, but Vera knew that she'd fallen hard for this adventurous man from Chicago.

"Hey, this evening was great." Sam pushed back from the table. "I believe you like Mexican food better than anything else in the world."

"Most people either love it or hate it," Vera said. "I'm numbered among the lovers."

A grin spread across Sam's face. "Glad to hear that you're a lover."

She smiled and tried to stop turning crimson. "You know what I mean."

Sam grinned. "Let's go, Vera." He stood up and took her hand. "We have a special surprise at my place."

Ten minutes later, Sam pulled into the driveway at Windsor Arms Apartments and helped Vera out of the car.

"You'll like my place," Sam said. "And it's even clean today!"

Vera raised an eyebrow. "Oh, really?"

Sam laughed nervously. "Come on in." He led the way.

The apartment was filled with lots of books, pictures on the wall, but not much furniture—just a couple of chairs. In one corner of the living room stood a large computer on a desk especially constructed for such equipment. As Vera wandered around the room, studying Sam's decor, some of the pictures fascinated her while others seemed strange.

"Some of your art is, well, *different*," Vera said.

Sam pointed to a swirling figure arising in a wind of brilliant colors; little was distinct except the face. "That's one of my Mexican favorites. It's called *Sunrise of Mexico* and was painted by Siqueiros. Of course, it's a print."

"And what is this one over here?"

"That's Tamayo's painting called *The Heavens*. You can see the stars in movement."

Vera nodded. "Yes. Sure. I tend to be more on the realistic side."

Sam smiled. "You'll like this one better." He pointed to a print behind Vera. "Edward Hopper's one of my favorite artists. This picture is called *Sunday*. Like it?"

"Sure." Vera smiled. "It looks like an empty Sunday afternoon in Shelton, Iowa." She shook her head. "I think this is more the style that fits me." Vera glanced around the room again. "You certainly have sophisticated tastes."

"I like art." Sam pointed to a chair next to his computer. "Now let's play with my word processor. Sit down."

Vera sat down and leaned over the top of the desk. "Hmm. Interesting."

Sam abruptly swung her around and put his arms around her shoulders. "You are quite lovely. Do you know that's a fact?" He leaned over, kissing her with warmth and passion.

Vera opened her eyes slowly. "Is that the way you always begin your computer lessons?"

"No. Just for my best pupils." Sam pushed her hair out of her eyes. "Let's see what we can find on my computer." He turned on the switch and watched the screen warm up. "Did I tell you that this machine talks?"

Vera shook her head. "No."

"Quite amazing. Watch."

"Really?"

Sam started pressing keys. "Are you ready?"

"I guess so."

"Here's a special entry." Sam held down the shift key and pressed the F10 button. A message appeared.

"What?" Vera leaned closer to make sure her eyes weren't deceiving her. She read out loud, "I love you. Will you marry me?" She abruptly stopped.

"The computer is talking to you," Sam said.

Stunned, Vera shook her head. "Computers don't talk."

"They speak what somebody else has made them say."

Vera blinked several times and only looked at him.

Sam's eyes took on the intense gaze Vera would come to know well. "My computer is speaking for me and you need to answer."

Vera searched his face, filled with innocence and expectancy. She could feel her heart beating louder and louder. She kissed him gently and spoke softly, "Yes, Sam. I will marry you." They kissed again, for a long time. Vera finally drew back, looking into his eyes. "I love you, Sam."

The warmth of the memory kept tugging at Vera's heart. From her window she could see that the sky had begun to lighten and the night would soon be over. Vera closed her eyes and tried to go back to sleep.

11

By late Thursday afternoon, the rawness of Vera's anxiety rose to almost unbearable levels. She needed information; she needed details. What had Sam been working on? Why had his plane crashed? Where was his body? She repeatedly called the police station, but Chief Harrison's secretary reported that he was "in conference." She tried the Harrison home but no one answered. By six o'clock, panic settled in and for a few moments Vera feared she might slip over the edge. She finally retreated to Sam's office to struggle with her emotions alone.

The home office felt like the one room where Sam might emerge from behind a curtain or jump out of a closet any minute. Sam's presence was all over the place. Pictures, awards, and mementos from chasing criminals lay on shelves and tabletops and hung on the walls. A commemorative award from the

Rotary Club thanked Sam for public service. In the corner was a small file cabinet filled with notations and photos from cases. A new computer and matching printer sat on the desk, just as Sam had left them a couple of days earlier. His marred chair stood in front of the small desk where he always worked. Vera could almost feel Sam in the room with her.

She sat down at his desk and tried to remember something Sam had once told her. "Think of the worst that can happen," Sam had said, "then decide what you'd do under the toughest circumstances. Then you will be able to face your worst fears, no matter how big they are. Usually, things won't turn out as bad as you first thought." It seemed like the right thing to do now. Vera reached for a pencil.

A notepad Sam kept near the phone would work. Vera tried to consider what might prove to be the worst experience that she and Cara would have to face. Lack of money? Losing the house? Well, the family savings account would take them through a couple of months, but then they would need income—desperately. It was a good thing that Newton had offered her a job. Working as a private investigator was no longer an exercise in self-improvement—it was necessary. The car was paid for, and they could make that old thing last a long time. She put the pencil down and tried to think. What did she *really* need?

Only one thing mattered at that moment. Vera wanted to know what had happened to Sam. She wanted to stand at the crash site, feel it, smell the dirt on the ground, see the twisted wreckage of the airplane, to know without question that Sam was gone. Obviously, Harrison was avoiding her. Whatever crazy mess had occurred, the police chief probably wouldn't tell her the full facts, and the complete story was exactly what she needed.

Vera leaned back in Sam's chair. What was it that Harrison

had told her about the crash? The chief had said that the airplane crashed in a field north of Culpeper, Virginia, and he mentioned Highway 29. Vera wrote these facts down on the notepad. The airplane had been heading for Dulles Airport. She scribbled this information across the paper. This set of facts framed the biggest problem Vera had to face. Maybe the fragmented pieces floating around in her mind would come together if she could stand on the ground where her husband had died. Vera folded the piece of paper and put it in her pocket.

Thirty minutes later the phone rang and Cara answered. "Mom," she called, "it's the police chief."

Vera picked up the telephone in Sam's office.

"I'm sorry I didn't call earlier," Harrison said. "We've had problems getting information. You'll remember the CIA isn't known for public disclosure. We still don't have any information on what type of airplane they were flying."

"I see," Vera's voice went flat. She instantly recognized that Harrison shouldn't have had any trouble calling the local airport to find out what airplane they'd used. He wasn't playing straight.

"We are still trying to find the confirmations that you need and will continue to do so."

Vera looked at the notepad in front of her. "I believe you said that the wreck happened just north of Culpeper, Virginia, off Highway 29. Am I correct?"

"Uh . . . yes. I believe they crashed about five miles north of the town, a short distance off the highway. At least that's the information I have."

Grabbing a pencil, Vera scribbled the mileage down on her husband's notepad. "Thank you." She realized her voice probably sounded hard and ungrateful. She needed to lighten up a tad. "When might I hear from you again, Chief Harrison?" Again too formal.

"I'm not sure, Vera. However, as soon as I hear anything, I'll be back in touch with you."

"Thank you. I'll be here waiting." Vera dropped the phone into the cradle.

Harrison's message came across about like Dick Simmons's had yesterday: *Just the facts, ma'am,* but very few of those.

The more Vera thought about Harrison's phone call, the more disturbed she felt. She sat back in Sam's chair. At least the solitude felt like a shield, keeping others at an emotionally safe distance.

About twenty minutes later Cara knocked on the office door. "Mom? You in there?"

After a long hesitation, she answered. "Yes."

"A man's out here to talk with you. Says his name is Newton. Ace Newton."

"Oh, yes!" In that instant the fragments in Vera's thinking came together in her mind. She knew exactly what she needed to do. "Please bring him back here. I'd prefer to talk to Ace alone in this office."

Moments later Ace Newton walked in with his hair plastered down, wearing his usual brown pilot's jacket draped around his paunchy stomach. "Vera, I just heard the terrible news." He extended his hand. "What in the world happened?"

"Please sit down." Vera shook his hand. "I appreciate your coming, Ace."

"I couldn't believe the report I received a short time ago. Sam died in an airplane crash?" His voice dropped. "Can't be true!"

Vera slid to the edge of her chair. "Ace, I really don't know what's going on. As bizarre as it sounds, Sam apparently was on some type of special assignment with the CIA. Can you believe it?"

"CIA?" Newton's voice rose again. "You're kidding!"

Vera shook her head. "I wish I were. The trouble is that I can't get any clear information from the police department. Of course, I'm sharing confidential information because you're a detective . . . and a friend. I know you'll hold it close to the vest."

Newton's eyes narrowed and he lowered his head, like a bull preparing to charge. "They won't tell you *anything?*"

"Virtually nothing, but I don't think kicking their doors down will make any difference."

Newton leaned far back in his chair and crossed his arms over his chest. "Naw, you can't win by being tough with the P.D. They're masters at acting dumb."

"But something has come to mind that Cara and I need. Harrison told me where the airplane crash occurred. Can you help me find the place?"

Newton rubbed his chin for a moment and frowned. "Where did it happen?"

"Virginia. A town I never heard of called Culpeper, off of Highway 29. They were flying a private airplane toward Dulles Airport."

"Culpeper? Hmm. Must be somewhere close to Charlottesville. I got a buddy there. The town's on 29 and is close to the home of Thomas Jefferson. Visited the area once."

"Could you help me fly up there tomorrow morning? I want to actually see the site of the airplane crash."

Newton took a deep breath. "You're talking about a long, fast trip and a considerable amount of expense to boot. I don't know. We'll need to take a commercial flight to Washington, D.C., then a private plane to Culpeper."

"You're the private investigator, Ace. You told me that most of your work was boring. I don't think this twist in your life will put you to sleep."

"Vera, Sam was always a good friend, and we're looking at your starting to work with me next week. I'll do whatever I can to help you." Ace rubbed his neck. "I'm not sure what's possible. Like I said, we're talking some money here because we need to have a perspective from the air first."

Vera nodded. "We don't have much, Ace. But I think it would help Cara and me to know for a fact what happened to Sam. I've got enough money in savings to cover the costs and keep me going for a little while. If you can do anything to make this trip possible, we'd be more than grateful."

Newton stood up slowly. "You must be ready to leave as soon as I tell you, and I'll need you to cover my expenses. Beyond that, the trip will cost whatever we can knock down and I'll go for the lowest dollar." He opened the office door. "I'll try to get us out of here as early as possible in the morning."

Vera took a deep breath. "Ace, you're the first piece of good news I've had all day."

12

VERA SLOAN SLUMPED NEXT TO THE WINDOW as the 737 descended into Dulles Airport. Cara sat next to her, with Ace Newton on the outside by the aisle. Although Cara had held Vera's hand for the entire trip, neither had said much. Talking seemed too difficult. The dull hum of the airplane's engines sounded beneath the other passengers' chatter.

"We will be landing in Washington, D.C., momentarily," the pilot announced over the intercom. "Thank you for flying with American Airlines today. Remember us when you have the opportunity of flying again."

"Oh, Lord," Vera prayed under her breath with her head turned toward the window, "please, please help us." The roar of the airplane's engines drowned out her voice. "We need You to lead us to the exact place where Sam died and to support us when we stand at that awful spot. Help us get through these next few days. Please sustain Cara through this terrible time. In Jesus' name. Amen."

"We will be on the ground in less than five minutes," the flight attendant's voice said over the speakers.

Vera didn't move. When they had first entered the airplane, apprehension about flying had almost overwhelmed her. If Sam had died in a crash, they certainly could as well. For the first thirty minutes of the flight, Vera feared becoming so frightened that she might vomit. *Maybe dying wouldn't be so bad after all,* she thought. The fear hadn't left her but she'd finally shifted into neutral and kept praying through the entire trip.

"Vera, I've got some information for you." Ace Newton leaned forward and started giving her the first definite instructions of the entire trip. "We'll walk over to a side hangar where my friend Oswald Rufisen works. As a child he was a Polish refugee and he's become a great pilot. He's not charging us a dime for his time, just the cost of the fuel."

"Thank you," Vera muttered. She again realized how emotionally wrung out she was. Something deep inside her had hit the emotions-off switch, sending her into numbness. "I appreciate everything you have done."

"I have a shortcut for us when the airplane touches down," Ace continued. "You and Cara follow me and we'll get out to the adjacent hangar quickly."

Vera nodded and looked at Cara, sitting in her seat like a piece of stone. Her sad face had the same undone look that Vera felt. Her misery was clear.

The airplane hit the runway with a gentle bounce and rolled down the tarmac. Confusing possibilities tore at Vera's mind. She suddenly wanted to get on a return airplane and fly straight back to Colorado Springs without even peeling back the curtain on this horrible airplane crash. Yet Cara and she needed to see the final truth, and there didn't seem to be any other way than to look at the terrible wreckage. She'd stay.

As the airplane pulled up to the terminal, Vera abruptly remembered a tractor wreck on her family's farm in Shelton, Iowa, years ago.

On the side of one of those black-dirt cornfields, her father, Henri, had hit a sinkhole and the John Deere tractor flipped into it with Henri sitting behind the wheel. The hired man ran back to the house to tell Vera's mother, Maria, to call for help.

During February, Iowa's cold winds still blew more than an occasional flurry of snow while farmers plowed. No one needed to tell Maria or Vera what happened when tractors fell on people. Vera could still hear her mother's frightened calls for help on the telephone. Vera had panicked.

She had rushed out the back door of their white farmhouse and run like a racehorse to find the field with the upside-down tractor. She had only to cut across the field behind their house to see the front wheels sticking up out of the dirt hole and the large back tires nearly out of sight. The sight of the wreck had gagged her, leaving her feeling weak and wobbly.

Vera expected to have the same reaction when she saw the airplane wreckage where Sam had gone down. Everything about the crash sounded horrible beyond belief. In Henri's case, it turned out that a bank of unusually soft dirt had softened the crash and her father came away with only an injured foot. Obviously, this was not possible when a jet smashed into the ground.

Ace quickly maneuvered Vera and Cara through the terminal and out a back door. Ten minutes later they walked into the front office of a plain hangar housing smaller aircraft. A man with receding white hair stood in the back, wearing a flight jacket much like the one Ace wore all the time.

"Hey, Ossie!" Ace waved at the tall man. "We're here."

Ace trotted ahead of Vera and Cara, giving his friend a hug. For a few moments, the two men talked by themselves before Ace brought Oswald over. Ace's smile had turned into a frown.

"Want you to meet my friend Oswald Rufisen. Ossie, please meet Vera and Cara Sloan."

The Polish pilot nodded respectfully. "My pleasure," he said with a slight accent.

"Uh, Vera," Ace rubbed his flight jacket nervously. "You're sure you've got the directions right?"

"I gave you what Chief Harrison told me. The crash occurred five miles north of Culpeper, off Highway 29."

Ace and Ossie exchanged a puzzled glance.

"That's *exactly* what Harrison told me on the phone," Vera insisted.

Rufisen pursed his lips and looked down at the cement.

Ace nodded his head hesitantly. "I see." He looked back at Rufisen. "I guess that's where we need to look."

"Okay." Rufisen shrugged and pointed to his small airplane, a white Cessna 340. "Let's get in and see what we can find."

Something's wrong, Vera thought. *This Rufisen guy doesn't look like he wants to fly. I wonder what he told Ace?* She reached out to grab Newton's flight jacket but he was too far ahead of her.

Once they were beside the plane, Ossie offered Cara his hand and helped her inside. Ace had gone around to the other side and Vera had no choice but to follow her daughter.

"I'll have us out of here as fast as the tower will let us take off," Ossie said.

Vera settled back in her seat, watching Ace sitting in the

copilot's seat studying a map. She had no choice but to quietly allow the two men to be in charge of the flight.

"How fast does this airplane go?" Cara asked.

Ossie smiled. "We can cruise at around 220 miles an hour if we're not fighting a head wind."

"From the map I'd guess that the crash site is about fifty miles from here," Ace said. "We'll try the view from the air first, before we get a car."

"Yes," Rufisen answered, pushing the airplane's motors to full propulsion. "Shouldn't take long. We'll fly in a straight line until we get past Manassas, and then we follow Highway 28 until we switch over to 29. Got it?"

Ace nodded his head. The airplane rolled down the runway and quickly took off.

As the Cessna hummed over the Virginia countryside, no one said much. In a short while the busy four-lane stretch of Highway 29 opened up beneath them.

Rufisen broke the silence. "We're high enough to see quite a ways. At this point we are approximately five miles north of Culpeper." He pointed out the window. "You can see the town down there. Basically just another little Virginia burg. I'm going to drop lower." The airplane gradually descended and slowed.

Vera pressed her face against the window, expecting to see the twisted wreckage down beneath their airplane. But nothing except open fields unfolded in all directions. "I don't see anything," she said.

"I don't either," Cara added.

"I'll keep flying due west," Ossie said. "Keep looking."

Vera and Cara watched carefully but saw nothing irregular or unusual.

"I'm going to turn around and come back, as we are getting

out of the range you described," Rufisen advised. "Let's take another run over the area. I'll go east of Highway 29 this time."

For the next ten minutes, the airplane cruised back and forth, crisscrossing Highway 29. The Cessna even flew five miles south of Culpeper. Nothing unexpected appeared.

Vera leaned forward in her seat. "I don't understand!"

Rufisen looked at Newton and raised his eyebrows. "You want to tell her?"

Ace turned around in his seat. "Vera, yesterday I asked Ossie to identify where the airplane went down so we'd save time today. Back at the airport he told me that there'd been no report of any airplanes going down in the entire area, or in the whole state. No crashes have been reported anywhere around Culpeper in years—if ever. But the only way to be sure was to fly out and see for ourselves."

Vera took a quick, sharp breath and blinked nervously several times. "I don't understand," she repeated to herself.

"Neither do we."

13

RUFISEN PULLED THE CESSNA INTO THE hangar and his crew got out, reassembling inside a small coffee shop at the rear of the building. Vera and Ace sat down with Cara while Ossie got the adults coffee and the teenager a soda.

Ace took a long sip of coffee and looked at Vera. "What do you think?" he finally asked.

Vera shook her head. "I'm totally stunned. Blown away. What can I say?"

Ossie sat down and ran his hand through his white hair. "Look, when Ace asked about a plane crash, I didn't have any idea what he was talking about. Out here in the hangar, we would have been among the first to hear of a crash. I read the newspapers and called a couple of local television stations. I can tell you emphatically that no airplanes have gone down in this area in a long time. I even checked further before you arrived this morning. Nothing."

Cara cuddled next to her mother and took Vera's hand again. The teenager appeared to be no more than a frightened child.

"Vera, I know you're in shock, but what can you make of this situation?" Ace said.

"I don't think that Chief Harrison has completely leveled with me, but I have no doubt he believed that an airplane had crashed. Obviously, even government intelligence couldn't move the wreckage this quickly. As I recall, he got that information from a communiqué sent by a secret government agency to his office. Why would such an agency deceive the local police chief?"

Ace pursed his lips. "I certainly don't know."

Cara took a sip of her drink and stared straight ahead.

Finally, Rufisen pushed a local newspaper forward. "Here's the paper I checked. An airplane crash anywhere is always big news. You can look for yourself, but there's nothing in here to tell us one thing."

Ignoring the newspaper, Vera stood up and started walking around the table. "I'm supposed to be trained to deal with situations like this one, but right now I'm not even sure what my name is." She stopped. "Ace, I don't believe that a police agency would release a death report if it wasn't true." Vera kept pacing. "Obviously, we don't have an airplane crash, but I'd bet Sam was shot or died in some other way that they'd have an even harder time explaining right now." She stopped and leaned over the table. "I believe we can safely conclude that Sam is gone, but the problem is that we have no idea how it happened. Everyone agree?"

Ossie held up his hand. "Look, I'm just a pilot. I don't

want to get involved in any funny business. Politics and crime frighten me." He started backing away. "Count me out of this conversation." Rufisen turned and walked out of the coffee shop.

"He only promised to fly us out there," Ace offered apologetically.

"Sure," Vera said. "No hard feelings."

Ace leaned back in his chair and wiped the corners of his mouth. "I hate to say the words, Vera, but if what you've said so far is true, there's a considerable amount of danger floating around out there that could affect all of us. I didn't even bring a gun with me."

Cara jumped slightly and her eyes widened.

Vera took a deep breath and sighed. "You took the words right out of my mouth, Ace. I was going to suggest that the possibility of a personal threat was certainly feasible. Something is obviously being covered up here." She sat down at the table and ran her hands through her reddish hair. "We've got to be very careful that we don't stumble into something that could be even more hazardous for all of us."

"Mom," Cara almost whispered, "you're serious?"

"Yes, dear. I am."

"Sounds like we've become the prisoners that Solzhenitsyn describes in his book." Cara bit her lip. "Daddy's gone and now we're hanging by a thread—and we haven't done anything. Just like the Russian prisoners, we're caught up in a trap that grabs us without our understanding what's happened or where we're going. We're turning into creatures like the political puppets in *Ivan Denisovich*. Really scary."

Vera looked pained.

"We must be very careful until this puzzle is worked out,"

Ace added. "I don't want to be part of any more funerals for a long time."

Cara started crying.

"Oh, no!" Ace groaned. "I didn't mean to upset you, Cara."

Vera put her arm around her daughter's shoulders. "It's okay, Cara. We just have to talk about all the possibilities. You understand, don't you? We must be honest and up-front."

Cara nodded but kept crying. "I feel so helpless."

"Sure," Vera said. "I do, too, but remember what Reverend Dozier said when we were sitting in Daddy's office?"

Cara frowned.

"The minister told us that when we are the most helpless, we can find the help of God. When we've run out of our own capacity to solve the problem, the hand of God enters the scene on our behalf."

Cara nodded. "I remember those words."

"I guess that's where we are today, dear. None of us are clever enough to know what to do. We need the Lord's help."

Cara wiped the tears from her face. "Then I think we ought to pray."

Vera looked across at Ace. He didn't seem to be uncomfortable and was nodding. "Okay, dear. You want to pray for us?"

Cara closed her eyes. "Dear Father God, we really need Your help. Everything is in such confusion, and I can't see how it can work out right. We need You to come down here and get hold of all the pieces in this puzzle and make them fit together. Please help us. Amen."

Vera squeezed her daughter. "Amen," she echoed.

"Did the minister say anything else?" Ace asked.

"Yes," Vera answered. "He told us that the power of God isn't like a fly swatter smashing an insect. It's more like a dam on a lake that releases water slowly in order to make electricity. Omnipotence is the capacity to get a job done right. That's the brand of help we need right now."

"We've certainly got a job to do." Ace leaned over the table. "Now, I'm going to give you my opinion. I think that we need to sign you on as a company employee, Vera. You need to be a card-carrying professional investigator. I don't know what's ahead, but you've got to be ready to protect yourself while asking the hard questions. I think that's the best way for you to go."

Vera nodded. "I agree. I'm not going to let Chief Harrison or anyone else sandbag me. My husband simply isn't going to die and disappear into oblivion. You can bet on this, Ace. I'm going to pursue this crime, regardless of where it takes me."

Ace pursed his lips. "That's what I thought you'd say. Now, Vera, there's more that I've got to express. You're going to have to take on a new professionalism. Change your clothes. Fix yourself up. Get yourself back in touch with all that textbook knowledge you learned at college. You're going to be stretched farther than you ever dreamed possible."

For an instant Vera remembered the leap from being the little farm girl to the city woman Sam married. If anything, she'd have preferred to be a country girl. What Ace had just described was an even bigger leap, and Vera wasn't sure she had that much left in her. She stared at Ace.

Newton rubbed his mouth. "I'm willing to stand with you if you're ready to step into some big shoes."

Shoes! Vera remembered how important shoes had always been to Sam. *That's how he learned about what made people tick. Sam found studying people's shoes–where they'd walked, the wear and tear, the cost, and the shape—told him volumes about the person's character. Sam almost had a mystical twist about using shoes to track down the killer. He would expect me to wear big shoes,* she concluded.

"You ready to take that kind of stroll?" Ace asked.

"No," Vera said. "I'm not ready at all, but I don't think I have any alternatives. I will put on those shoes regardless of how poorly they fit."

14

FIVE HOURS AFTER THE DISCUSSION IN THE hangar, Vera, Cara, and Ace stepped off the airplane at the Colorado Springs terminal and walked down the hall toward the exit. Not much was discussed until after they had passed the security screening machines.

Then Vera slowed to a halt. "Ace, I'll be in your office on Monday morning, ready to go to work. I don't know where we're going. But I'll be prepared for a long and hard journey."

Ace looked down at the floor and nodded his head. "One way or another, I know we'll get this job done. We'll make it." Tears suddenly formed in his eyes and he abruptly reached out and hugged Vera. "I'm so, so sorry." He hurried away.

"Let's go, Cara." Vera put her arm around her daughter's shoulders. "Time to get home."

Vera drove from the Colorado Springs Municipal Airport

down Airport Road, west toward her house. For several miles neither she nor Cara spoke. Finally, Cara turned to her mother. "I've been thinking about our situation, Mom."

Vera looked at Cara, still wearing the same yellow sweatshirt she'd worn over her khaki chino pants for the last two days. She usually kept herself looking sharp, but lately her clothes appeared crumpled and wrinkled.

"I can't let you take on this battle by yourself. I want to help."

Vera took a deep breath. "Thank you, dear."

Vera turned onto Bijou Street and drove across the bridge over Monument Creek, continuing toward Twenty-third Street. She didn't say anything for several blocks. "You're asking a great deal," Vera finally answered. "I don't have any idea where all of this turmoil might take me. After all, Cara, you're only fifteen years old."

"I'm still asking you to let me be a part of this. And I'm nearly sixteen! That's why I'm asking for a promise. Mom, we're all that we've got."

"Yes," Vera answered. "You are right. I won't hold anything back or keep any secrets. Same for you?"

Cara forced a smile. "Sure thing."

On Saturday morning Vera walked into A Touch of Beauty Salon on Bijou Street, not far from her home. The sign on the plate-glass window promised:

MORE THAN A SALON!
BODY TREATMENTS, HAIR CARE, MAKEUP,
MASSAGE, NAILS, AND TONING FACIALS

The receptionist had said to show up at ten o'clock for her appointment, and Vera had come prepared for the works.

Earlier, Vera had paced back and forth worrying, wondering, pondering, struggling to know what to do next. One part of her mind said, *Hunker down and disappear from sight. Stay the way you are and don't fool with your appearance. Keep the predictable look. Lock the doors and don't come out until next spring.* But another voice shouted back, *No! Get yourself ready to take on whatever might come. Ace told you to look professional. If you don't take care of and protect yourself, no one else will. Buck up and get on with it!*

The latter idea prevailed.

When Vera had turned down the bedcovers, she found herself in tears. Every ounce of her body wanted to clutch Sam and hold him next to her, tight and close. She knew she hurt in a way that no beautician could cure.

Vera had slipped down by the side of her bed. "Oh, Lord, I don't know where in the world I'm going. I don't like to change my appearance, but I've got to be ready to face the world. Help me know how to walk through this jungle. I don't want to do anything that would offend You." Tears welled up in her eyes and she started crying again. "Amen," Vera finally whispered.

Somewhere in the black of night, she had drifted off. The next morning she got up and prepared for the trip to A Touch of Beauty for the grand makeover.

"I'm Vera Sloan," she told the lady sitting behind the front desk, "and I have an appointment at ten."

"Yes." The receptionist looked at her appointment book. "Charlize will be with you momentarily."

"Charlize?" Vera frowned.

The receptionist smiled and winked as if to hint that all the names in the place were pure showbiz. She handed Vera a book of hairstyles and suggested she look through it while waiting.

Vera started thumbing through the possibilities. She needed something that would work well with the quality and characteristics of her hair. The change should be stylish yet easy to care for. She finally found a photo of a cut she thought would work.

"Mrs. Sloan?"

Vera looked up. A tall, attractive woman who looked vaguely like Cameron Diaz stood above her.

"Yes, I'm Vera Sloan."

"Wonderful." Charlize twirled around and beckoned for Vera to follow her. "Come on back and let's start making you into a new woman. We'll come up with something that will stop your husband in his tracks."

Vera froze for a moment. She wanted to correct the woman but the words stuck in her throat. She gritted her teeth to keep from breaking into tears.

"You're a local person?" Charlize asked over her shoulder as she whirled her salon chair around.

"Yes."

"Glad you came in. I always love to work on new people." She slipped a nylon gown over Vera's clothes. "What do you have in mind?"

"I . . . I want to have a different look," Vera said hesitantly, slipping into the chair. "I have a picture of what I want."

Charlize narrowed her eyes and squinted for a moment at the photo. "Yes," she said slowly. "Yes. Quite a switch, but I believe that you'll be stunning. Good choice."

"I need to update my look—bring some style to my hair and makeup. I have a new job."

"Hey, that doll is Lauren Holly!" Charlize held the picture up to the light. "Does she ever look great! She's so glamorous."

Vera almost reached up to grab the picture back. Looking like a movie star was the last thing she had in mind. Who knew what people might say? Then again, maybe that was what she needed.

"We should do your eyebrows, Vera. They need to be shaped. Okay?"

"I guess. Sure."

"Look, sweetie, you seem to be a little nervous about this process." Charlize sat down on a stool next to the chair. "Am I reading you right?"

"I grew up in a rather simple country environment," Vera confessed. "I guess I never really completely cut that old rope."

"Do you want to?"

Vera nodded slowly and then spoke determinedly. "Yes, I must. I need to look professional."

"Then why don't you let me take what you've said so far, and see what I can do?" Charlize grinned. "We need to cut your hair quite a bit shorter to get this Lauren Holly look. I think I'd razor the nape of your hair so that it hugs your head." Charlize started walking around Vera, lifting her hair here and there. "I'll need to slice the top and front layers into wider sections so they'll overhang the close-cut back a bit. I'll leave the bangs irregular in length to add a little softness. Sound acceptable?"

Vera took a deep breath. "I think so. I hope my daughter likes the change."

"Right. She'll think that a movie star came home tonight. We'll also work on some new makeup to fit your hairstyle." Charlize went to work at a fast, steady pace. Vera closed her eyes.

Two hours later, Charlize turned Vera slowly around

toward the mirror so that she could see the completed look for the first time.

"That's me?" Vera gasped.

"Striking, isn't it?"

"I . . . I look great! I love the cut."

Charlize smiled wryly. "Honey, when I work on 'em, they always come out enchanting. You're a drop-dead, knockout-gorgeous redhead."

"Oh my!" Vera could see that her heart-shaped mouth had taken on a new depth and dimension of color. The tinted shadow around her blue eyes made them sparkle with a new brilliance and her skin radiated a soft glow.

"The next step is inside your head, Vera. You've got to start thinking of yourself as attractive instead of plain. You look like a sleek professional, so now you need to develop the eyes of a woman who's seen it all—and then some. Okay?"

Vera swallowed hard. "Sure."

"Your next step is to get some clothes to go with the look, Vera. Then you'll be ready to hit the office. I love your eyebrows!"

"You've done a great job, Charlize." Vera pulled out her checkbook. "I'll be back for the touch-up."

"Sure thing." Charlize took the check. "You call and I'll be here waiting."

Vera hurried out of the salon and drove home to pick up Cara. Thirty minutes later she drove into the nearest shopping center. She wanted to shop both Vanity and Jerome's Apparel stores, as well as a Petite Sophisticate outlet that ought to have clothes that would especially fit her. What would normally have been a party—buying a new wardrobe—now felt more like a grim job to be completed. Sam's death had changed everything in her life. Yet Cara helped to keep her upbeat.

"I can't wait to see what the new Vera is going to dress like," Cara said. "Oh, man! I think your hair is a total knockout."

"Thanks, dear. I've got a definite idea of what I want. Shouldn't take us long."

"You kidding? It'll take me ten hours!"

"Not today, Cara. Let's hit it."

Vera moved through the stores like a whirlwind, quickly finding a couple of suits that would give her the business-woman look. Cara discovered some turtleneck sweaters that offered her more options. A couple of pairs of pants fit in well. She was spending far more money than usual, but looking sophisticated was essential at this point.

"Mom, I think these outfits are great," Cara concluded. "Let's try the next store."

"Okay. Let's move."

Vera finally found the high-fashion style that would equip her to go anywhere she wanted. A leather jacket gave a chic look to the ponyskin skirt and long-sleeve T-shirt. She also threw in another business suit. A new pair of knee-high boots and a leather bucket tote finished the outfits. Vera Leestma had forever disappeared; Vera Sloan emerged with more than a touch of savoir faire elegance.

Come Monday morning she would walk into the agency wearing that red suit, her updated makeup, and a fresh haircut. Ace Newton wouldn't have any question that he had a *new* partner.

15

THE FREEZING MORNING WIND WHISTLED down the streets of Colorado Springs, blowing puffs of snow across the hood of Vera Sloan's car. At nine o'clock the temperature hovered around ten degrees. Vera turned her car into an empty parking space in front of Ace Newton's All-City Confidential Agency. Her new knee-high leather boots felt warm and reassuring. She pulled her long, black wool coat closer and hurried inside.

Newton was talking on the telephone and didn't look up. "Be with you in a minute," he shouted from his office.

Vera stood in the reception area, looking over the scene. The offices weren't large, but there was a second office area next to Ace and a desk out front for the secretary. The floor plan should prove adequate for everyone's needs. Vera liked what she saw.

"Sorry for the wait," Ace called from his office, hanging up the phone. "How can I help you, ma'am?" He walked into the outer area.

"Help me? You're kidding!"

Newton's mouth dropped. "Holy moly! Is that you, Vera, hiding under that short hair?"

"What do you think?" Vera smiled.

"Man alive! I wouldn't have recognized you walking down the street! Have you ever done a job on yourself."

"I look okay?" Vera's smile began turning into a frown.

"You're the one who's kidding. You're a knockout."

Vera grinned. "Great." She nodded her head resolutely. "I'm ready to go to work, Ace. Of course, we both know that my primary interest is working on what happened to Sam."

Ace pursed his lips. "It's been a short time, Vera. I take it that you've put all the funeral arrangements on hold."

"Yes, I talked with Reverend Dozier and we have an understanding. The first moment that we have something tangible, he's ready to hold the services. For the time being we'll wait."

"Cara's okay with that approach?"

"Cara's not okay about anything, but she's with me as long as I keep her abreast of what's happening. I'll have to involve her more than I'd like."

Ace studied Vera's face. "I guess the real question is whether you're ready to begin working today."

Vera looked down at the floor. "No, Ace, I'm not, but I don't have any alternative. If nothing else, I must stay busy. As long as I keep moving, I don't cry. Understand?"

Ace nodded. "Sure. But, Vera, I've been going over my books during the weekend. I'm sorry to tell you that I can't pay you until you start generating income for the office. I'm delighted to consider you an employee, but I can't cut you a paycheck unless you're making money for the agency."

Vera nodded. "I understand, but I've got to keep moving. Right now I've got to make sure that I know what happened to my husband. For a couple of weeks I can live without a paycheck." She forced a smile.

"Okay." Ace pulled at his chin. "It's a deal." He turned and beckoned for her to follow. "Come on back to my office." Ace walked inside and pulled up a chair. "Let's get started."

Vera sat down. "I'm ready."

"You passed the dress test. In addition to looking professional, the way you dress should make you look in control. That's the first button we've got to hit every day. Even if you're dealing with low-life scum, they've got to think that you're in the driver's seat. You're okay on that score."

"How about a secretary?" Vera pointed over her shoulder. "Who runs the front office?"

"I have a lady named Sally Armfield who comes in twice a week and does the dictation as well as the paperwork. You'll like Sally. She's around fifty and easygoing."

"Good. We'll get acquainted later in the week."

"You've got a permit to carry a concealed weapon?"

Vera nodded.

"Most of the time I don't carry a weapon, but who knows where this trip is going to take you. I'd suggest that you carry one."

"Sure. I understand."

"I've got a small camcorder should it become necessary during surveillance work. I also have some bugging devices when they're needed."

"Got you covered on those fronts, Ace. I've learned how to use all those items."

"How about a raincoat?" Ace grinned.

"Raincoat? I've got one at home."

"How about something that will stop bullets?"

Vera's mouth dropped slightly. "You're kidding. My plastic coat only does well to stop the rain."

"I'm thinking about a Kevlar-lined raincoat with the capacity to stop a nine-millimeter slug. They cost more than a thousand bucks, but I'd assume your life is worth slightly more. Right?"

Vera coughed. "A *thousand* dollars?"

"Afraid so, but it only needs to work once, and you'll never be thinking about cashing in on the money-back guarantee. I know we're talking some expense here, but I think this is what you want in your backseat."

Vera nodded. "You bet."

"Later in the week I'll go over the electronic paraphernalia that I keep in the back room. We've got bugs, sweepers, long-distance parabolic and directional microphones. I've even got debugging equipment. Everything we could need."

"Okay." Vera leaned back in her chair. "Sounds like you're equipped for much more than you indicated the other day while we were eating lunch."

"I was a bit on the modest side, but the truth is still that most of what I do, day in and day out, is far more on the boring end of the scale."

Vera pushed her short red hair back. "Sam's situation won't be. I'm sure of that fact. You ready to talk about what I should do to pursue his case?"

Ace pushed back from his desk and stuck his long legs out in front of him. "Oh, man. We're talking a toughie, Vera." He crossed his arms over his round stomach. "Well, you already know the police aren't going to help you much. What do you know about the case Sam was working?"

"Literally nothing. Nothing at all."

"Hmm, that was what I was afraid you'd say." Ace opened his bottom desk drawer and pulled out a newspaper. "I've been thinking about the circumstances surrounding the telephone call he received early on Monday morning. Have you given any thought to that?"

"No, I haven't."

"One big event happened on Monday morning." Newton shoved the paper across the desk. "Look at Tuesday's front-page stories and tell me what you see."

Vera quickly skimmed the stories. "Not much here about international news," she said. "Story about a skiing accident. A bad car wreck happened out on the interstate. Here's a story about a bank president dying of a heart attack, but I don't see—"

"Go back, Vera. Look at that last story again."

Vera started reading the story out loud. "George Alexander was found dead in the parking lot—"

"Stop." Ace held up his hand. "When did this man die?"

"Well, I'll be. That's not very long before someone called Sam and he ran out of the house."

"Vera, we don't know if there's any relationship between this man and Sam's disappearance, but it's the most significant event I can find that fits your timetable."

Vera looked thoughtful. "I don't have any idea who this Alexander is, except that I've seen his name in the papers occasionally."

"Okay." Ace pulled his chair closer. "We need to search for a connection."

"All yesterday afternoon I thought about what Sam might have been doing that he hadn't talked to me about. I thought about searching his office for any possibilities, but I decided to wait until after we talked this morning. Now I'm ready to take the house apart."

"Good. I want you to start searching at home, because we can't go to Sam's office at the police department. You need to hit the bedroom, the closets, any unexpected place where Sam could have hidden anything. Since his assignment was top secret, he wouldn't have left material lying around on his desk. I'm hoping that he didn't keep all of his special notes or work materials downtown. Can you search his home office today?"

"Absolutely. I'll start on it immediately."

"Keep this name of George Alexander clearly in mind."

Vera stood up. "Cara's coming home during the noon hour. She wanted a breather from school in case things got overwhelming. She can help me."

Ace nodded. "All right. This is how every case begins. We just go in and start looking."

16

TWENTY MINUTES AFTER LEAVING THE ALL-City Confidential offices, Vera pulled up in her driveway. As she turned off the car, she stared at the garage. Possibly that was the place where she ought to begin before searching Sam's office when Cara came home. She still was bundled up—she might as well tackle the coldest location first.

For the next thirty minutes, Vera poked and probed around the two-car garage, looking in boxes, behind a worktable, and through an upright storage cabinet. She found nothing unusual. She did discover her blender, which she hadn't been able to locate for a month, and a couple of towels from the kitchen. Sam must have used them for some project or another and not put them back where they belonged.

Vera closed the door to the garage and took off her coat. Working in the warmer indoors would be a big plus. She started walking from room to room, looking in every corner, searching for some hidden nook where Sam might have stashed some of his notes. Everything seemed so familiar and obvious that she feared overlooking an important clue.

On the other hand, how in the world did she know that he had *ever* left anything concealed around their house? The whole idea was only a thought that started with her conversation with Ace Newton. Maybe she wasn't doing anything but chasing a wild goose.

Still, Vera returned to the closet by the front door and started looking again. *Nothing in there; back to the bedroom.* She got down on her hands and knees and peered under the bed, behind the dresser drawers, in the back of the closet; she handled all of Sam's clothes. Nothing. Absolutely nothing.

Vera walked into the kitchen. It had been so unlike Sam not even to give her a hint of what he was doing. Sure, the police department had its code of confidentiality, but she'd helped him on three cases and her input had made an important difference. Moreover, they'd talked confidentially many times, but Sam hadn't even given her the first clue about this secret case. Chief Harrison hadn't called her in days, which meant that he wasn't prepared to leave anything on the table for her to consider.

Vera poured a cup of coffee and picked up her Bible. She flipped through the book of Psalms, stopping on Psalm 34. For a moment the silence cleared her mind, and then she started reading the verses. Near the end of the chapter, a couple of lines leaped out at her. She read out loud:

> The LORD is close to the brokenhearted
> and saves those who are crushed in spirit.

A righteous man may have many troubles,
but the LORD delivers him from them all;
he protects all his bones,
not one of them will be broken.

Vera laid the Bible on the table. "Oh, Lord," she prayed, "thank You for this promise. I need You to be close to me. I am truly numbered among the crushed in spirit. This verse declares that righteous people have troubles, and that's where Cara and I are today. But the promise is that You will deliver us. We really need Your help. In Jesus' name. Amen."

For a few minutes Vera wept quietly, but she finally got up and emptied her cup in the sink. Then she searched the kitchen, taking drawers out of the cabinets, looking at the back of the woodwork, probing through the pantry, checking every angle, but again she found nothing that she didn't expect. Sam simply hadn't hidden anything in the kitchen.

Vera glanced at the wall clock. Cara would be coming home soon, and she would need to eat quickly so she could help Vera search Sam's office. A little soup and a sandwich ought to be enough. Vera grabbed a can of Campbell's chicken noodle soup from the pantry as well as lettuce, tomatoes, and bologna out of the refrigerator. In ten minutes she had everything prepared and two plates set on the table. The smell of the soup simmering on the stove offered its own consolation.

Vera sat down to wait for Cara and looked at Pikes Peak looming beyond their backyard. The glory of the magnificent snow-covered mountain always offered encouragement. "I will extol the LORD at all times," the psalmist had written, and that was the way Vera felt looking at the tree-covered slopes.

"I'm home, Mom!" Cara bounded through the back door and into the kitchen. "I'm glad you're here."

Vera kissed her daughter. "How'd it go this morning?"

Cara sighed. "Everyone was more than nice to me. One teacher went out of her way to express her sympathy. A couple of times I thought I might cry, but I got by well enough." Cara sat down at the table. "By lunchtime I knew I needed to come home. The extreme niceness of my friends started annoying me. I got nervous."

"Sure. Glad you came, Cara. I want you to eat quickly and help me before you go back to school. I've been taking the house apart looking for some clue, a hint, anything that your father might have hidden around here that would tell us more about the case he was pursuing. I've waited to start on the most important area—his office. Could you help me?"

"Excellent, Mother! That's exactly what I want to do." Cara sipped the soup and started eating her sandwich. "Won't take me long."

During lunch Vera described the sort of material that they were looking for. As soon as they finished, Vera and Cara went back to Sam's office and started searching.

"I want you to begin on the left half of the room and I'll take the right," Vera said. "Remember: don't overlook anything."

Vera looked at the computer, the most likely place for Sam to have hidden data. She'd save the main drive for a hard look after Cara went back to school.

"Mother," Cara said, "would Dad have possibly put something on the underside of a table or a desk?"

"Your guess is as good as mine, Cara. I wouldn't discount anything as a possibility."

Vera started opening desk drawers, inspecting the contents

carefully, and then pulled the drawers completely out to look at the inside of the desk. Again, most of what she saw was, unfortunately, familiar. Routine papers, pens, paper clips. Nothing exceptional.

"I think that . . . maybe . . . possibly . . . I've found something," Cara said as she tugged on something.

Vera whirled around. "What?"

Cara lay on her back, her hands wrapped around something on the underside of the printer table.

"What did you find?"

"Ummph! Just a moment." Cara changed positions. "The edge of a computer disk is sticking out but wedged between the pieces of wood."

Vera got down on her knees and ran her hand along the edge. "Yes, I can feel it. Cara, run into the kitchen and get a screwdriver." Vera pushed upward gently while waiting for the implement.

"Here you are, Mother."

Vera pried up gently, pulling the disk at the same time. "I got it!" She pulled out the disk. "No one would put a disk under a tabletop by mistake. I'm sure your father hid this."

Cara sat down at the computer and immediately fired it up. "Let's see what's here." The menu opened, and Vera pushed the disk into the floppy-drive slot, watching for the disk directory to come up on the screen.

"Wow!" Cara exclaimed. "Can you believe it? *Look at this!*"

17

VERA AND CARA STARED AT THE COMPUTER, struggling to understand the names listed on the screen. The headings didn't make any sense.

Vera moved her finger down the screen. "What a strange set of names! *Irneh* and *Airam?* What in the world do those designations mean?"

Cara scratched her head and stared at the screen. "Daddy and I talked about computer stuff all the time. I'm trying to remember anything unusual that he told me about titling."

"Look at this one. *Arev?* Here's another. *Arac?* Maybe it's a foreign title of someone or someplace."

Cara kept staring; then a smile started spreading across her face. "Mom, remember how Dad liked to play games with people's names?" Cara put her finger on the names Vera had just questioned. "Look again. What do you see?"

Vera blinked several times. "The whole thing's a total mystery to me."

"Look again. I remember what he often did." Cara grinned broadly. "*Arev* ought to ring a bell with you."

Vera shook her head. "Sorry. No lights went on."

"Think about it, Mom."

Vera sighed. "Sorry. I don't see it."

"*Arac* is *Cara* spelled backward! *Arev* is *Vera* spelled the same way. Get it? Dad has spelled our family names in reverse. That's how he camouflaged these files. Simple but effective!"

Vera's mouth dropped. "You're absolutely right. *Irneh* is my father Henri's name. *Airam* is my mother, Maria. But our problem is that this is nothing but a list of names. There's no material here."

"I think that Dad must have been saving this as a secret directory of some sort," Cara mused. "Trouble is, we need to find out how to get to where these names are leading us."

"I don't understand."

Cara kept staring at the screen. "Nobody was better at using a computer than Dad. He taught me stuff that my teacher at school didn't even know."

"So?" Vera sighed in exasperation.

"So, I need to become a hacker of sorts," Cara answered. "Let me show you something that Dad taught me." Cara reached down to the hard drive and rebooted the computer. For a moment she watched the screen. "When the log-in prompt comes up, I'll hit *Cancel.*" She quickly typed on the plastic keys. "All this does is disable passwords."

Vera watched Cara type, wait for the machine to process, then type some more. "What exactly are you doing?"

"I'm trying to get to a place on the disk where we can use

these names we found. I think Dad created a secret place for the information the names represent."

"Hurry."

Cara typed quickly, using the machine like a professional. "Here we go," she said. "Okay, Mom. Let's see what happens when we bring this material up." Cara hit the top file name, *Irneh,* and immediately the file opened.

"Yeah!" Vera clapped her hands. "You've done it!"

"How strange." Cara leaned forward, staring at the screen. "This looks like a series of letters written from someone named Ivan Bashilov to George Alexander."

Vera rocked backward. "Alexander! That's one of the names we're looking for."

Cara looked more closely at the screen. "This material seems to be a copy of a letter about banking. The Bashilov guy is telling this George Alexander how to handle large sums of money."

Vera pounded on the desk. "We've found it, Cara! Alexander died last Monday morning of a heart attack. No question about it: your father was doing some kind of investigation on Alexander. Bashilov will prove to be an important aspect of this case. Way to go, Cara!"

"Mother, I hate to tell you, but I've got to go back to school. I'm going to be late if I don't leave quickly."

"Sure, dear. I understand. Why don't you hurry back and I'll keep working on what's in these documents."

"Okay, Mom. I'll be eager to know what else you find out. And I think your office search is over—I doubt that there would be another disk hidden around here, since so much material can be crammed into only one of these things."

"Cara, I'd guess that we've hit the jackpot. Thanks a million."

Cara hugged her mother. "Feels like I did something that

truly counts. I can face the rest of the afternoon now." She hurried out of the room.

"I'll see you tonight," Vera called after her. "Take care, dear!" The front door slammed. Vera turned back to the computer and started reading every letter several times. For the next half hour, she studied the file's contents.

This Bashilov character must have been bringing in the money by the truckload. We're talking hundreds of thousands of dollars!

All of Ivan Bashilov's correspondence was from the same address: the Samson Building on Ninety-sixth Street in New York City. *Looks like Bashilov lives in the Big Apple,* she mused. *He obviously stayed close to the place where they keep the big money.*

Vera started accessing other files. Slowly the system that Sam used began to emerge. He had taken the roles that people played in the Sloan family to designate the type of material he was filing. Because Henri was the grandfather, all data centering on Bashilov had been filed under that name. The designation meant that the Russian was the leading figure of the money operation. She found under *Arev,* her name spelled backward, elaborate descriptions of George Alexander and his investments in the Colorado Springs area. Sam must have seen the bank president as the mother of the operation.

Vera started making notes on what Sam had written in each of these files. Apparently Alexander had been investing Bashilov's money as well as handling his funds as a banker. The bank president had bought up a number of business and land holdings around the Colorado Springs area as well as in Utah and Wyoming. He seemed to have bought property with funds transferred from Switzerland and then transferred the property titles into Bashilov's name. The system had a number of ins and outs, but the bottom line appeared to be that the

Russian was investing a great deal of the money in assets that should appreciate in price, maybe turn out to be hedges against inflation.

But why would Sam be investigating this twist in Alexander's business? Vera asked herself. *I can't see anything wrong here.* She turned to other files.

Eventually, a file named *Mas* surfaced, which was filled with dates and notations. Sam had kept a running record of what he was observing and discovering. He had apparently tapped into both the e-mail system that Alexander used as well as a dedicated fax line. The earliest entry indicated that Sam had started working on this case as far back as last April, and Sam had maintained a constant observation of Alexander well into the fall of that year. Sam appeared to have compiled an incredible amount of information, including everything about the man, just about down to the size of his underwear.

On the screen appeared pictures of the Investor's Bank building, Alexander's home and wife, and a nice big photo of sweet-looking George Alexander himself, who appeared about as villainous as one of Cara's schoolmates. His round face and balding head made him look like a caricature of a banker. Expensively dressed, Alexander didn't seem to be much more than an average local investment counselor.

Bashilov's picture popped up—an ugly guy who might raise havoc whenever and wherever he got the chance. He had a neck like a bull with a head as slick as a billiard ball. Vera could believe this creep had the capacity to be the source of real, old-fashioned trouble.

"But how was Sam caught up in this operation?" Vera pondered out loud. She started back through Sam's notations, reading them carefully and methodically.

Vera quickly realized that Sam had apparently discovered an important difference between what Alexander spent and the actual amount of money given to the sellers. He noted that about $200,000 to $250,000 had disappeared from the Russian's account.

Slowly Vera began to wonder if Sam had worked his way into some kind of personal relationship with Alexander. The banker appeared to have trusted him. Sam's notations left Vera with a strange, uneasy feeling.

How bizarre. Vera turned away from the computer and looked out the window. *How extremely unusual. Doesn't seem like the way a policeman usually operates.* Vera rubbed her forehead and stared out at the street. "Not at all," she whispered.

She looked back at the next entry on the screen.

PEAK NATIONAL BANK. DENVER.
$200,000.00
106006779:0404014320. SAM SLOAN.

Vera blinked several times, then rubbed her eyes. She couldn't believe what she was seeing.

For several minutes Vera tried to bring other meanings to the material she had been reading. A terrible accusation kept pushing to the surface. She couldn't deny it any longer.

Vera gasped. "No! It couldn't be!" She covered her mouth with her hand. "Lord, please forbid it!"

But the implication had become clear in her mind. What if Sam *had been* working both sides of the street? Taking money? Hiding it? Such large amounts of money had been flowing through Alexander's bank and out into properties that it wouldn't have been hard to dip into an overflowing pot. What if Sam had started double-dipping? Even the hint of such an idea sent ice racing through her veins. She froze in the chair and couldn't move.

Sam wouldn't steal! Vera shook her head, but her mind wouldn't stop repeating the disturbing thought. *Or would he? Could he have been offering undercover protection to the banker? What if he ran out of their house because something had happened to Alexander and it ruined the business deal they had been operating? Sam might have found himself in double jeopardy.* Her breathing started coming hard and fast.

Nothing about the scheme made any sense to her. The mere thought of Sam on the wrong side of the law left her disoriented and out of sync with the world she had known forever. She kept breathing rapidly.

I can't tell anyone about this possibility, she thought. *I've got to protect Sam's reputation. I can't let his memory be smeared in any way. Even the thought makes me feel ill. Got to let it cool. Settle for a while. I sure can't tell Ace Newton. I've got to handle this completely on my own.*

Vera's isolation deepened, becoming hideously empty and threatening. She started to walk out of the office, but her legs turned to spaghetti and she started slipping down to her knees. After a moment, Vera sprawled out on the carpet, sobbing as if her heart had broken into pieces.

18

DICK SIMMONS AND BASIL ABBAS HAD SPENT nearly an hour driving from Colorado Springs to the edge of Denver. Taking Interstate 25, they drove through Littleton, passing the Inverness Golf Club and heading north. Chief Harrison had asked them to check out a peculiar lead and keep the inquiry on the quiet side. Simmons had looked askance. It was not how he liked to play the game, but he kept his mouth shut.

Simmons turned his plain brown Dodge back to the east on Ohio Avenue and pulled into a parking lot on Downing Street. In front of him was a neighborhood Peak National Bank situated in a conventional blond-brick building.

"This looks like the place," Basil said.

"Sure does. Let's go in." Simmons led the way.

"Is the manager here today?" Simmons asked the receptionist. "I need to speak to him or her."

"Yes." The lady pointed to an enclosed desk area. "She's in there. Her name is Marilyn Stout."

"Thanks." Simmons walked to the door of the office. "Ms. Stout, may I have a moment of your time?"

The attractive, middle-aged lady looked up. "Certainly. What can I do for you gentlemen?"

Simmons held out his badge. "I'm Dick Simmons with the Colorado Springs Police, and this is my partner, Detective Abbas. May we ask you several questions?"

The woman's eyes widened. "Yes. Of course."

"I need you to reference an account for us." Simmons pushed a piece of paper across the desk. "We want to know if there is any money in an account with that name and number."

Marilyn Stout looked at the scribbling for a moment and then turned to her desk computer and started typing. "S-a-m S-l-o-a-n." She looked at the numbers again. "1-0-6-0-0-6-7-7-9." She typed quickly. "Ah, yes. Here it is." The woman leaned forward. "There is quite a bit of money."

"How much?"

"Two hundred thousand dollars," she said quietly.

Simmons walked around the desk and looked over her shoulder. "You're not kidding. Can you print out a copy of this material?"

"Yes." Stout started typing again.

"Who is allowed to write checks on this account?" Basil asked. "I mean, who has access to this money?"

"Only Mr. Sloan."

"Hmm, interesting. I'd appreciate your keeping this inquiry confidential."

The woman nodded her head. "You can count on me." She handed the printout to Simmons.

"We appreciate your help." Simmons turned and marched out of the bank, with Abbas close behind. He immediately walked across the street and jumped into his car.

For several minutes he sat behind the wheel, staring at the amazing amount of money that Sam Sloan had deposited in the Peak Bank. "I wonder—"

"Don't wonder," Basil interrupted. "Check it out."

"Yeah," Dick said. "Let's try a long shot."

"I'm ready."

Dick flipped on his cell telephone and punched in the number of Ace Newton's All-City Confidential Agency. The secretary answered and quickly put him through to Newton.

"Ace?" Simmons began. "I got a question for you."

"Simmons, don't you ever tell anybody your name?"

"I'm in a hurry," the detective answered. "I need a little confidential insight. Can you tell me anything about Vera Sloan?"

"*Anything?* Come on. You're kidding me."

"I want to know what kind of financial shape she's in."

"Why?" Ace asked. "You going to take up an offering for her down there at the police station?"

"Come on, Newton. I'm asking you a serious, confidential question."

"Well," Newton hedged. "I don't know much about the Sloans' private world, but I know that she had to go to work for me. They don't have any more money than any other cop does, if that's what you mean."

"No signs that she's got anything stashed away?"

"Are you kidding me, Simmons? The woman is straight as an arrow. No, Vera Sloan is struggling to make ends meet."

"Thanks, Ace. Let's keep this conversation between the two of us."

"Sure."

Simmons hung up. "Now, ain't this a strange, smelly kettle of fish? Vera doesn't seem to know anything about this bank account. Nothing."

Basil pushed the long strand of hair out of his eyes and stared straight ahead. "I don't know," he muttered. "I simply don't know."

"Doesn't look good for Sam."

"As Saint Origen once said, 'Don't make a hasty judgment lest you fall into sin.'"

"What? Origen said that?"

"No, but he should have."

By the middle of Monday afternoon, Vera decided that she should call Ace Newton with a report of what she had found in the office. Knowing that she was making progress would buy her more time to think through what to do next. She dialed All-City.

"That's right, Ace." Vera pressed the telephone closer to her ear. "I found enough of Sam's notes to know that he was definitely working on the Alexander situation. The bank president is our link to what Sam was doing for the CIA. I have his computer files open in front of me right now."

After a long pause, Ace said, "Exceptional, Vera. You've done better than I thought you would."

"It will take me the rest of the afternoon to work on this material." Vera looked around the office that she had cleaned, dusted, arranged, and rearranged a million times. An emotional heaviness pressed against her chest.

"Sure. Stay with it until you've got some sense of where the next step will take us."

"Okay." Vera relaxed slightly. At least Newton wasn't pushing her to return to the office. "I'll keep going."

"Vera." Ace hesitated, then asked, "You and Sam got any savings put back anywhere? I mean some real money."

"Come on, Ace. I'm working for you because we don't have much put back. Like I told you, I can't afford to go more than a couple of weeks without a paycheck. No, I don't have a hidden stash." Her stomach tightened, but it was the truth.

"See you in the morning, Vera." Ace sounded distant.

"I will be there." Vera hung up. At least she had the rest of the afternoon, that evening, and early tomorrow morning to think about what she would tell Newton. But the pressure was far from gone. Vera pushed the telephone back on the desk and looked out the window at the scene on Twenty-third Street.

Cars occasionally cruised past their house. The temperature hadn't risen and it was still freezing outside. A stretch of sparkling snow ran down over the gutter and into the street. *Good day to make a snowman,* Vera thought, *and Sam had always loved doing that with Cara.*

Vera rubbed the side of her face nervously. Maybe Sam hadn't done anything more than the job that the CIA gave him to do. The data wasn't clear, but it had given her a strong impression that Sam had been walking on the wrong side of the street, which wasn't the right place for a stroll.

Vera kept staring out over the snow-covered lawn. The uniformity of the unending expanse of whiteness had a flatness that left her feeling empty. She needed a miracle—an answer to drop out of the sky.

Vera had pressed Reverend Dozier to tell her why the

tragedy happened and in turn, he'd said that the issue was *how they used* what had occurred. Well, she wasn't going to let all the good things Sam had done over many years of hard service be ruined by what seemed to have evolved from nothing but the terrible pressure of the moment.

Maybe Sam was caught in a bind about which I know nothing, Vera thought. *Possibly there's a circumstance that explains why he needed the extra cash. I'm sure if Sam were here, he'd tell me and everything would abruptly make sense. At least there'd be an explanation . . . but I don't even have an idea of why he used Peak National Bank to hide the money. Nothing.*

But Sam wasn't there and wouldn't be ever again. And that was the rub. Vera had no alternative but to act on her own. She couldn't even tell Cara, lest she say something under some unexpected circumstance that might throw everything into turmoil. It could happen at school, with one of her friends, in front of Ace Newton or a cop—anywhere. No, Vera would have to harbor the story as if it were nothing but her own darkest secret.

She decided to finish searching the office, in case any more clues were available. When nothing turned up, she returned to the computer files, checking out what had been said, to whom, about what—the whole nine yards. After thirty minutes of reading, one idea became crystal clear: this Bashilov character had an office in New York City in something called the Samson Building. If she wanted to find Bashilov, that was the place to look!

Vera jumped up from the desk and hurried across the room to start rummaging through Sam's set of reference books, looking for his atlas of the United States. When Vera found the book on the bottom shelf, she quickly thumbed through the pages until she found a detailed map of New York City. Sure enough! Ninety-sixth Street cut through Central Park on the north side.

If she flew into LaGuardia Airport, it should not take much time to cross over the East River and run down Park Avenue where the Samson Building was situated. She could find out in a hurry who Ivan Bashilov was.

Vera stared out the office window again. Cara would insist on going. Taking Cara out of school was filled with complicated issues, but Vera knew that her fifteen-year-old daughter wouldn't sit still while she flew by herself across half the United States to make sense out of what had happened to Sam. At the least, Cara would scream if she didn't go with Vera on the start of this trip. Vera would have to negotiate.

Compromise? Stealing? Negotiating? Where in the world would this roller coaster stop? Vera shuddered. Each inch of the trail violated her values, ideals, hopes. How must this look in the sight of the Almighty?

And where was God in all of this turmoil? Reverend Dozier had said that God's purposes weren't as easy to fathom as humans might think. He'd put that on the mild side! If omnipotence had the capacity to achieve a purpose, where in the world was God in this struggle? Vera found it difficult to see any rhyme or reason to their mess.

Anger started to boil again, and Vera felt like she was standing on the edge of an emotional explosion. "Got to keep my head," she groaned. "Can't let myself blow up and slide over the edge. If I crater, all is lost."

Tears started running down her cheeks. Every thought felt excruciating. A throbbing lump rose in her throat and Vera could no longer avoid the real pain that hovered behind her little aches and nagging woes. Her husband was gone forever, and she felt like her heart and mind would shrivel into nothing. Depression surged like an angry army on the march.

19

SEVERAL HOURS LATER, VERA HAD COMPOSED herself. When Cara came home from school, she wanted to know what Vera had discovered.

"I checked out the entire office," Vera explained, "and you were right: I didn't find any other disks or data. I think the one disk was all Sam hid in there."

"Hmm." Cara sat down at the kitchen table. "I'd hoped that you would find something more."

"So did I, but I think the material on that one disk covered everything that your father was doing."

Cara began drumming her fingers on the kitchen table. "What are we going to do next, Mom?"

"We?"

Cara looked up with a raised eyebrow. "I believe that we were in a 'we process' from the get-go. At least that's what you promised me. Right?" Cara leaned over and raised both eyebrows.

Vera studied her daughter's eyes. The defiant, stubborn intention that always clashed with Sam's ideas was written all over Cara's face. She wouldn't give an inch.

"Yes." Vera sighed. "I agree."

"Then as I said, what are *we* going to do next?" Cara leaned back in her chair.

Vera ran her tongue across her teeth and rubbed her forehead. "I think that I need to go to New York City. It's a big trip, but I don't see much alternative."

"Oh!" Cara's eyes lit up. "I'd like to go there."

"Yeah, that's what I thought you'd say." Vera shook her head. "Cara, I'm not sure what we're doing. Do you understand? I could be walking off the end of a gangplank."

Cara nodded soberly. "Mom, I do realize that we're not running off on a pleasure junket. Yes, I know that this entire business could turn out to be dangerous."

"After all, we're trying to find out who killed your father." Vera looked as if she might cry. "My best guess is that we'll need to fly to New York City quickly to see if we can run down this Bashilov man that was on the computer files. After that, I don't know what we'll do."

Cara pursed her lips. "I understand."

"And I don't think that you can be out of school more than a few days. If you go with me, we have to have an agreement that you'll come back when I tell you—no fierce arguments. Got it?"

Cara wiggled uncomfortably in her chair. "That's pushing the envelope, Mom. How can I agree to a situation that hasn't happened yet?"

"Because you can't miss but a limited amount of school, that's how. You either agree now or you're not going, young lady."

Cara rubbed her eyes. "This is truly unfair."

"I'm not interested in being equitable. I'm only concerned with keeping you informed, as I promised, and your keeping up with your schoolwork." Vera leaned closer to Cara's face. "Do we have an agreement or not?"

Cara shrugged. "I guess I have to agree."

"Good, because I'm too upset to get into one of those shouting matches that you often had with your father. If we're both in agreement, then we can go forward."

"When would we leave?"

"I think immediately."

"Immediately?" Cara's eyes widened.

"Time is of the essence, Cara. We need to act as quickly as possible."

20

VERA PULLED BACK THE BEDSPREAD AND LAY down, trying to drift off to sleep. She'd found it difficult the night before and didn't expect to slumber better tonight. The pain she felt during the day turned worse when darkness fell.

Her bed felt warm and comforting, but was still half-empty. That special vacancy hurt the most. The everlasting vacuum Sam left filled Vera with despair. She reached over and felt the soft pillow next to her head. His fragrance was still on the pillowcase. Maybe if she remembered good things, the night would pass faster. Vera stared at Sam's picture sitting on the nightstand.

Sam had always been such an adventurous bundle of lightning. His police work suited him: Sam could walk in and out of deadly situations like Batman swinging in on a rope, saving the victim and then flying back to safety. The Sloans had had their arguments over some of those escapades, and Sam's risk taking could make Vera angry. But her life never lacked excitement. Sam filled every day with new promise.

Vera remembered his coming into their small apartment in Denver years ago and flopping down in the chair against the wall. He dropped a newspaper and stretched out his legs across the bare wooden floor in their bedroom. Cara was only a baby then, asleep in her crib in the next room. The room and apartment were sparsely furnished.

"Got an idea!" Sam said enthusiastically. "Want to hear it?"

Vera remembered pushing herself up in bed and noticing how Sam's eyes had started to sparkle. For days they had been dull and somewhat on the lifeless side. "As always," Vera said.

"You know that I'm not happy with my job," Sam had said. "In fact, I really haven't told you about how much I find the work to be plain boring. I didn't want to upset you or anything."

Vera pulled her knees up under her chin and studied his face. Sam looked more excited than she'd seen him in weeks.

"It's not that I don't like working with computers. After all, I do have a college degree in the subject. But I find doing nothing but hitting the plastic keys hour after hour gets so monotonous, so predictable, that by the end of the day, I think I'm going to go absolutely and totally nuts."

Vera nodded her head. "I understand."

"I mean the job pays well—better, in fact, than what I'll probably find somewhere else. But I think if I keep doing this work—well, the idea just depresses me."

Sam looked as handsome as the day Vera had first seen him in the Subway restaurant. His brown hair had thinned a tad, but he still had those big, blue eyes that gave his face a look of innocence.

"I'm not saying that I want to quit tomorrow morning," Sam continued, "but I sure need to think about the possibility for the next day. I just don't think that working at Motorola is right for me."

"Okay, Mr. Tarzan, what jungle are we supposed to set out to explore for this abrupt change of direction in our lives?"

Sam smiled that sly little grin that meant he'd been waiting for her question. Vera had learned to read his little maneuvers and knew when he was taking her down a path that he'd already mapped out.

"I know this is going to surprise you." Sam picked up the newspaper off the floor. "I found this ad in the *Rocky Mountain News* today." He thumbed back to the classified pages. "Really surprised me." Sam folded the paper back and held up a page with a box circled with a black marker.

"What is it, Sam?"

Sam started reading. "The Colorado Springs Police Department is seeking new personnel at all levels for duty in this area. Applications can be sent or made in person at the police offices on Nevada Street." He lowered the paper. "Don't you think that sounds exciting?"

"No," Vera said. "The question is, do *you* think that sounds exciting? I hadn't planned to apply for a job."

Sam had grinned sheepishly. "Vera, I didn't say it out loud earlier because I thought it would sound too immature. But I always wanted to be a policeman. Must have thought about it a hundred times when I was a little guy."

"Cowboy, chief, fireman, police. That's sort of the order for boys to think about the future. Sam, you stopped on police. That's what you're telling me?"

Sam shook his head slowly. "Strange, isn't it? But it's true. I think I got into computers because the emphasis was on solving problems. Figuring out mysteries always intrigued me and I thought computers would be like that. Turns out that they're more routine than I thought."

"So, the next step is for us to bundle everything up and trudge down to Colorado Springs?"

"I thought maybe it would be better for me to take a trip down there first and get a feel for the lay of the land."

"And when would you go?"

"Tomorrow morning. I already took the day off."

Vera burst into laugher. "You come in here like this is an idea that just started rolling around in your head, when in fact you've already gotten tomorrow off? Sam, you try to play me like a piano. I'm just not sure whether this is a sonata or a rock-and-roll number."

"Well," Sam twisted uneasily in the chair. "I'm simply making an inquiry."

"Really?" Vera noticed that Sam's eyes shifted toward the floor. "Why is it that I get the feeling you've been working on this far longer than the last couple of days?"

"You know that I try to check things out carefully so I don't get us in a bind," Sam said slowly as he started folding the newspaper. "I don't want to fly off on some tangent that would cost us financially."

Vera thought for a moment. "You've already checked out this possibility. Haven't you?"

Sam raised his eyebrows. "I did look into what was happening with the Denver Police Department. They told me the best openings were down in the Springs."

Vera laughed again. "The truth is that you've been considering this option for some time."

"I wouldn't put it quite in those terms."

Vera leaned forward against her knees. "What would be your way of stating it?"

Sam got up and moved to the edge of the bed. He took Vera's hand. "I really want to try this line of work," he said. "Dear, if it doesn't work out, I can always get another job in the computer industry. The demand is going to grow and I will always know how to make those machines tick, but this is what I want to do." He squeezed her hand.

Vera looked up through the darkness around her at the ceiling above her head. Sam had never looked back once he applied for the job. He enjoyed detective work more than anything else in his life. The investigations, the chase, the catch—the whole process fit him like a glove. The unexpected changes, twists, and turns were the most enjoyable part of the job. Vera's problem then became getting him to come home from the job without bringing everything he was working on with him.

Vera knew that she'd done the right thing in encouraging Sam to pursue the job. Everything they'd hoped for seemed to fall in place, and Colorado Springs had proved to be a good place to live. Whatever problems they had faced weren't worth mentioning. The trouble was now that Sam was gone, the void left a hole in her heart the size of Texas.

21

SLOWLY THE SUN ROSE THROUGH THE HAZE hovering over Colorado Springs on Tuesday morning. The bite of winter still clutched the mountain region in bitter cold. Television's first news of the day didn't offer any relief for the week, but then again, Vera expected to leave for New York City that afternoon. The weather on the East Coast promised to be somewhat warmer.

Vera reached across the bed and felt the emptiness on the other side. Sleeping by herself wasn't anything new. Many times Sam had been gone overnight, but knowing she was alone forever cut through Vera like a knife. The new day felt equally empty.

Cara slowly stuck her head around the door to Vera's bedroom. "You awake?"

"Yes."

"We're really going to leave this afternoon?" Cara slipped inside, still wearing her pajamas.

"We are. Have you packed your bag?"

"I did last night."

Vera sat up and threw the covers back. "I want you to go to school this morning like today is any ordinary day. I'll send a note to your teachers so they'll excuse you for the rest of the week." Vera stretched and crawled out of bed. "I'll see if Ace Newton can take both of us to the airport this afternoon. You be out in front of the building ready to roll at two o'clock sharp."

Cara nodded. "Okay."

"And make sure you've got your school assignments at least through the first of next week."

"Oh, come on, Mom. I don't want to worry about—"

"Yes, you do!" Vera said firmly. "We're not flying off on a vacation. You make sure that you've got everything you should be studying."

"I will," Cara said quietly and started out of the room. "You okay this morning?" She gazed over her shoulder with a longing, lost look.

Vera held out her arms. "Come here." She hugged her daughter tightly. "No. Neither of us is in good shape this morning, but we have to go on, don't we?"

Cara sighed. "I guess so, but it sure is hard."

Vera held Cara closer. "I know you're a grown-up fifteen-year-old, but I love you, sweetie. We'll be all right." She tried to sound confident. "We're going to find out what happened to your dad. We'll find the broken pieces. You'll see."

Cara squeezed her mother's hand and left the room quickly. Vera could see the tiny trail of tears running down her face. Watching Cara vanish through the door, she took a deep, long breath and started making her bed. The day would be demanding, and she needed to be ready. She had to maintain a composed appearance.

At nine o'clock Vera quietly walked into the downtown offices of the All-City Confidential Agency. Ace Newton wasn't there yet but a woman was sitting behind the front desk, typing.

"You must be Sally Armfield," Vera said.

The woman looked up in surprise. "Yes. I'm Sally."

"I'm Vera Sloan." She extended her hand.

"Oh, my goodness!" The woman jumped up and ran toward Vera with her arms open. "You're the poor dear who lost her husband." Sally hugged Vera. "Bless you."

"Thank . . . uh, thank you," Vera stammered.

"Bless your heart. Ace told me about your husband's death. I was so saddened. Please sit down, Vera. I want to get to know you."

"I appreciate your kind words." Vera edged into the chair in the waiting room. "We're beginning to get our lives somewhat reordered. I have a fifteen-year-old daughter named Cara."

"That's exactly what Ace said. What a lovely name. He said she was a little beauty."

"Cara is an attractive child—I mean, young woman."

"They grow up so fast." Sally pursed her lips and shook her head. "Gets scary the way time passes so fast. I have two, you know. A boy and a girl. Both grown, though. Out of the house."

"Oh." Vera forced a smile. "Your husband works here in the Springs?"

"He does." Sally beamed. "Runs the Texaco filling station

over there on Thirty-first Street, right off the Interstate 24 exit. You know, going up toward Manitou Springs."

"Yes. Certainly." Vera kept smiling but wondered how much information Ace really did entrust to this woman. She chattered like a sports announcer. What if Ace had let something slip?

"Jack keeps their cars' tanks filled and I try to keep all the typing and paperwork complete down here. Sure is a lot of material to sort out and fix."

Vera nodded. "Know when Ace will be here?"

"He called me at home earlier this morning and said he had to have breakfast with a man. Should be here any moment."

"Good. I'll go back to my office and take care of some details. I won't bother you any longer. Please call me when he comes in."

"Oh, no! No bother at all." Sally turned back to her computer. "I love to talk."

Vera smiled again but hurried back to her office, which was next to Ace's. While there wasn't anything on the desk or in the room for her to do, she wanted to be careful about what she said to Mrs. Armfield until she and Ace had talked at some length. Confidentiality never was a small issue.

After hanging her coat on the rack next to the wall, Vera sat down before her empty desk. Nothing to do but stare at the desktop and worry over what Sally Armfield knew about her problems. Probably a lot!

Feeling paranoid was a new twist in Vera's world. Doubt and distrust were a strong temptation.

Vera heard the front door open. "Sally, how are you this morning?" Ace's voice echoed down the hall.

"Ah, Newton's here!" Vera said to herself and grabbed a notebook lying on top of the desk.

"Your new employee has arrived," Sally's voice boomed down the hall.

"Not 'employee,'" Vera mumbled under her breath. "Private investigator!" She hurried out of the office. Someone had to correct the secretary's mistake.

Seconds later Vera walked into Newton's office. "Good morning, Ace."

"Vera! Come in." Ace motioned for her to take a chair. "Close the door behind you."

Vera relaxed. Shutting the door was a good sign.

"I had breakfast this morning with an old friend of yours." Ace took off his brown leather flight jacket and hung it on a coatrack behind his desk. "Dick Simmons."

"Simmons!" Vera's mouth dropped slightly. "You know Dick?"

"About as long as I knew your husband. We all worked together at the station house down there on Nevada Street."

"I'll be darned."

Ace sat down behind his desk. "I wanted to see what Dick might tell me about Sam's disappearance. We talked about everything from trout fishing to deer hunting, but Simmons doesn't seem to know one crying thing about what's happened to Sam. Appears that the police chief has made it clear that they're not even to discuss the matter around the station. Simmons talks like he's totally mystified about Sam's disappearance."

"Well, that was the impression that Dick left with me, but I didn't know if he was lying or not."

"He could be misleading us," Ace continued, "but I don't think so. Some of what he said about money bothered me. My bottom line is that Simmons is in the dark on this one."

"Money?" Vera crossed her arms over her chest and tried to look blank. *Does Dick Simmons know about the secret bank account? Does he suspect Sam of wrongdoing too?* "Did he say anything about what the police chief knows?"

"No, Simmons didn't, but I got the impression from him that Harrison's knowledge is also rather limited." Ace pushed back from his desk and stretched his legs out in front of him. "Mighty strange situation going on down there."

Vera decided to let the money issue go. She didn't want to draw attention to it. She looked over her shoulder. "What does Mrs. Armfield know about my problems?"

"Sally?" Ace shook his head. "Virtually nothing more than that Sam died. I don't talk business with Sally. In fact, I haven't really told her that you're coming to work as a private investigator."

Vera relaxed. "Good. When I arrived this morning, she was cordial and talkative. I didn't know what to expect. She does need to know that I'm an investigator—not the janitor."

Newton laughed. "Sally's a great secretary but that's as far as it goes. I'll let her know what you do."

Vera pulled her chair up closer to Ace's desk. She knew it was time to level with him. "I need to go to New York City."

Ace's eyes widened. "The Big Apple?"

"All the correspondence that I found on Sam's computer indicated that George Alexander had been in constant contact with a man who has offices on Ninety-sixth Street on Manhattan Island. The character's name is Ivan Bashilov, and he's a mean-looking individual."

"Bashilov? Sounds Russian."

"From his letters, I'm sure that he is. Because we can't find out anything from the local police, and the CIA sure isn't going to divulge any confidences, I need to go to the big city and run down this Russian."

Ace pursed his lips and scowled. "Vera, New York City can be a wicked place."

Vera felt a slight sting in Newton's words. She didn't like the implication that she was in over her head, but it was better than trying to skirt around her suspicions about Sam having his hand in the cookie jar. She didn't say anything but nodded her agreement.

"You sure you want to run around up there by yourself?"

"Cara's going with me."

"Cara? Now there's real muscle to pull you out of any hole you fall in. I'm sure that sweet little fifteen-year-old child can kick fannies like any big-time pro wrestler."

"I understand," Vera said soberly, "but I promised her that I wouldn't cut her out of the pursuit. I can't leave her behind."

Ace raised an eyebrow. "You've got enough problems without dragging a teenager around behind you."

"Yes." Vera looked Ace square in the eye. "But I don't have any choice, Ace."

"Here you are on your second day at work and you're getting ready to function like a longtime professional cop." Newton shook his head. "We're talking tough and dangerous work here."

Vera felt the biting edge in his voice again and knew Ace was right. The fact was, she was in over her head—so far that she could easily drown on this assignment. For a few moments Vera silently thought about what he'd said. The truth was that she had to do everything possible to protect Sam's reputation, and there simply wasn't any alternative to this trip. Out of the corner of her eye she could see Newton studying her. She needed to respond professionally to what he'd said.

"Ace, you are absolutely correct about the problems, but that's the business we're in. People hire us to go places and do things that they're afraid to attempt. Actually, I don't see any other possibility than going to New York City and running this information down. I am prepared to face the consequences."

"You talk like a character out of the movies, Vera." Newton sounded disgusted. "Let's just keep this on a personal basis. Obviously, you're going to go regardless of what I say." He tilted his head down and glared at her. "And take your teenage daughter with you."

Vera bit her lip but didn't say anything.

"Okay. What do you need me to do?"

"I'll call as often as I can. I have a reservation at the Renaissance Hotel at the corner of Twelfth and Lenox Avenue, north of the Russian's office. If we keep in touch at least once a day, that contact will offer an important safety factor."

"Safety factor? Yeah, give me half a day of travel time and I can show up some day or the other in case someone starts shooting at you."

"You might call the local cops in New York City."

Ace closed his eyes and gritted his teeth.

"You can keep me informed on what's unfolding in Colorado Springs, and I'll make sure that you know the score in New York City. After all, Dick Simmons might come up with further information."

"Simmons seems to be about as well informed as a chimpanzee. I doubt it."

"You have to remember, Ace. I have a college degree in this subject and—"

"And nothing, Vera. You're looking at a hard-core effort here that could push you off the top of the mountain. Don't overestimate what your academic background has given you. It's one thing to wow me when you're looking for a job but another thing when you're pounding the pavement in New York City."

Vera wanted to argue but there wasn't any point. Newton was totally correct and Sam had been too. She needed five years of experience on the police force to take on such a difficult assignment. She quietly nodded.

Newton opened the bottom drawer of his desk. "I want you to take this cell phone. It's small enough to hide in your pocket. I'll tell you now: don't hesitate to call me at a moment's notice. You understand?"

"Yes, I do."

"And don't you get into any of this heroic nonsense that doesn't do anything but get people killed. You reading me clearly on this one as well?"

"Yes, I am."

"All right!" Newton frowned and shook his head angrily. "Good heavens. Your wandering off in that huge city is nuts. Totally nuts." He pounded his desk. "I swear. You seem to be running this place instead of me." Ace stood up and started pacing. "This afternoon I'll bring you a small bulletproof vest, in case you need extra protection. You should have purchased that Kevlar-lined raincoat."

"Yes, I should have," Vera said quietly. "Thank you."

He glanced around his desk with a wild-eyed look. "I want you to remember that this was your idea, not mine. Understand?"

Vera nodded.

Newton scratched his head. "Anything else that you want me to do?"

"Could you take me to the airport this afternoon?"

"Heavens, now I'm your taxi driver!" Newton got up and put his brown leather jacket back on. "No!" He clomped out of his private office and then stopped before reaching the front door. "What time?"

"Could you come by my house at one-thirty?"

Newton shook his head. "I guess." He stomped out of the building without saying a word, slamming the agency's front door behind him.

Vera watched as he walked down the street. He was one irritated detective. Not a good way to start her second day at the office.

22

AT PRECISELY 1:30 ON TUESDAY AFTERNOON, Ace Newton pulled up in his Ford pickup in front of Vera Sloan's one-story house on Twenty-third Street. Before he could turn the engine off, Vera stepped out the back door, carrying two suitcases.

"Hey, let me help you." Ace leaped out of the truck. "The luggage looks heavy."

Ace appeared to have cooled off from their morning discussion. Vera kept walking, swinging the bags in front of her. "You're going to miss my fashion show, Ace. I've got new clothes packed in here that I would have worn this week."

"Somebody as small as you will break your back lugging those things." He grabbed the suitcases and swung them into the back of the pickup.

"No trouble carrying them," Vera said defiantly.

Ace shrugged. "Don't kid me!"

"My, my. You've brought your best car."

"I always drive my pickup when I want to make sure no one is following me. Throws 'em off track. I'd assume that someone might be watching you this afternoon."

Vera hopped into the cab. "I doubt it. Let's hit the road. We don't have much time."

Newton reached behind the front seat. "I want you to put this in your suitcase before you go into the airport. If you think that you could get into a place where shooting might occur, this vest could save your life. It will stop a bullet. You might get knocked down, but you won't get killed." He shoved it into her hands. "Keep it handy. I also prepared you a little bag of arsenals that you might need along the way. There's an electronic stethoscope, a phone tap, pocket bugs, and other equipment of that order. Just in case."

"Thank you, Ace." Vera folded the vest. "I know that you're worried about me, and I promise to pay careful attention to what I'm doing." She stuck the bag in the top of her tote purse.

Newton started backing out. "You'd better, because you've got a daughter who's already lost one parent." He looked at her hard. "As I have told you before, we don't need any more deaths."

Vera only nodded.

"All right. I'll go by the school and pick up Cara." Newton shifted into low and started up the street. He looked at Vera carefully. "Can I ask you a personal question?"

"Sure."

"You got enough money to take care of you in New York City?" Newton stared straight ahead.

Vera took a deep breath. "You know we don't have any big savings. I've already spent more than I normally would to take on this new job, but I'm taking enough money with me to do whatever is necessary to find out what happened to Sam. I've got credit cards. I can live with it."

Newton nodded his head. "Yeah, that's about what I thought." The pickup zoomed on down the street. "If you run low, call me."

As promised, Cara was waiting in front of the school, and they quickly left for the airport. While they cruised across town, Newton fired off an endless stream of advice and instructions, most of which Vera already knew and some that she'd never follow, but Ace's monologue passed the time getting to the airport.

Newton pulled up in front of the entrance to the terminal and Vera hurriedly packed the black bulletproof vest in her luggage. Then he zoomed away and she walked in with Cara. Forty-five minutes later their airplane lifted off for New York City.

As the Boeing 737 glided above the clouds, Vera kept thinking about what her minister and Basil Abbas had said last week. Abbas had warned her to be aware of the attack of evil. Dozier had said that in the midst of their helplessness, the help of God would come. If there ever was a time when she felt helpless, it was now. She felt as if her life had turned into an abstraction not tied to anything physical or enduring. She and Cara would probably return in a couple of days, having never found Ivan Bashilov, and the whole pursuit would come to a boring end. The CIA and Chief Harrison would continue to be nothing more than walls of silence, offering no help at all.

Cara leaned over, trying to talk above the roar of the airplane's engines. "Mom, we're going to look for this Russian person. Right?"

"That's our objective."

"And you have the man's address?"

Vera nodded. "Shouldn't be hard to find the place. It's in the center of Manhattan Island."

"You really think the guy is a Russian?"

"In his letters he made references to places in Russia, like the province of Chechnya and the town of Khankala. Obviously, the man's name is Russian. Bashilov fits our expectations. I think we can make a fairly solid assumption that his nationality is Russian."

"Hmm." Cara leaned back in her seat. "Very fascinating."

"Why?"

"Well, I started out studying this book by Alexander Solzhenitsyn about Russians and now we're chasing a real-life Russian."

"You find that fascinating? I think it's more terrifying."

Cara stared thoughtfully out the airplane window. "I wonder if this Bashilov is anything like the people in my story."

Vera studied Cara for a moment. That strange hybrid—a fifteen-year-old going on twenty-five—was back. Cara certainly looked old enough and at times seemed to be mature, but then she'd quickly slip back into that early adolescent mode. She'd never be able to deal with the possibility that her father had done something illegal. The probability had to be kept from her at all costs.

"The men in Solzhenitsyn's story struggled through similar terrible circumstances," Cara explained. "Most of them didn't do anything more than try to survive in an impoverished country. Maybe this Bashilov is like one of these men."

Vera didn't want to answer. Comparing him to innocent human beings made her job more difficult.

"The hero of this story is named Shukhov. The circumstances of the camp have forced him to live like an animal. Really tough, huh?"

Vera still said nothing. In their world they had plenty. Economic need couldn't have forced Sam to take the money. What could have pushed him over the edge even to consider stealing? And it was a significant amount of money!

"When the day in the prison camp started it was twenty below zero. Can you imagine anything that cold?"

Vera could. She had stomped across the mountains north of Colorado Springs when the snow and the wind were at severe temperatures. Winters could get tough above the Springs.

"Shukhov got sick and needed to go to the infirmary. Even going in for help was filled with problems because nobody trusted anybody else."

"Cara, why do you think people trust each other?"

The young girl looked puzzled. "I guess," she finally said, "it's because they know each other well enough that they can predict and believe in what the other person will do."

Vera looked back out the airplane window. If she had ever believed anything about Sam, it was that he would do the right thing in all situations. She had been willing to trust him with her life, and now she had a tough, heartrending situation to face. What if he hadn't been trustworthy?

Maybe I've been wrong all these years, she thought. *But how could it be? Sam and I have argued and had our disagreements, but I knew him like the back of my hand. I never saw him do anything that wasn't righteous and good. We went to church, prayed, even had a spiritual life together. How could he possibly steal and I not know it?*

"I think that the harsh struggles these Russian men faced forced them to do things they would never have done on a normal day," Cara continued. "Maybe any of us would become capable of criminal acts under the same circumstances."

"Possibly," Vera answered. "I don't know."

Cara leaned over. "You seem upset."

"I guess . . . this whole experience wears on me."

"Of course, but you also look like you are really worrying. Are you afraid?"

"Afraid?" Vera nodded her head. "Yes, I have a considerable amount of fear about what is ahead for us."

"New York frightens you?"

"No, dear. New York City is filled with many fine, good people. You know that I've been there before."

"Then what's bothering you, Mom?"

Vera pursed her lips but hesitated. "I guess I'm afraid of what we might find."

"Yeah, I know." Cara reached over and took her mother's hand. "Do you think that Daddy might still be alive?"

"I'd like to think so, Cara, but that wouldn't be realistic. I suppose that one of my fears is not being able to find out anything about what happened to him."

"Why would anyone want to kill my father?"

Vera shuddered. Through the years crooks had threatened Sam, but no one took them seriously. Sometimes the people Sam arrested even ended up becoming his friends. The only plausible reason for his death was that he had been involved some way in taking money.

"I don't know," Vera lied.

23

CARA WATCHED HER MOTHER CAREFULLY OUT of the corner of her eye as the Boeing 737 circled above New York City, waiting for the final signal from the control tower to land. Vera looked drawn and distressed, and she kept moving her hands around in her lap, squeezing them, rubbing and pulling at her fingers. Her mouth looked set in a determined way. Periodically, the muscles on the side of her jaw rippled as if she were grinding her teeth. Cara's mother stared straight ahead.

She doesn't ever seem to cry, Cara thought. *Like she's doing it for me . . . or maybe she's just out of touch with how bad she hurts. I think she's fighting against allowing herself to feel the depth of her pain. She acted too casual, lighthearted around that Newton guy. I know that ha-ha stuff was a front. She worries me.*

"Do you have your seat belt fastened?" Vera asked.

"Sure." Cara pointed at her buckle. "Everything is ready."

"Good," Vera answered but didn't smile.

What in the world are we going to do? Cara pondered. *I don't have the slightest idea how she's going to run this man down. Makes my skin crawl. I certainly hope she has a plan.*

"We've now been cleared for our final approach," the pilot announced over the intercom. "We will be on the ground shortly."

I actually wish we were still at home. I don't like this situation. I don't have any idea what we're doing or how Mom will handle it all, Cara thought.

"Keep close to me when we land," Vera said into Cara's ear. The airplane slowed and started to descend. "Losing you in LaGuardia Airport would be a disaster."

I'm not going to lose her in a crowded airport! Come on! Cara looked carefully at Vera again. *I wonder what she's thinking. She seems even more tense than I noticed earlier this morning. Really upset.*

The airplane settled over the runway. Vera grabbed the two ends of the seat's arms, pressing her fingers against the metal guard.

Mom has no idea that she's wound up tighter than a drum, Cara realized. *I wonder what's on her mind right now.*

The airplane hit the ground and bounced a couple of times before the pilot threw the engines into reverse and the passengers lurched forward slightly in their seats. The plane slowed quickly.

"Mother, I'd like to ask you a question."

"Sure." Vera kept looking straight ahead.

"What if you find this man and he turns out to be a crook, a criminal, a really bad guy?"

"I don't understand your question, Cara."

"What would you do if he turned out to be carrying *a gun?*"

Vera stared out the window for a moment. "I don't know."

She swallowed hard. "I guess I'll have to cross that bridge when I come to it."

"Or jump off it."

Vera didn't answer.

Cara studied her mother's eyes. She looked unsure of herself, which was unusual for her.

"Well," Vera seemed to be thinking out loud. "I will make sure that I examine my gun in my luggage as soon as we get checked in at the hotel. Then again, if it's too late tonight, I'll have to do that first thing in the morning. I'll take care of any problems." Her voice trailed away.

Cara knew her mother could be a very determined person. She'd taken on college almost like cleaning their house and made things work out fine, but her voice sounded different now. More uncertain and pressured.

"We could run into trouble, couldn't we, Mom?"

Vera nodded.

I've got to pay close attention to all the details, Cara decided. *I don't want to add to the pressure she's under, but I've got to make sure she doesn't make any mistakes that would get us into big-time trouble.*

"We're here," Vera stated. "Remember, stay close and we'll get our luggage first."

"Sure, Mom. Don't worry. I'll stay with you every step of the way."

Darkness had fallen by the time Vera and Cara got a taxi and started toward the hotel. The night was cold and a salty smell lingered in the air.

"Where you babes headed?" the cab driver asked.

"The Renaissance Hotel on Lenox Avenue in Manhattan, please," Vera answered.

"Yeah, sure." The driver hit the gas pedal and the car shot out into traffic. "You ain't from around here. Right?" He glanced at them in the rearview mirror.

"No, we're not," Vera answered.

"Yeah, you don't sound like New Yorkers," the driver said as he careened back and forth between cars. "Got a different accent."

Vera didn't say anything.

"Where you from?" the driver persisted. "What part of the ol' USA?"

"Colorado Springs!" Cara shouted over the seat and then realized that her mother was giving her a severe "shut your mouth" look.

"Colorado Springs. The other side of the world. Big mountains and all."

"Yeah," Vera said. "Out west."

"You see those mountains from your house?"

Cara glanced at her mother. She didn't seem to be giving her the shut-up expression anymore. "Yes. We see them every day."

"Now ain't that somethin'?" the driver mused. "Never been on the other side of New Jersey myself. Got no idea what a Rocky Mountain must look like."

"They're really big," Cara chattered. "You'd like them."

"Sure would." The driver grinned. "I'm sure I would."

Vera didn't say anything. Bright lights and billboards flashed past. Vera kept looking out the window, watching the amazing array of endless streets filled with a thousand different types of businesses. The taxi driver seemed to have slipped out of the role of inquisitor and let the talk go. Twenty minutes passed.

"Hey!" The driver pointed out the front window. "There's the Renaissance. Right over there."

Cara glanced at the taxi's meter. "Look at that, Mom. It's going to cost us thirty dollars!"

"That's my best bargain price," the driver quipped.

Vera looked at her daughter harshly. "Thank you," she answered the man and pulled out her billfold to pay him.

As the taxi sped away, Vera hissed, "*Please!* You're in the big city now. We pay the bill without flinching. Okay?"

Cara nodded apologetically.

Ten minutes later Vera and Cara were settling into a room on the hotel's eighth floor overlooking the city.

"Mom, this city is really huge. Oh, man! Look at the cars down there!"

"Uh-huh." Vera lifted some items from her suitcase and took them into the bathroom.

"I mean, you ought to see the cars speeding up and down the street. Awesome numbers."

Vera came out of the bathroom and pointed at a chair next to a small desk. "Sit down, Cara. I want to talk to you."

"Sure, Mom."

"Cara, I remember well the first couple of times that I came to New York City. Once I was with my father and the next time in a school group. I had to learn the ways of this place. We're in a city that's completely different from Colorado Springs. You can't open the door of this room to anyone who doesn't work for the hotel." Vera looked at her daughter. "Do you understand me?"

"Yes."

"And I don't want you walking around outside in the street by yourself. I'm going to have to make some trips around the city alone. During those times I want you to sit in here and do your schoolwork. Do we have a firm understanding?"

"Sure." Cara shrugged.

"Good. I've got a lot on my mind, and I must figure out what I'm going to do." Vera got up and walked toward the door. "I need some time to be alone. I'm going out for a walk and I'll be back after a while. Are you comfortable with all I've said?"

"I understand." Cara smiled reassuringly.

"Okay." Vera shut the door behind her and stepped out into the long corridor.

Vera knew that Cara was standing on the other side of the locked door slowly surveying the silent room. The room would look extremely empty. Vera suddenly felt very, very alone.

She started down the hall.

24

VERA WALKED DOWN THE LONG HALL, worrying about Cara. Could her daughter endure these first moments in a New York City hotel, sitting alone by herself? Would she do as Vera had instructed and stay put? Vera believed she would. In the end she didn't see any alternative but to get away to be by herself and think. She had no reason not to trust Cara.

Thick carpeting swallowed the sounds of her feet shuffling across the corridor and down the hall. The elevator door opened, and within moments, Vera walked out into the foyer of the Renaissance Hotel.

Wherever she looked, people seemed to be wandering around in strange, meaningless patterns, coming and going. Even at this hour of the night, they were meandering off into who knows where. No one seemed even to notice Vera's existence. All those other journeys only happened to crisscross with hers in this foyer at this moment. The disconnected nature of things left her once again with the realization that she had to find her way through this city—and the mystery of Sam's death and dealings—completely by herself.

She walked out into the street. A cold wind blew up the boulevard, and she wished she'd worn a heavier coat but kept walking. A block away, she gave up the evening stroll and wandered into a small coffee shop.

"What can I get for you, ma'am?" a woman asked with a Latino accent.

"Coffee is fine."

"Sure thing." The woman turned to the coffeepot and quickly poured a cup.

Vera walked to a corner booth and sat down. She dropped a couple of artificial sweeteners in her coffee and stirred the steaming brew. Ever since Ace Newton had suggested that she take a bulletproof vest and an assortment of technical tools, the danger of the trip had bothered her. The mere thought of his telling her to be prepared lest she get shot chilled everything in her. Vera realized that with her inexperience, she could walk into trouble and never see it coming. It was more than a little sobering.

And what about Sam's reputation? Could she really do anything that would protect him from disgrace? At first the idea had seemed as simple as making breakfast. Now it was clearly a difficult and serious matter. Possibly all that she would do was make matters worse. Everything would have to be worked out gingerly, a step at a time. Vera shuddered even though the café was warm.

Setting her coffee cup down slowly, Vera firmly took hold of the tabletop with her fingers, as if to steady herself. The time had come to push the grief and fears aside. Vera had to get hold of her feelings. She had a mountain to climb that demanded every ounce of her energy and concentration. No longer could she let the gnawing loss of her husband undercut her ability to focus on her job. Anxiety over what might happen couldn't be allowed to rob her of the sharpness she needed to face this task.

Basil Abbas had clearly warned her about the creeping intrusion of evil. Vera's perspective could become distorted before she knew what hit her. He had made it clear that she must keep her mind clearly focused on what was to be accomplished. Now was the time to get things straight.

I must remember exactly why I'm up here, Vera thought. *There's too much at stake for me not to take control of what happens next. I'm in New York City to find out what happened to my husband and why he had $200,000 stashed away in that bank! That's what I've got to start doing come tomorrow morning, regardless of what gets in my path.* Vera let go of the tabletop and relaxed.

Vera glanced at her watch. She had forgotten to change it when they passed through two time zones. The jolting truth glared back at her from her wrist. It was three o'clock in the morning in Colorado Springs! Vera grabbed her purse to hurry back to the hotel.

Halfway out of the booth, Vera stopped. "Wait a minute!" she exclaimed as the fullness of the realization shook her. The waitress turned around and looked her way. Vera slid back down in the seat and smiled weakly at the woman. *I'm here to catch a murderer! This is no small-time operation. There's a crime to be solved. I've got to discover who is out there killing people! My grief and personal struggle have to be set aside. Everything goes on hold until I get back to Colorado Springs.*

Vera shook her head and buried her face in her hands. "I'm

here for much more than I've let myself recognize," she muttered under her breath. "Time to get tough."

The first sunlight of morning peered through a slit in the curtains of the hotel room and awakened Vera. The night before, Cara had already gone to sleep when Vera came back to the hotel, but it hadn't been easy for Vera to fall asleep. Only in the latest hour of night had she finally dozed off. As the day broke, she lay in bed thinking about what she must do next.

"Lord, I feel extremely strange about this entire business," she prayed under her breath. "I'm not even sure how to proceed. Please keep me from stepping off into something that would turn out wrong. If anything, I need You to come out from behind that tree and give me concrete direction. Please help me find my way."

She had one clear step to take today: she needed to walk to the address where Bashilov's offices were located and find out what was there. This was the place to begin! Reverend Dozier had promised that God helped the helpless. She now fully qualified for divine intervention. The time had come for the assistance to show up.

Trying to avoid waking Cara, Vera got out of bed quietly and slipped into the bathroom. Thirty minutes later, she opened the door and peeked out. Cara was still sleeping like a baby. Vera tiptoed back to her end of the room, where she quickly dressed. What she needed today was the knockout, Big Apple look.

"Mom, you going someplace?"

Vera froze. She had thought Cara was still asleep.

"Just getting dressed, dear."

"Not trying to sneak off on your old buddy, are you?"

"No, of course not."

Cara inched out of bed. "Good. Because I need to go with you this morning. Right?"

Vera took a deep breath. "I guess."

"Excellent. Won't take me long to take a shower." Cara slipped into the bathroom and shut the door.

"Darn!" Vera said under her breath. *I was afraid this would happen. No alternative but to wait on her to get ready.*

Ten minutes later, Cara came out of the bathroom. "See how fast I can be?"

"When you want to."

"Let's get some breakfast and then we can—"

"Hang on just a minute, young lady. I believe that you are here with me and not the other way around." Vera picked up the telephone. "You're going my way, not vice versa. Right?"

Cara nodded reluctantly.

"Concierge? Yes, this is Vera Sloan in room 859. Do you know if there is a small restaurant in the area with a simple breakfast?" Vera listened for a moment. "Yes, I'm aware that you have a restaurant downstairs, but I'm looking for something more basic." Vera listened again. "Just two blocks south? Wonderful. Thank you." She hung up.

"A *small* restaurant?" Cara asked.

"Yes. Now let's back up. I believe the procedure is that you follow me around."

"Yes, ma'am."

"Cara, I want you to pay attention. Watch. Notice if you see the same people twice. Look behind us. Don't let someone tail us. Understand?"

Cara nodded her head.

"You're a part of this escapade because I need you to be my extra set of ears and eyes. Don't let me down."

"I won't. I promise."

"Okay, grab your coat and let's go."

"Yes, ma'am." Cara picked up her coat.

Turning her back on her daughter, Vera stuffed her pistol into her large purse, along with some of the accessories that Ace had sent with her. At least she had a few basic items should she need to do any electronic surveillance.

Retracing her steps from the night before, Vera quickly guided Cara through the hotel foyer and out into the street. Only a block away she found the small café the concierge had recommended. They stopped and had a quick breakfast.

"Mom, do you know where we're going?" Cara set her orange juice glass on the table.

"I think I know where to begin. Got to take this one day at a time, dear."

"I'm ready to roll." Cara pushed back from the table. "Time to move."

Yes," Vera said, "it's definitely time to move on."

25

VERA HURRIED OUT OF THE RESTAURANT with Cara trailing behind her. "Come on. We've got to hurry."

"What's the rush?" Cara asked when they were back on the street. "We're not chasing the clock."

"There's lots to be done today," Vera answered abruptly. "You've got to keep up with me."

Cara nodded. "I understand."

Vera looked up and down the street. "Just stay with me." She picked up her pace. "Keep your eyes open and don't let anything slip by you."

"You bet. I'm paying total attention."

Many of the pedestrians looked affluent, but some appeared to be street people. Most were indifferent and made no eye contact. A few looked tough. Vera kept walking down the busy street with her eyes fixed straight ahead. About a block from the restaurant she stopped and studied the gang of boys coming toward them.

Cara nudged her. "Mom, those guys look really tough. Should we cross the street?"

"No," Vera replied and walked toward the group of boys. "They're just kids."

Cara stared in horror as Vera walked into the middle of the five teenagers and past them. *"Mom!"* she hissed.

The youths looked like they were in their late teens. They were wearing baggy jeans with long, shiny chains dropping down their pants legs. They wore baseball caps backward. A couple of the boys looked puzzled, but none spoke. One whistled.

Vera smiled and kept walking.

Cara stared with eyes the size of half-dollars. She walked far around the boys. When they had passed the group, Cara said, "I thought they'd grab you or something terrible. Really, Mother!"

"Not on a busy street like this one. Keep your cool, Cara. Don't be intimidated."

"They could have shot you!" Cara protested.

Vera ran her hands along the side of her purse, feeling the weapon inside. She said nothing.

"Oh, man!" Cara shook her head. "This is craziness."

"They frightened you, didn't they, Cara?"

"Look. I'm no child," Cara said defiantly, "but those guys were thugs. I'm not interested in getting into some hassle with a street gang."

"Good," Vera answered. "That attitude will keep you out of trouble. Don't forget it, Cara. You do remember that I've got a gun, don't you?"

"Yeah. You said so on the plane."

"The gun will help us if we need it. We're going to walk for a while. The office of this Bashilov guy isn't too far from here and the exercise will do both of us some good. Keep up with me—I want to walk a little faster." She picked up the pace.

Cara fell in with her mother, scurrying past the crowds of people walking toward them. For a block she didn't do anything but try to maintain her mother's fast clip. She kept shaking her head. "You know, I wouldn't have walked through those guys in Colorado Springs!"

"Really? Well, we're not in Colorado Springs." Vera picked up her stride. "Makes a difference."

Finally, Cara leaned over. "Mom, who do you really think this Russian guy is?"

"I don't know."

"But what's your hunch? What do you expect? You've got to have some idea."

Vera looked at her daughter. "We're here because someone is responsible for the death of your father, and this man looks like he's probably right at the center of the problem. At the least, that's where we must begin. We'll have to be cautious in how we find out who he is."

Cara kept walking faster. "Maybe we won't want to meet him face-to-face."

Vera kept walking. "I doubt it," she finally said.

Cara's questions ceased and they kept marching down Lenox Avenue. Vera stared straight ahead, thinking about what her daughter had said. Cara's questions only added to her apprehension. In ten minutes they stood at the corner of Ninety-sixth Street and Park Avenue.

"There it is." Vera pointed across the street. "See the sign above the door? The Samson Building. That's the one we've been looking for. Big place."

Cara stared. "Yeah! Wow."

Vera studied the building. "We're going to cross the street here," she instructed. "When we get to the other side, you stand on the corner and watch outside. I'm going inside to survey the listing of who has offices in there. You watch the people coming and going from the building. Simply stand outside and look casual. Keep the distressed look off your face. Got it?"

"Anything I should look for?"

"Know what a Russian looks like?"

"No."

Vera smiled. "Neither do I. Just pay attention, Cara. That's the point. Who knows what may happen? Your job is to be an observer right now. That's all. Just stand out here with your eyes wide open."

Cara took a deep breath. "Okay. I'll do my best."

"Let's go."

Vera took the lead, and when she hit the curb, she continued in a steady pace straight into the tall building. A large glass directory hung in the center between the elevators. Vera quickly surveyed the long line of *B*s but nothing even close to Bashilov appeared.

Hmm, Vera fretted. *Not what I expected.* She reached in her purse and fished out a list of names and addresses that she had made before leaving Colorado Springs. On the top of one of the letters had been the heading *Ukraine Imports Company* with the Samson Building address. Vera went back to the directory again, starting from the bottom with her index finger.

There it is! Vera thought. *Bigger than life!* She turned around and hurried outside.

Cara still stood next to the traffic light, staring at the front door of the Samson Building with the intensity of a police dog. People surged past her, apparently not noticing Cara's harsh gawk.

"I found the business!" Vera said. "It's in there."

"What are you going to do?" Cara's eyes got bigger. "That place could be full of crazies. Crooks. Who knows what?"

Vera took a deep breath. "This is what we came for. I want you to go in that street café and drink a Coke or something. Just wait patiently for me. I'm going in to find out."

26

VERA TOOK THE ELEVATOR TO THE TENTH floor, trusting that Cara would stay put in the small café. Anything could happen, and she needed to be sure that her daughter stayed in the background. It was Vera's job to check out the clues, and Cara's to stay out of the way—and out of danger.

The elevator door opened and Vera found herself looking down another long corridor. No one was in sight, so she started following the door numbers to her right. The directory had said that Ukraine Imports was located in Suite 1015, which appeared to be around the corner. The carpet felt thick and expensive. The offices looked well kept and some had been freshly painted. The Samson Building had to have cost a fortune; the Ukraine Imports people must have money.

Vera reached the corner and peered around, but no one was in the hall. She studied the large door labeled *1015*. Across the massive oak frame, *Ukraine Imports* had been printed in gold and black. *Expensive looking*, Vera thought. Beneath the company logo was the name of Ivan Trudoff, but no one else. In the computer letters, Bashilov sounded like the guy that ran the show, so his name should be public, obvious. Why wasn't he listed?

Slipping toward the door, Vera felt nervous. What might she find on the other side? How would she actually start her investigation of this mysterious business and its owner? Vera took a deep breath and slowly reached for the doorknob. What in the world would she say to whoever might be on the other side?

The inside of the office was decorated lavishly. The material on the couches looked like silk and the draperies were gorgeous. Rather than regular tile, the floors were covered with rich carpet. Whatever Ukraine Imports was, the company appeared to be doing a booming business. A man in a dark-brown trench coat sat on a couch reading a magazine. A secretary sat behind a reception desk, reading a newspaper. When Vera approached her, the woman looked up with a startled expression.

Vera thought quickly, then asked, "Is this the office of Ukraine Exports?"

The receptionist looked at her quizzically. "No," she replied. "This is Ukraine *Imports.*"

Mr. Trench Coat lowered the magazine and stared at Vera.

"Hmm," Vera rubbed her chin. "I must have gotten something mixed up." She smiled at the woman's surprised face. "You don't export Russian items?"

The receptionist shook her head. "Just import them."

"Well, what a surprise. Let me try another angle. Do you have an employee here by the name of Bashilov?"

Mr. Trench Coat dropped his magazine.

The receptionist shook her head casually. "Never heard of such a guy."

"How strange." Vera pursed her lips thoughtfully and glanced at the man sitting on the couch. "I wouldn't have any idea where to look next."

"Neither would I," the receptionist said. She went back to her newspaper.

"How unexpected," Vera said. She looked at the receptionist and added, "Hope I didn't bother you."

"No trouble," the receptionist answered in a flat voice.

Mr. Trench Coat kept staring at her.

Vera retreated slowly, trying to find some angle, some point of inquiry, something that might give her leverage to ask another question. The receptionist had been about as responsive as an answering machine.

"Well, I suppose I'll try some other offices on down the hall." Vera turned toward the door. The sinking feeling of failure hit her in the pit of her stomach.

Suddenly the door behind the secretary opened and a heavyset man walked out. He didn't look at either the man in the trench coat or Vera. His shoulders and neck were massive, and his head was shaved. He approached the receptionist's desk. "Have you finished with those letters?" he barked with a heavy accent.

The woman quickly stashed the newspaper. "Just about. I'll have them back there to you in a few moments."

"Make it quick," the man snapped. "I don't have all day."

"Certainly." The receptionist turned to a computer screen and began typing.

The muscular man went back into his office without even noticing Vera. He shut the door firmly.

Vera's mouth dropped. She stared in disbelief, her heart

pounding. Her mouth went dry. She'd seen that man before—on the computer disk that Sam hid. He was Bashilov!

Vera suddenly noticed that Mr. Trench Coat had picked up his magazine and started reading, but he kept peeking at her out of the corner of his eye. He seemed to be scrutinizing her.

Nothing made any sense. The receptionist had sounded like she genuinely had no idea who Bashilov was, but she'd spoken to this man as if she'd worked for him for a considerable amount of time.

"Something else you need?" The receptionist stopped typing and looked at Vera.

"Excuse me." Vera forced a smile. "Could you tell me who that man was?"

"Him? That's Mr. Trudoff. Ivan Trudoff. He owns Ukraine Imports."

"I see," Vera mouthed the words more than spoke them. "Thank you."

"Sure." The receptionist tilted her head as if waiting for a response or expecting Vera to hit the road.

Without saying anything, Vera closed the door behind her and hurried to the elevator.

Trudoff? Vera thought. *Bashilov? Was the receptionist tricking me? And why did Mr. Trench Coat keep watching me? What in the world is going on in that office?*

Vera stopped at the corner of the hallway and glanced around. No one was in sight. She pulled out the telephone that Newton had given her and punched in his number.

"Ace Newton here."

"Ace," she whispered. "It's me, Vera. Can you hear me all right?"

"Barely. Can you talk louder?"

"I don't want to. Listen to me carefully. I need you to go on the Internet, the special software you've got, whatever, and trace information on a guy named Ivan Trudoff. I'm not sure how he's related to Bashilov, but I need to know everything you can find. I'm sure he's a Russian."

"I'll try," Newton answered. "How quick do you need this stuff?"

"By tomorrow morning if possible."

"That's cutting it close. I don't know if I can find out anything by then, but I'll do my best."

"Great. Take care." Vera clicked the phone off. No one had come out of any of the offices. She hurried to the elevator.

The elevator door closed in front of her and Vera pressed the button for the lobby. She kept thinking about the man in the brown trench coat. She exited the elevator and lobby, and crossed the street to the café.

Cara was sitting in a window booth, watching everyone who went past. Her eyes lit up when Vera approached. Vera sat down beside Cara but didn't say anything.

"Mom! What'd you find out?" Cara pulled on her coat sleeve. "Come on!"

"I don't know, dear." Vera stared out the window at the Samson Building. "I don't have any idea at all, but I want you to go back to the hotel. I've got to follow a lead."

"Oh, no!" Cara protested. "I have to go with you!"

Vera leaned forward and looked hard in her daughter's eyes. "Remember what I told you? You take a taxi straight back up this street to the Renaissance. I'm sure you've got plenty of schoolwork to do."

Cara took a deep breath, as if she were building up a forceful response. Then she stood and stomped out of the café.

Vera watched Cara until she successfully hailed a cab, then sat back in the booth. *Okay, Mr. Trench Coat,* she thought. *Come back out. You seemed to enjoy watching me like a hawk. Now let's see where you go.*

27

For fifteen minutes Vera tried to relax in the café booth. She kept watching the Samson Building, hoping that the man she'd seen in the Ukraine Imports offices would soon come out of the front door. Every few minutes she glanced at her watch. Suddenly she looked up to see the man in the brown trench coat zoom past her. Vera quickly dropped a few dollars on the table to pay her bill and tip and slipped out of the café. She located the tall, thin man and began to follow from about thirty feet behind.

Mr. Trench Coat kept looking down and counting something in an envelope that looked like small sheets of paper—maybe money. He was so absorbed in tabulating whatever it was that he didn't look around, so Vera walked in a straight line behind the man, matching his pace step-by-step.

His coat's got a European style to it, she thought. *He's not a local.*

The shoe heels don't look American. Too blocky. No style. Haircut's on the shabby side. Rough looking. This guy is an import. Shipped in from somewhere. Russia?

At the corner of Ninety-sixth and Park, the man abruptly headed for Second Avenue. He still didn't seem to notice anyone around him, but Vera didn't want to take any chances.

I'll stay on the opposite side of the street, making it more difficult for him to spot me, she thought. Vera picked up speed, staying parallel but slightly behind the man.

She could see his unruly hair bouncing in the breeze as he maintained a brisk clip. The man obviously knew exactly where he was going.

Oh, my gosh! Vera exclaimed silently. *That's a subway sign ahead.*

The guy was going for the underground train. She abruptly ran out in the street, hoping to cross and keep him from losing her on the subway.

A taxi driver squealed to a halt only two feet from Vera and shook his fist out the window. "Watch out, you idiot! You'll get run over!"

"Sorry." Vera kept trotting across the street, watching Mr. Trench Coat. She didn't want to let him out of her sight and couldn't be slowed down. The tall man disappeared down the stairs into the terminals that ran under the city.

Just what I feared! Vera puffed and hurried down the same stairs. She didn't see the man again until she turned the last corner. About thirty feet ahead, he dropped a slug in the turnstile and walked to the left.

"Oh, no!" Vera gasped. *I don't have subway fare.* She rushed to the cashier window, watching her man disappear down an escalator.

"Five fares." Vera slapped a ten-dollar bill in front of the operator at the window.

Without even looking at her, a dark-complexioned youth pushed the brass tokens and her change forward. Vera grabbed the coins, scurried toward the entrance, and ran down the escalator.

At the bottom of the steps, two long corridors opened in front of her. The wall sign said one route led to Battery Park, and the other line ran north to Yonkers. Vera's mouth dropped. The tall man had disappeared and she had only seconds to decide which way to go.

Vera remembered a map that she'd seen of Manhattan. The expensive apartments tended to be at the tip of the island. "There wouldn't be as much of a possibility of his having an apartment down there as if he went north," she thought out loud. "I'll try Yonkers." She ran down the tunnel.

The sounds of cars and trains rumbling above added to Vera's nervousness. The tunnel smelled musty. She came to a small flight of steps and hurried up. Ten feet ahead the tunnel opened onto a track.

Vera slowed down, trying to look less conspicuous, but her heart kept pounding. She felt sweaty. Still, she tried to look composed. The entry tunnel ended and maybe fifty or sixty people were standing alongside a track. Nobody paid any attention to her as she tried to search subtly for the trench-coated man. Vera inched through the crowd.

She finally saw the man ten feet ahead of her, standing by himself and still looking inside the envelope. Vera whirled around, fearing he would see her. Standing with her back to him, she slowly scooted away.

Got to keep downrange from this guy, she decided. *Far enough away to get in another coach. The one next to his. Don't want to be obvious. Lord, help me disappear in this crowd!* She stepped closer to five women standing together. Not far away she could hear the clatter of the coaches flying toward them. Vera braced herself.

The subway train hurled into the terminal stop as if it might go on through, then stopped on a dime. For the first time, Vera's suspect looked around. He didn't seem to notice her and jumped on the car in front of him. Vera quickly got on the following coach. All of the seats were taken so she stood in the aisle and grabbed the metal rail above her head. The train pulled out and shot toward upper Manhattan Island and Yonkers.

For five minutes Vera clung to the handhold as the car jerked back and forth. The angle allowed her to look through the glass on the doors at the end of the cars and watch her man in the next coach. He had put the envelope in his pocket and now seemed more intent on where he was going.

From her vantage point, Vera could study the man's appearance. His face was pale and drawn. He had long fingers and narrow hands that seemed strangely fixed like weapons. The tall, thin man looked like one big stick of dynamite, primed and ready to explode in an instant. The longer Vera considered his composure, the more she realized that he wasn't relaxed but sat in a tense, rigid posture.

The train slowed and the man leaped to his feet, lining up to get out. The sign on the wall read *Crotona Park.* Vera stepped into place, ready to move when the door opened. Mr. Trench Coat was the second one off the car and turned immediately to his left. Dozens of people were lined up to get on the train, so Vera had to struggle to get off. Taller than most of the people walking around him, the mysterious man proved fairly easy to see from a distance. He took the stairs up to the ground level and disappeared around the corner.

No! No! Vera said to herself. *Can't let him get out of my sight.* She hurried up the steps but several people were coming down and slowed her. When she reached the landing, the man was nowhere in sight. "He's gone!" Vera gasped. She started walking slowly through the mob of people pressing to get on the subway. The station felt more like a riot than the site of public transportation.

Vera kept pushing forward. To the side of the crowd she could see a row of telephones. Out of the corner of her eye, Vera caught sight of the back of a dark brown coat next to the telephones. She stopped and looked again. It was the man, using the phone! Vera caught her breath.

To one side of the multitude moving past, Vera saw a large black scarf that someone had dropped. She quickly scooped up the cloth and threw it over her head. The opaque material proved long enough to fall over Vera's head and shoulders while keeping her face fairly well concealed. Without slowing her pace, Vera walked over to the phone stall and picked up the phone next to the man. She pushed in a quarter, glancing at him, but he didn't turn around.

"*Dah, dah!*" the man barked into the phone.

Vera kept her back turned but leaned toward him with her ear turned in his direction.

"Prahsteeteh, eezveeneetheh." The man shrugged and tossed a hand up in the air. "Yes. I speak de Engleesh. Dis is Senka Volo calling."

Vera pulled the receiver away from her ear. "Yes, I'd like to speak with Mr. Jones," she said in low, muffled tones.

"The boss paid me," Volo continued. "De man paid me in dollars."

Vera leaned closer to him.

"No problem. More business come sooner. De Colorado matter is settled."

Vera caught her breath.

"He likes de way I do things. Good money there."

"Thank you," Vera said abruptly into the silent receiver to keep the appearance of a phone call going. "Yes, but I can't wait much longer. Thank you."

"Be there tomorrow. Yes. *Spahseebah.*" He glanced at her.

Vera stared at the wall to avoid the man's catching any glimpse of her face. She was far, far too close for comfort. She waited for Volo to say something else. He must be getting instructions. "Thank you," Vera said into the silent phone. "Yes, I appreciate your efforts." She slowly turned again to check. Senka Volo had slipped away!

Vera slammed the receiver down and frantically looked up and down the corridor crammed with people. Down at the far end she caught a brief glimpse of the tall man in the brown coat rushing through the door.

Vera started pushing her way out into the herd, trying to get through the people before her suspect got away.

"Hey, that's my head scarf!" A heavyset woman suddenly blocked Vera's advance.

"What?" Vera tried to look around her.

"I dropped that scarf just a few minutes ago." The fat-faced woman pushed her hand in Vera's chest. "I want it back!"

"The scarf?" Vera looked down at her shoulders. "Sure." She pulled the black cloth off her head and shoved it at the woman. "It's yours." She tried to get past her.

"You trying to steal this wrap or something?" The large woman looked ready to punch Vera.

"Sorry." Vera twisted out of her grasp and quickly pushed into the line of people.

"You come back here!" the woman called, but the private investigator kept hurrying toward the front door.

Vera burst out onto the street filled with people. Taxis were lined up along the curb. Cars buzzed down the street. Wherever Vera looked, she saw nothing but a sea of people marching down the street. In the endless parade, she could not see any dark brown trench coats. *He's gone!* she thought disappointedly. *I've lost him.* Vera ran her hand nervously through her hair. She started back inside the Crotona Park station and stopped.

Colorado! she thought. *This foreign joker wouldn't have come up with that comment on my state out of nowhere in a thousand years! At least I know his name is Senka Volo and he's tied to this operation in some way or another.*

28

VERA GRABBED A TAXI IN FRONT OF THE Crotona Park subway station. On her way back to the hotel, she pulled out her cellular telephone and called Cara.

"You doing okay, kid?"

"Mom, are you serious? I'm sitting here having the greatest experience of my life reading my schoolbooks. *Sure.*"

Vera laughed. "Listen, I'll be back there in ten minutes or so. Why don't you meet me downstairs in the restaurant near the front door? Go ahead and order something for lunch. I'll let you know what's happened so far."

"I'll be there."

Cara hung up and Vera leaned back against the seat. She missed Sam terribly. If only he were there to tell her what to do next. Vera felt tears starting to well up and she swallowed quickly.

She had to keep herself together. That was the only way she

was going to get anything done. This wasn't the time to break down. She took a deep breath.

The taxi sped on, turning onto Lenox and dropping her off in front of the Renaissance Hotel. She went into the restaurant. Sure enough, Cara was sitting there by herself, halfway through eating a hamburger.

Cara looks like she's twenty, Vera thought. *She's a gorgeous young woman.*

Cara waved. "What'd you find out?"

Vera sat down. "Quite a morning!" She put down her tote bag with the gun and the phone beside the table. "I've had a difficult day so far."

"What happened?"

"I didn't tell you the details back in the street café, but the secretary at Ukraine Imports didn't seem to know Bashilov exists. Then this man came out of the boss's office with the totally bald head, the big neck, the frightening look, everything except the right name. She called him *Trudoff.*"

Cara shook her head. "Sounds confusing."

Vera nodded her head. "You bet."

"And you're not sure what's going on?"

"Yes and no," Vera answered. "I'm not sure about the man in that office. Maybe Trudoff, maybe Bashilov. Possibly one guy with two names. But I followed another man waiting in the reception area, and he proved to have real possibilities. I think the Ukraine Imports office is definitely part of this puzzle."

"Excellent," Cara said. "I knew you'd figure something out."

Vera shrugged. "Yes, I made progress, but I don't know where any of this is going. The secretary could be deceiving me, but she didn't seem like that sort of person. She just seemed indifferent."

Cara nodded and looked out the window at the people

walking down the street. "Sure are a lot of people going up and down these streets." Her voice trailed away.

Vera studied her face. Cara looked lonely and lost in this gigantic city of twelve million. If Vera let herself go, she would feel the same way. "Awfully big place, isn't it?"

Cara nodded her head. "Sure is."

"You miss your father, don't you?"

Cara bit her lip. "Yeah. I do." A tear slowly meandered down her cheek.

Vera took her hand. "I do, too, dear. We just have to keep on pushing to get through all this mess. We have to keep on trying to get at the truth."

"Mom, sometimes things don't make good sense. Even doing my schoolwork feels meaningless. I wanted to come here, but now I feel as out of place as a tennis ball at a basketball game. Crazy, isn't it?"

Vera squeezed her daughter's hand again. "The world's like that, Cara. We have to go on under difficult circumstances. We don't have any other choice."

She nodded. "I know, Mom." She finished her lunch and pushed the plate back.

"Cara, I've got to think by myself again. I want you to go back to the room and stay there until I come up. I've got to figure out what I'm going to do next."

"Mom, you promised that I could be a part of everything that happens."

"You will be, but I need to be alone now, okay?" Vera answered. "I'm not hungry, but I'll have some coffee. Please go back and study some more, and I'll return after I've thought about this problem."

"Wouldn't it be better if I—"

"No," Vera cut her off. "It wouldn't. I will see you later."

Vera watched her daughter head for the elevator. For a long time she sat, lost in thought.

This town may be New York City, Vera thought, *but it feels more and more like a labyrinth of confusion where nobody knows what's going on or how long they might stay alive.*

For five minutes Vera sat alone and sipped a cup of coffee. Everything in her head felt scrambled and out of order. How in the world could she put the pieces of the puzzle together? She'd learned something today, but what?

An image came back to Vera. She could once again envision her minister in Colorado Springs sitting across from her. He'd said that the issue wasn't what had happened as much as what she chose to make of the tragedy. God had given her the capacity to rebuild the scattered parts of her life, and that was her task at this moment. Surely, providence would lead her through this twisted place!

Vera knew that the man the receptionist had identified as Trudoff had clearly been called Bashilov on all the correspondence they had found on Sam's computer. The only conclusion was that Bashilov and Trudoff were the same person. But why did he use two names? And was he tied to what happened to Sam?

"Care for me to fill your cup?" the waitress asked.

Vera jumped. "Oh! I didn't see you coming. Yes. Sure." She pushed the cup toward the waitress.

"Call if you need anything." The young woman walked away.

Vera looked out the restaurant window again. A rush of cold wind whistled down the street, blowing and stirring up the dead leaves and twigs along the curb. A few flakes of snow drifted past and Vera felt the cold. Winter was far from over.

Vera sipped her coffee again and thought about what she'd learned. Everything indicated that this Ivan Trudoff character had the money and resources to do whatever he wanted. The decor of the lavish office clearly told that story. He could be responsible for Sam's death. If the two had clashed over money—and they apparently dealt with enormous sums—Trudoff could have arranged for Sam to die.

Part of the reason that I'm here is to protect my husband's reputation, Vera thought. *I can't let this killer get away with murdering both Sam and his history.*

The words hurt when she thought them. Even if Sam had been stealing money—or at least taking money illegally—she wasn't going to let his good name be tarnished by some aspect of a story that no one would ever fully understand. After all, who in Colorado Springs would ever hear of this Bashilov character? He'd simply continue living in luxury in New York City while hundreds of people who loved Sam would be disillusioned. And worst of all, Cara would be devastated!

Then there was this Senka Volo character. Who knew what this guy was about? He'd certainly eavesdropped on her conversation with the receptionist, and he knew something about Colorado. Whoever he was, Mr. Trench Coat must be watched—that is, if she ever saw him again.

Vera reached down and felt the outline of the gun in her purse. She believed she had the capacity to pull the trigger. But could she—really? Could she shoot Bashilov or Volo if necessary? Even the idea froze everything inside her. She shuddered again.

Vera realized Christians weren't supposed to kill. Certainly, they were forbidden to murder. She had to protect herself, but she didn't want to be in the business of shooting at anybody.

The telephone in her purse began ringing. Vera rummaged through her tote bag until she found the phone.

"Vera, it's Ace. How are things going?"

"It's a struggle, Ace. I don't really know what to do next."

"Yeah, I understand. Vera, I had to pull a bunch of strings but I've gathered some data for you on this Ivan Trudoff guy."

"Excellent!"

"The man survived World War II under the worst of circumstances," Ace began, "but I don't have any insight on what he did during that period. Turns out that he's got a truckload of brains and in 1960 ended up at the Moscow University, studying law. He became a member of the Communist Party and got himself into the government of Mikhail Gorbachev. By 1989, though, the old party line was clearly going down the toilet."

"Hmm. Sounds like I've got a bright boy here who knows how to get close to the action."

"Right. Any fool could see that things weren't going the way Marx predicted."

"What happened to Trudoff in this shuffle?"

"Best as I can tell, he may have started messing with crime. There appears to have been a hasty exit from the Russian government. At the least, the State Department has a big black mark behind this man's name. He's used an alias in the past. I think you could be dealing with a big-time crook here. I'd stay out of this man's way. He's got to be highly dangerous."

"Thank you, Ace. You've helped me a great deal."

"Got any more to tell me?"

"No, not right now."

"Stay in touch with me."

"I will." Vera clicked the phone off and stared at the table. What in the world had she gotten herself into?

29

AT THE COLORADO SPRINGS POLICE DEPARTMENT, Chief Al Harrison stood at his third-story window, looking over the downtown area and waiting for the other detectives to arrive. In front of him lay the snow-covered Acacia Park with the bronze statue of General Palmer, one of the founders of Colorado Springs, standing at the entrance. People hurried up and down the city street while the high mountains' cold winds blew snow in every direction. Harrison kept thinking about the report lying on his desk. He glanced at his watch. *One o'clock. Everyone should be back from lunch.*

"Chief, you called a meeting?" Dick Simmons walked in wearing a blazing-red tie.

Harrison looked over his shoulder. "You planning to start a forest fire with that new tie?"

"Just a little something to warm me up on this cold day." Simmons grinned.

The police chief shook his head. "I swear, Simmons. You've got more flashy colored ties in your closet than anyone else on the planet."

"I try to stay on top of the trends." Simmons kept smiling a smug grin. "This is one of the latest. Got to look my best when I run down vicious criminals."

Harrison rolled his eyes. "Where are the rest of the officers?"

"They're coming. Ought to be here any moment." Dick looked around the office and out the front door to make sure that no one was listening. "After checking on the $200,000 deposit at Peak National Bank, I wondered if you'd heard anything additional about Sam Sloan's situation?"

Harrison squinted. "I thought I told you not to ask any questions on that issue."

"Sure, but right now it's just me and you."

"Don't push your luck, Simmons."

"Sorry," a policeman said, rushing into the room, "I got delayed on an emergency phone call."

"Your hundred and one calls are always emergencies, Smith," the police chief grumbled. "Sit down."

Two more officers filed into the room, including Basil Abbas. Harrison made a quick survey of the group. "Looks like everybody's here. Sit down." He pointed at the door. "Simmons, shut the door. This is a confidential conference."

Simmons quickly obeyed and silence fell over the room.

Harrison picked up several identical reports lying on his desk. "This is top-secret information for the time being, so don't anyone leave this room and talk about what you're about to read." He started handing out the copies. "Make a hasty scan of this material and then we'll discuss it."

Each officer took a copy and immediately started reading. Harrison went back to the window and watched the street below him.

Dick Simmons was the first to speak. "Hey, this is an autopsy of that George Alexander guy, the president of the bank!"

"Yeah, I thought he died of a heart attack," Smith added.

Harrison turned around slowly. "But what does that autopsy say?"

Simmons laid his copy on the small table next to him. "The picture I get is that Alexander died of a heart attack all right, but it wasn't natural. I mean, something caused his heart to quit thumping. You might say that it was induced."

"Exactly," Harrison answered. "Now, did you get what caused the man's death?"

Simmons picked up the copy again and started reading.

"Let me make this simple, boys." The police chief walked over and sat down at his desk. "Did any of you notice the welt described on Alexander's neck on the morning that the body was found?"

A couple of the officers nodded.

"Although nothing was said or released to the newspapers," Harrison continued, "Alexander's wife had no knowledge of any wound, knot, or welt on the man's body when he left home that morning. Something caused the swelling to occur after Alexander left his house. When I learned what I just told you, I asked the coroner's office to thoroughly run this problem down."

"What did they find?" Basil Abbas asked.

"The coroner checked this thing out carefully and came to the conclusion that it was caused by a low-caliber pellet, from an air gun like a small Crossman air pistol. It was compact but strong enough to leave a painful sting, and quiet enough not to be heard at any distance. In other words, the coroner's opinion was that Alexander got shot in the neck before he died, and that's tied to what killed the man."

The officers looked at each other with puzzled faces. Dick Simmons frowned. "No one indicated any of this to us earlier."

"Or none of you caught it." The chief's voice sounded caustic. He leaned over the desk. "Now, I understand that Sam Sloan was among the first people to look at the body. Right?"

A young policeman near the rear of the room held up his hand. "I guess that's why I'm here. I called Sloan at home because he was the first detective that came to my mind. I mean, everybody knows Sam does a good job, and I just thought—"

"Okay," the chief said, cutting him off, "I get the picture. You called Sloan because you thought he was competent."

"That's about it," the policeman said sheepishly. "Nothing personal about any of it. I didn't mean to throw a kink in department policy."

Harrison stared at the young officer in front of him. "Except that you did violate policy procedure by not calling here first." The chief turned to look at all the officers. "This matter is still of a completely confidential nature, and I don't want talk anywhere outside of this room. Got me?"

Four heads nodded.

"Okay," the chief said. "Simmons and Abbas will stay. The rest of you go back to your duties."

Two policemen got up and hurried out.

"All right," Harrison continued, "read this autopsy report again and let's make sure that we're all on the same page."

"I thought this man's funeral had already been held," Simmons said.

"They had a memorial service because they didn't want any information flying around about something strange killing Alexander," Harrison said. "But I had an understanding with the widow that there'd be no burial until after this autopsy was completed. It can take as long as a week to fully test what might have been in the stomach. The truth is, Alexander's body is still down at the morgue."

Simmons gave Abbas a surprised look.

"Yeah, I understand. Neither of you was in on this situation." Harrison leaned back in his chair and crossed his arms over his chest. "No one knows because I'm the only other person in the department who had any idea that something illegal was going on with the bank president. Sloan had been working this case and he was under no one in the city police force but my office. Unusual procedure, but it was all approved by me."

Simmons took a deep breath. "I see." He raised both eyebrows. "How come you're bringing us in at this late hour?"

"I think I'm going to need some help before long," the chief admitted. "You're two of the most trusted men we've got."

Simmons grinned. "Nice to know that you have a high opinion of us."

"I didn't say that I did!" Harrison barked. "I said you were trusted. Don't get ahead of yourself, Dick."

Dick held up the report. "The best that I can make out of this medical mumbo jumbo is that they found traces of something called 'prussic acid' in Alexander's stomach."

"And in his lungs," Abbas added. "What is prussic acid?"

"Causes your blood vessels to constrict radically," the chief explained. "Do you also notice that the coroner found tiny pieces of broken glass in the man's face? Here's the bottom line. Someone threw prussic acid in Alexander's face. He both smelled and swallowed the stuff. The dose was so strong that he died quickly. I'd say that the air pistol in some way or other broke a vial of the acid and sprayed our good bank president. The man was murdered."

Abbas took a deep breath but said nothing.

The police chief got up and walked back to the office window. "I'm sure that Sam guessed there was a problem, but best as I can tell, he didn't talk to anyone."

Both detectives nodded.

"Simmons, I want you to go out there and find Vera Sloan. Sam wouldn't admit it, but I know that he and his wife talked a considerable amount about the cases he was working. See if Sam said something—anything—to his wife. I want to know what *she knows*. Got me?"

"Yes, sir, I'll do it as quickly as possible."

"Have either of you mentioned to anyone what you discovered at the Peak Bank about Sam Sloan's deposit?"

"No, sir."

"Don't." Harrison nodded toward the door. "Keep your mouths shut, but see if you can find out anything on what's happening with Sam's wife. You can go now."

30

IVAN TRUDOFF SHUT HIS OFFICE DOOR BEHIND him and cursed. The secretary was an idiot! A fool! He had given her those letters to be typed in plenty of time for her to have them done by now. The stupid woman should have handed them to him immediately when he walked out to her desk.

Of course, dullness was what he had wanted when he hired a secretary. If there was anything he didn't need, it was someone bright enough to be searching through the files or finding his sequestered hidden file system. A self-indulgent twit served his purposes best. And that's what he had. He cursed again.

Trudoff glanced at his wristwatch. The bookkeeper should be coming up the back steps in a few moments. Nikita Grishin, the accountant, took care of intimate contacts with the banks and financial negotiations with contractors for Ukraine Imports' "heavier" products. He had first met Grishin when both men worked for Gorbachev's government in the Soviet Union. Like himself, Grishin had barely survived the World War II assaults of the Nazis. In time, Grishin became one of Trudoff's closest associates.

The Russian sat down at his desk and quickly rummaged through some financial papers and his last correspondence with Yossi Abu Medien. He drummed on the desk with his fingers. He didn't like Senka Volo's caveats. Trudoff picked up the phone and pressed the intercom button.

"Hello," the secretary answered.

"Come in here immediately."

"Yes, sir."

Trudoff laid down the phone and stared at the door.

The secretary bounced in with several sheets of paper in her hand. "Got a couple of those letters done, but I don't have—"

"Sit down," Trudoff said, cutting her off.

"Sure thing." The woman slid into the chair opposite his desk and smiled a silly grin. "What ya need?"

"Some woman come in here this morning?"

"Yeah. Said she was looking for the Ukraine Exports Company. I told her that she had the wrong place."

Trudoff stared at the woman.

"I did something wrong?" The secretary shrugged.

"Was she looking for a man?"

The receptionist twisted her mouth. "Well," she paused and scratched her head, "there was some strange name."

"Was it Bashilov?"

The woman frowned. "Oh, it sounded close to that name, but I don't think that was it."

Trudoff leaned over his desk and glowered. "Volo heard

you talking with her, and he was sure she was looking for a man named Bashilov."

"Volo was sitting clear on the other side of the room, and I doubt if that jerk could have heard anything the woman said clearly." The receptionist shrugged again. "I think he must have mixed up the names because I don't remember the woman asking for a Bashilov. Seemed more like *Boslop,* or maybe *Bashelou.*"

Trudoff cracked his knuckles. The corners of his mouth dropped. "You got hearing problems?"

"Of course not," the woman snapped. "I'm telling you the story like I experienced it."

Trudoff leaned back in his chair. "When anybody comes in here, I want to know about it. Understand?"

"Sure."

Ivan reached over and took the letters. "Okay. You think about that name and see if you can recall it with more certainty."

"You know, it really wasn't anything." The receptionist stood up. "Simply mistaken identity. Got the wrong office. Your friend Volo's got a big nose and a huge mouth." She walked to the door.

Trudoff's eyes narrowed to slits. He watched the door shut behind her. "The woman has the brains of a goat," he muttered to himself.

For the next five minutes Trudoff scribbled the name *Bashilov* over and over on the pad lying in front of him. Years spent working for the Communists and with the KGB had taught Ivan Trudoff to assume nothing. Every step in his journey was calculated, measured, observed, or no action was taken. A simple procedure like constantly checking on what the people around him were doing had saved his life many times. The name was important. No one came into his office looking for any name even close to Bashilov by accident.

Trudoff glanced at his wristwatch. Maybe after lunch Grishin would show. No problem. Twelve o'clock always meant working out in the sealed gymnasium he had assembled next to his office. Each day the receptionist would leave for lunch, locking the front door behind her, and Ivan slipped into the concealed former office next to his.

Time to start the exercise, he thought. *Yes, the ignorant woman will leave momentarily. I can begin early.*

Walking briskly across the room, Trudoff pushed a button under a shelf on his bookcase. Immediately, a wall panel that had previously been a doorway into the side office slid open, revealing the inside of the adjacent room as a weight-lifting gym. Along the side walls stood Trudoff's confidential files. Once he shut the sliding entry, he was in a room that virtually no one knew existed. Secrecy was as natural to Trudoff as eating breakfast. The only place that he completely relaxed was inside his hidden gym.

"Magnificent!" Ivan mumbled to himself, watching the panel close behind him. "Always works."

In one end of the room, a shower had been installed, and across the adjacent wall, a full-length mirror where Ivan could observe himself working out. He immediately began stripping down to his boxer shorts.

For a moment Trudoff stared into the mirror. At five feet, eight inches, he was not tall for the size of his chest and arms. Weight lifting had developed Ivan into a bull with seventeen-inch biceps, a fifty-inch chest, and a seventeen-inch neck. For a moment he studied himself. Trudoff's round face and double chin, as well as his shaggy eyebrows, looked typical enough, but shaving his head gave him a sinister look he liked. After all, he could let his coarse black hair grow out anytime. His slightly flattened nose made him look somewhat like a boxer. Three teeth on the left side of his mouth had been completely capped with silver, a distinguishing mark not so easily covered.

"Not bad!" he said to himself, glancing in the mirror.

Trudoff sat down on the chest-press machine and began his strenuous, fast-paced routine. He grunted, pressing the heavy pads on the chest machine forward. "A-a-a-h!" he shouted, sending three hundred pounds away from his body.

The sudden thrust of the large amount of weight unlocked a hidden room in his memory, touching a long-forgotten nerve. He didn't like the emergence of those terrifying old memories.

In 1944 a remnant of the Nazi army had appeared out of nowhere and overwhelmed his village, the burg of Pskov. He had been only three years old but he could vividly remember the screams and shouts of the villagers. People ran in every direction, trying to avoid the horde of thieves and cutthroats marching in with strings of ammunition hanging around their necks. Ivan remembered the Waffen-SS machine-gun crews rolling in on trucks, firing their endless stream of terror at anything that walked or moved.

His mother kept screaming, "Ivan! Little Ivan! Where are you?" Trudoff's mother had pushed the bedroom door open and found him curled up by the bed against the wall, covering his head in terror. Suddenly Ivan's grandfather rushed in behind his mother and pushed her aside.

"Get out!" Grandfather had cried. "We must run at once!"

At that moment a machine-gun crew pulled up outside the Trudoff house and opened fire, sending shots through the window. Grandfather had suddenly shaken in a spastic dance of death, then dropped to the floor. An instant later an explosion rocked the little house, bringing the roof crashing down. Smoke and dust nearly suffocated Ivan. Even now, decades later, Trudoff remembered frantically pushing and pulling to get the pieces of plaster away from his face. Trudoff was sure that he would die. Minutes later, Ivan's mother pulled a hunk of the wall back and lifted him out of what had promised to be his tomb. His mother's face was brown from dust and soot and her clothes hung limply from her shoulders, torn to shreds. Ivan never saw his grandfather again.

Trudoff stood up slowly and walked over to the leg-press machine. Recollections made him want to do erratic, crazy things. He shook his head and continued exercising even harder for the next forty-five minutes.

31

AT 12:58, IVAN TRUDOFF CLOSED THE clandestine panel door to his gym and returned to his desk. Predictably, the secretary would show up five minutes late and the afternoon grind would begin again. He delighted in catching her tardiness and rubbing her nose in such sloppy performance.

Suddenly the back door to Trudoff's office opened, interrupting his thoughts, and Nikita Grishin walked in. Like Trudoff, Grishin was a stocky man. But his shape was due to fat, not muscle. His cheeks jiggled when he walked, and his hands were the size of half-hams.

"Hail, Comrade!" Grishin mockingly saluted as if addressing a commissar. "I trust you already filled your palm with rubles this day."

"You are a comic today? You are also late."

Nikita shook his head. "What else can one be in a world filled with fools and idiots? I was delayed at the bank."

"Ah, fools and idiots! You took the words right out of my mouth. Sounds like you've been talking with my receptionist already."

Grishin's slitlike eyes narrowed even farther. "I have enough problems without getting into some meaningless conversation with her."

"Come on," Trudoff mocked. "Surely she is no worse than the secretaries we had to put up with in the Kremlin's offices."

"Really?" Grishin raised an eyebrow. "I wasn't aware that there was much difference."

Trudoff chuckled and walked around his desk. He sat down opposite Grishin. "I believe you've been having conversations with the Bank of New York City. Correct?"

Nikita Grishin shook his head and the fat around his neck quivered. "I have been listening more than talking." He scowled. "If you know what I mean."

Trudoff studied Nikita's face carefully. He had learned to read the simple twitches, the lines, a few muscular movements in Grishin's usually stoic face. Today the man didn't look happy. "What's going on?" Ivan asked.

"Bank regulators are tightening the reins on how accounts operate," Nikita said bluntly. "For some reason, they are particularly interested in funds that are transferred in from abroad." He drummed on the desk with his fingers. "Particularly the former Soviet Union countries."

Ivan took a deep breath. "So?"

"We are becoming their main source of interest." The corners of Grishin's mouth dropped and hardened. "The large amounts of our transactions have caught their eyes."

Trudoff could feel anger starting to boil. "What do you mean?"

"We are moving millions of dollars around the world." Grishin folded his arms over his fat chest. "These transactions begin in foreign accounts. Everyone is afraid of getting caught up in the drug money business and big sums automatically catch the eye of bank officials. But I believe we may also have attracted political attention."

Ivan stared across the room out the window that overlooked Manhattan. For a moment he ground his teeth. "I wonder if that fool George Alexander in Colorado Springs was involved in any of this."

Nikita shook his head. "I don't think so. That gluttonous incompetent simply wanted to steal from us. His actions didn't fit into this scheme of things."

Trudoff slumped back in his chair. "I don't like the sound of this. We came to this country because it is the most powerful in the world. We thought it would provide a safe haven for our business transactions."

"Yes, but the nation is also highly regulated. The Americans are no fools, and bank officials at high levels are not easily corrupted." Nikita rolled out a fat lip.

Trudoff folded his hands across his chest and cracked his knuckles. "I don't like the sound of *any* of this report," he spoke sullenly. "Any of it!"

"You think that I enjoy the problem?" Nikita leaned into the desk.

Trudoff rubbed his mouth nervously. "Have you talked with anyone about this matter?"

"No one. Only you."

"I am surrounded by nothing but difficulties!" Ivan pounded

the top of the desk. "Problems! Do you hear me?" He was shouting now. "I'm sick of it!" He stood and started pacing around the room. "Nikita, we came here to get out of a world ruled by people shooting each other in dark alleys, and now we again find ourselves pressed down similar city streets. It makes me extremely angry."

Nikita Grishin kept his arms folded over his chest and his face set resolutely. Fat rolled over the side of his collar. He said nothing.

"I suppose we can always call on the services of my associate Senka Volo," Ivan threatened. "He seems to be the most successful in dealing with these unexpected glitches in our operation."

Nikita turned uncomfortably in his chair. "We can't go on killing everyone who gets in our way. Sooner or later those deaths will catch up with us."

"No!" Trudoff shouted. "We aren't going to be controlled by a worthless political system! The Nazis aren't going to be allowed to come marching in here again, regardless of whether they are wearing black uniforms or red, white, and blue. No one is going to run my life." He suddenly stopped and grabbed a vase of flowers sitting on a small stand next to the windows. With one mighty heave, Ivan threw the flowers across the room, smashing them against the wall. "They can shoot me before I will buckle to these manipulating swine!"

The vase shattered against the wall, and water splashed against the wallpaper. White flowers fell across the rug. Nikita stared with his mouth open. Immediately the outer office door opened.

"Hey, everything okay in here?" the receptionist asked.

Trudoff whirled around. "Didn't I tell you *never* to enter this room without knocking?"

The woman looked at the broken vase, the flowers scattered on the carpet, and at Grishin sitting in the chair. "Oh, I didn't know anyone was here." She blinked several times. "Sorry," the receptionist said apologetically. "I just thought that maybe you'd hurt yourself."

"Out!" Trudoff screamed. "Get out of here!"

The receptionist disappeared instantly, slamming the door behind her.

"There's another one that Senka Volvo can take care of," Trudoff growled. "Kill all of them!"

Nikita Grishin looked at the floor. "I know that you don't like what I've told you, but I have been completely honest, Ivan. You know that I don't play games."

Ivan shook his head. "Yes, yes. Of course." He sighed.

"I will be going now, but I will keep working on the complications. I have not given up hope, but we must be careful."

Trudoff nodded. "Certainly. Take care, my friend."

Nikita waved and disappeared out the back door.

With his hands behind his back, Trudoff stared down at the street far below him, thinking out loud. "That woman who came in here this morning . . . whatever her name is . . . has got to be investigated. Maybe she's part of this problem."

No one comes in here asking for information, he thought. *I must find out more about who this person is.*

32

Vera and Cara started back up Lenox Avenue. On each side of the thoroughfare, expensive stores flashed their elegant wares. Sophisticated clothing and fur coats filled their windows.

"I must, in some way, get inside the world of this Ivan Trudoff, or Bashilov, character if I'm going to answer any of my questions," Vera said.

"How would you do that?"

"I'm not sure," Vera answered, "but I've got to work my way inside that business office. I must do something to get this clown to talk while not exposing my hand. That's a big problem!"

"Thanks for letting me come with you. We'll find a way."

"Sure."

For several moments, Vera thought about going back to Trudoff's offices at night. Picking locks was an art Sam had taught her. The tools were in her purse. She could break in and search the place. During her college studies, she'd learned a number of approaches to searching for evidence: the spiral method, a grid approach, a strip or line search. Any of them would work on Trudoff's offices, but Vera would have to pay careful attention to make sure she didn't get caught. At the least, she'd collect evidence about who the man was.

Cara broke the silence. "You know we could get in big legal trouble for breaking into Trudoff's place."

"Yes, breaking into his office wouldn't accomplish anything if I got caught. Surely the office must be wired with a security system. If we didn't disable the device, we'd probably have the police all over us in thirty seconds."

"No kidding!"

"But then again, maybe we wouldn't!" Vera stopped walking. "I can't decide what to do without taking a long, hard look at the place." She abruptly picked up her pace. "Why not? If I case the building carefully, something unexpected might turn up. Who says that we can't break in?"

"You don't mean that!" Cara gasped.

Vera started walking faster.

Ace glanced at his watch. In thirty minutes he would leave the All-City Confidential Agency and head for home. Out in the reception area, he could hear Sally Armfield typing up what he'd dictated for that day. By the next morning he'd be able to submit two survey forms to the Colorado Springs companies wanting data on their prospective employees. He had checked the courthouse and the credit bureau, gone over their driving records. Their histories were clean. Both men had quite a bit of debt, but who didn't? They should be good employees.

The front door opened and a man asked Sally, "Is Ace Newton here?"

"Sure," the secretary said. "He's in his office. Let me ring him."

Ace listened for a moment. It wasn't easy to hear clearly, but he recognized the voice. He jumped out of his desk chair and rushed into the front reception area. "Hey, Dick."

"Ace Newton!" Dick Simmons said. "As I live and breathe. Didn't mean to interrupt your nap."

"Don't josh me." Newton shook Simmons's hand. "I'm surprised that they'd let a cop loose on the streets after 4:30. Dangerous for the citizens."

"I've been sent out here to make sure that you're not still peddling drugs to grade-school children."

Sally Armfield's mouth dropped.

"He's kidding, Sally." Newton patted the secretary on the shoulder. "Don't take this man seriously. Understand? He's mentally incompetent."

"Of course," Simmons added. "Ace sells only to the kids' parents."

They laughed and then Simmons asked, "You got a minute?"

"For you? Not on your life." Newton grinned and pointed over his shoulder. "Come on back."

They walked into Newton's office, and Ace closed the door behind them.

"This place is secure?" Simmons asked.

Ace grinned. "Sure . . . until I push the tape-recorder button under the desk with my big toe."

Simmons's flat laugh lacked feeling. "Yeah, sure. I want to make sure that we're not overheard."

"You're safe." Ace pointed at the desk chair. "Sit down and take a load off your feet."

"I want to talk about this Sam Sloan problem." Dick sat down. "How's his wife holding up emotionally?"

"Vera's struggling to know what's coming off. In fact, you're about the first person from the police department who's even expressed any interest in a week." He raised his eyebrows mockingly. "I'm sure Chief Harrison sent you down here just to ask me that question."

Simmons twisted awkwardly in his chair. "Believe it or not, Harrison did send me over here."

Newton laughed. "I bet he did."

Simmons scooted up closer to Newton's desk. "We're talking as old buddies, good times here, Ace. Whatever we say can't go any farther than this room today. Okay?"

"Depends." Ace's smile faded. "Vera's an employee now. I'd probably have to talk with her. Can't promise that I wouldn't, but everyone else will be out of the loop."

Dick rubbed his mouth for a moment. "I can live with that possibility."

Ace leaned back in the chair. "Okay, partner. Shoot."

"We know that Sam talked with Vera more than he should have when he was working cases. She helped him solve a couple of those big murders. Sam wouldn't admit it because he didn't want Vera drawn into some courtroom fight, but I know that he confided in her all the time."

Newton didn't answer. He only nodded his head knowingly.

"Turns out that Sam was involved with this case where

the bank president got murdered. George Alexander was the man's name."

Ace froze in his chair, trying not to convey the charge of energy that he felt. He'd certainly been right in his hunch about Sam's being in some way involved in the investigation of the bank president's death. Ace just nodded.

"I need to know if Sloan told his wife anything about what he learned about the man's death."

"Let's see here." Ace casually stretched his legs out in front of him. "Maybe we can trade a little information. You tell me something; I'll tell you something."

"You're on." Simmons put his elbows on Ace's desk.

"You say that Alexander was murdered? Got that right?"

"I didn't tell you that, but if you want to draw that conclusion, you'd be dead center on target."

Ace nodded his head. "Has Sam turned up?" he asked. "I mean, does anybody know where his body is?"

Simmons shook his head. "Harrison is tighter than a clam. Isn't saying anything except that Alexander was murdered."

"Hmm." Newton pursed his lips. "Don't know what to make of all this, but I can tell you absolutely that Vera knew nothing about Sam's involvement in this case until after he was gone. Sloan didn't tell her one crying thing. You talked to Vera about any of this?"

Simmons scratched his head. "Interesting. No, I haven't been out to the Sloans' house all week. Never saw a case quite like this one. Nothing is making much sense. The police chief was only hoping that Vera knew something."

Newton shook his head. "Not on your life. She got nothing from Sam personally."

"Okay, I appreciate the confidential information." Simmons stood up to leave. "Thanks, Ace."

"No problem." Ace watched him walk out, still pondering the fact that the police didn't have the slightest idea that Vera was in New York City, working to solve this very case.

33

Darkness had begun to settle over New York City and the evening traffic picked up. Cold wind whistled down the street, making Vera shiver. She stood opposite the Samson Building, surveying the area while Cara sat in the street café, drinking hot chocolate. A building that size, and with such wealthy tenants, had to have security alarms in the offices. They would have to deal with that problem. The matter was now a *they* issue—Vera had promised Cara that she would be included in the investigation and this was where the promise had taken her. No turning back now.

A telephone began to ring persistently. Vera looked around. No pay phones were in sight. The ringing continued. She abruptly realized the noise was coming from her purse and immediately began digging for the cellular telephone that Ace Newton had given her.

"Hello?"

"Vera, is that you?"

"Yeah. Sure." Vera immediately recognized Newton's voice.

"Where are you?"

"Standing on a street corner in the middle of New York City."

"My gosh! You're still alive and working on the job."

"Where'd you expect me to be? Sitting in a bar, talking to the locals?"

Newton laughed. "New York City must be treating you fairly decent."

"You're kidding."

"Listen, Vera. Dick Simmons just left my office minutes ago with some information you ought to know."

Vera pressed the phone closer to her ear. "What's he saying?"

"This is all on the q.t., but Dick confirmed that Sam was working on the death of George Alexander when he left town. And here's the big stuff: Simmons says that Alexander was murdered."

"My, my!"

"Vera, you're dealing with truly bad folks up there. They knew how to pull off a big-time killing when they knocked off the bank president. You've got to be very careful. Don't forget about that bulletproof vest I sent with you as well as the technical equipment. I'm telling you not to take chances, Vera."

For a moment Vera stared at her purse. She had the gun and some of the investigative accessories with her.

"What I'm telling you is that these people may well shoot first and ask questions later," Ace said. "Don't let yourself get cornered."

"I'll keep that clearly in mind."

"And don't hesitate to call me if you need help."

"Help?" Vera laughed. "Aren't you the guy who lectured me on the fact that it would take days to get you to New York City?"

"Don't be a smart mouth, Vera."

"I'll call you later tonight or first thing in the morning."

"Do that." Ace hung up.

Vera put the telephone back in her purse. *He would have a heart attack if he knew where I was standing right now—and what I'm about to do,* she thought. She abruptly remembered Basil Abbas's advice to guard against the attack of the evil one. She paused long enough to ask God for protection and wisdom, then snapped the purse shut and stepped out into the street.

She should have enough equipment to get started. Her ten-key set of lock picks ran the gamut from a diamond pick to a half-rake and a tubular-cylinder lock pick. The L-shaped or T-type lock picks usually did the job. It'd take a whale of a lock to keep her out. Cara was also carrying a small backpack with some basic bugging equipment.

Vera walked into the café. "Okay, Cara, it's time to go. Walk beside me. We want to look as inconspicuous as possible."

Cara took a last swallow. "I'm ready." She stood up looking more like an adult than she ever had in her life.

Vera smiled. "Dear, we will be all right."

Cara's grin had a slightly grim twist. "Thank you, Mom. I appreciate being able to go with you."

Vera hugged her. "Let's go."

A few people were still coming out of the building. Vera didn't see any security officers around, but she kept walking to keep from drawing attention to herself. Once inside the building, she and Cara took the elevator.

"We'll get off on the tenth floor," Vera told Cara. "Both of us must keep looking for something, some alternative to breaking in. Watch closely." The door opened and they stepped out.

A couple of businessmen were walking toward the elevator. Vera didn't want to look like a thief surveying the building, so she picked up her pace and walked past them without making eye contact. Once more she turned the corner and led the way to Suite 1015.

"Good heavens!" Vera gasped as she realized that the secretary could come barreling out, leaving work for the day. "Cara! Hurry up!" she whispered and walked away fast.

At the far end of the hall, Vera turned another corner and stopped in front of a small alcove. "We've got to try another angle." On each side were rest rooms and in the middle was an unmarked door. She tried the knob and found it to be locked.

"Looks like a dead end, Mom."

"Not necessarily. Usually these closets don't have very sophisticated locks." Vera started rummaging through her purse. "Let me see what I can do."

Cara glanced nervously up and down the hall. "I'll watch."

"What we have here is a lever-tumbler lock." Vera pulled a simple-looking key out of her purse. "They've been around a long time, but some of them have been vastly improved and aren't easy to pick." She inserted the key. "Let's hope this one is on the common end of things." Vera slowly turned the key. "I don't think I'll need to read this lock," she said to herself and kept pushing the key. "Feels like I can open it." A slight click echoed from the lock. "That's it!" She pulled the door open.

"You did it, Mom!"

"Shh!" Vera whispered. She peeked inside and discovered that she'd found the janitor's closet. Down the wall, wires and cables ran into a small receptor box. "The security system outlets!" Vera snapped her fingers. "We're really in business. Those wires are probably the power sources to the security system. At least it's a good guess. I'd bet they've got either passive infrared detectors or photoelectric cells of some variety in those offices. When I cut the wires, the system should be deactivated until the wires are reconnected." Vera slipped on a pair of rubber gloves and took out pliers with insulation around the handles. "I never take a chance with electricity," she told Cara. She reached up and carefully cut the wires.

"What's all this stuff?" Cara pointed to a four-wheeled cart in the closet.

"That's our cleaning equipment."

A small plastic mobile cart had dust cloths, paper towels, plastic trash-can liners, and an assortment of cleaning supplies. A vacuum cleaner had been positioned on the end of the cart. On the wall hanging next to the brooms, two long, blue dusters dangled from a nail. A cloth patch over the top pocket of each read *Samson Building.* The same patch was attached to the front of a blue baseball cap.

Vera took off her leather jacket, sticking it on the bottom shelf of the cart. She positioned her purse where she could grab the gun or any of the accessories if necessary. The blue duster wrapped around her clothes and tied at the waist.

"Put the other duster on, Cara. Make it quick."

Cara started wrapping it around her. "This smock will work."

"I buy all these stylish clothes only to end up looking like the local cleaning lady," Vera said. "Can you believe it? We come to New York City and end up dressed as if we were the janitorial crew."

Cara giggled. "Yeah, we'll look on the far-out side."

Trying to decide what to do next, Vera ran her hands

nervously through her hair and suddenly remembered that she had a stylish new haircut. Aside from the duster she was wearing, she didn't look anything like a cleaning lady. She picked up the baseball cap and put it on. She was relieved to find that it covered most of her hair.

Vera quickly pushed the cart out into the hall and made sure the cleaning-closet door wouldn't lock behind her. She slowly edged toward the suite. "Stay close to me, Cara. If someone shows up, start wiping the baseboards like we work here."

Ace was right, Vera thought. *Regardless of how attractive those drapes were, this guy kills people. I'm sure I wouldn't offer Bashilov, Trudoff, whoever, any challenge . . . unless I get the jump on him. Thank goodness Cara is here to run for help.*

Vera heard the elevator door open and knew someone could come around the corner in a flash. She dropped down on her hands and knees as if cleaning around the baseboard. "Down!" she ordered Cara. Two men walked around the corner. Neither man looked at them.

"Need to hurry," an American businessman in a sport coat said to the other man. "We're almost late."

"I told you we should go faster," the heavier-set man said with a thick Russian accent. "Alec, you don't know how to get anywhere on time." The voice faded. He shook his head and opened the door for the second man. They walked in quickly.

"The door's unlocked," Vera whispered to herself. "I could just walk in like those two guys did." She stood up and inched forward. *Heaven help me! I could be walking into a trap.*

Cara stared at her mother but didn't say anything.

Vera stopped the mobile cart next to the big oak door.

She prayed under her breath as she reached for the doorknob. It turned easily. Vera peered around the door but saw no one. "Stay outside and act like you're cleaning," she told Cara. "If you hear me yell or scream, run for the police."

Cara's face whitened.

Vera gently pushed the cleaning cart inside and grabbed a cloth. For a moment she stood perfectly still and listened but heard nothing. If no one else came in, she could examine the office carefully. Those two men had to have gone somewhere, and the only other door she could see was behind the receptionist's desk. The meeting had to be back in Trudoff's inner office.

Vera tiptoed closer to the receptionist's desk. No one was in sight and all the doors were closed. For the first time she noticed a set of file cabinets sitting to one side. She tried to open the drawers but the entire set was locked. Nothing about the desk area looked unusual or suspicious. The room didn't seem to be anything more than an average well-decorated outer office. She didn't have much time to find a clue.

On the desk was an intercom phone with a flashing red light. Maybe important phone numbers were stored in there somewhere. Vera carefully picked up the receiver and heard a voice. She pressed the phone closer to her ear. Men were talking.

"Ah khahchoo ehst . . . ehst lee pahbleezahstee khahroshly reestahrahn."

Trudoff must have left the conference call receiver turned on, Vera realized. *I'm listening to their conversation in the inner office!* Her mouth dropped. The voices were distant but she could make out what they were saying.

"We can discuss this further over supper tonight," an American voice said.

"There is nothing left to discuss," a heavily accented Russian man responded. "We must kill this man quickly."

Someone else answered something in Russian.

"Okay, okay," the American voice answered. "I've got the message. Whatever you say."

Vera hung up at once. *Kill someone? I've got to get out of here.* She turned over the phone receiver. She wanted to unscrew the bottom of the phone and attach a transmitter from her purse, but time was running out. She couldn't cut it this close. These men were as dangerous as she'd feared.

Vera put the phone down and headed for the door. She grabbed the dust cloth and pushed the cart in front of her. These men would come charging out of that office and she and Cara had best be on their way down the hall rather than found playing with the telephone. The door quietly clicked shut behind her as she left the office.

With a quickening pace, Vera pushed the cart ahead of her down the hall. Cara hurried behind her. They slipped around the far corner from the alcove and watched the door of 1015 from the shadows. Any minute, those men would come out and she wanted to see their faces.

For five minutes she watched without moving, but nothing happened. After twenty minutes, Vera slipped down the hall again. "Stay here, Cara. I'm going back to check the door." The men had sounded like they were on their way out. Why hadn't they come out the front door?

She put her hand gently on the big oak door. She still had on the duster and could pass for the building's cleaning help. Vera twisted the doorknob. It wouldn't budge. The door was locked.

Vera stared at the doorknob. Obviously, no one had come out. Someone must have locked it from the inside. She turned and started back down the hall, thinking about her situation.

There's got to be a back door, Vera concluded. *They took another way out.*

"Let's get out of here, Cara." Without hesitating, she rushed back to the cleaning closet and pushed the plastic cart inside. She hung up the blue duster and the baseball cap and put her coat back on. Cara did the same. Vera quickly reconnected the alarm wires. Shutting the door behind them, Vera and Cara scurried back to the elevator. If nothing else, they would find out about that parking garage.

The elevator door opened and two young women got off, speaking Spanish. Wearing blue jeans and T-shirts under their heavy coats, they certainly didn't look like secretaries for the tenth floor. Had to be the cleaning crew.

"Good luck," Vera quipped as they passed them.

The two women stopped and stared as the elevator door closed in front of Vera.

34

IVAN TRUDOFF WORKED HIS USUAL LATE HOURS, leaving the office well after the secretary had gone home and night had settled. International telephone calls occurred with clients in other time zones, and that dictated Trudoff's office hours. Transferring money across national barriers also operated on its own unique system of demands. When it came to making money, Trudoff did whatever was required.

The Russian didn't take his customary cab to the Plaza Hotel where he stayed. Instead, he walked into Central Park toward the Tavern on the Green restaurant. Wrapped in a heavy overcoat, Trudoff strode steadily into the thickly wooded park. The outside world of cabs and cars disappeared in the more serene ambience of a city park that looked like a mountain forest.

People thinned out and Trudoff stayed by himself on the

path winding toward the popular restaurant. He turned the corner and found two Latinos standing in front of him, blocking his way.

"*¿Qué pasa?*" The largest youth in a black leather jacket leered at Trudoff.

"*¿Su amigo?*" the other boy asked the first and started inching forward.

Trudoff stopped, eyeing the two carefully.

"You only speak English, big boy?" The younger kid in the leather jacket started circling to the left side.

"I think we can teach you a little something." The other boy started to move to the right.

Without blinking an eye, Trudoff reached under his arm and pulled out a Smith and Wesson Model 57 revolver. One bullet could stop an elephant. Trudoff aimed at the larger boy.

The Latino's eyes widened and his mouth dropped.

"Wait!" the smaller youth shouted. "Don't shoot!" He started backing away.

Trudoff watched the larger juvenile leap backward into the bushes. His companion started to run but tumbled down the side of the hill, rolling head over heels.

Trudoff laughed and glanced around the area, making sure no one was in sight. Guns alerted the police, and they wouldn't waste any time showing up. He walked a bit faster but not at a pace that would make him look as if he were fleeing. Expensive clothing ought to cover any questions. So much for the bad boys.

Trudoff walked casually into the Tavern on the Green. He always used this particular restaurant when running his armaments business. The maître d' immediately recognized him and rushed forward. "Ah, Mr. Bashilov, so good to see you again, sir."

"Thank you, James. I believe I have a party waiting for me."

"Indeed, sir. May I take your coat?"

"Of course." Ivan turned around for the head waiter to remove his overcoat.

"The coat will be waiting for you when you leave, Mr. Bashilov."

Trudoff smiled and slipped a ten-dollar bill into his hand. "Please make sure that we are not disturbed."

"Certainly." The maître d' kept bowing. "No problem. You'll find the man at your usual table."

Trudoff walked slowly through the restaurant with a magnificent stride. People turned and glanced as he passed. Ivan liked being noticed in an expensive restaurant.

At the back of the room an Arab recognized him and stood up. "Ah, Mr. Bashilov. Excellent to see you."

Trudoff smiled. "Yossi Abu Medien, my old friend."

The Arab extended his hand. "Good to see you again."

Trudoff shook hands, sat down, and shot a look at the menu. After a moment he closed the plastic cover and looked hard at the waiter. The man immediately stopped what he was doing and hurried to the table.

Trudoff looked at the Arab coldly. "You want nothing more?"

"Only the drink that I've already ordered." Abu Medien kept smiling. "My stomach is on the slight side today. Please order as you wish."

"Make it a filet mignon, medium rare, with a baked potato, as fast as possible," Trudoff told the waiter. "Thank you."

The man hurried away.

"Let us speak of business immediately," the Arab said nervously. Off in the distance the sound of police sirens filled the night. The Arab looked around frantically. "We've already corresponded about these matters at some length."

"You are in a hurry?" Trudoff smiled slightly. "Someone chasing you, Yossi?" Trudoff kept smiling but watched the man carefully, enjoying his nervousness.

The Arab fidgeted. "I find that if I stay on the move I have less troubles in this country."

Trudoff laughed. "I think it's the kind of business that you do. Maybe that is what makes your feet want to walk before your body is ready to go?"

Yossi laughed uncomfortably. The sound of the police sirens increased and he looked anxiously over his shoulder again. "See what I mean?"

Trudoff smiled. "As you say, let us get to the point. I am aware that Saudi Arabia contributes more than $25 million a year to PLO coffers. Colonel Khadafy shelled out at least $40 million to the Black September terrorists a number of years back." He leaned over and smiled. "Money should be no problem for you, Yossi."

The Arab's eyes narrowed. "The former Eastern Bloc countries have no trouble furnishing us with what is needed. Even a poor country like Bulgaria can produce some arms."

Trudoff shrugged. "Then go to them with your business. Why waste my time?"

Abu Medien glared. "I need the Soviet AK-47s, pistols, and grenades."

Trudoff raised his finger to his lips. "Shh! We must be cautious of what we say even in a place like this. Maybe the police have microphones under the table." He winked mockingly and chuckled.

"Can you produce these weapons for us or not?" the Arab persisted. "Especially at the price we need?"

"The matter must first be transacted with cash transfers of

moneys to my account in Switzerland. Our problem is that you want me to give them to you rather than arrive at a fair price."

"Your supper, Mr. Bashilov." The waiter set the steak in front of Trudoff. "Anything else?"

Trudoff smiled. "You have done well. Excellent timing and speed."

The waiter bowed politely and disappeared.

"We must agree on an acceptable price," Yossi pushed.

"The standard price." Trudoff smiled and began eating. "Yes, of course, I am one of the few people who can still deliver Russian weapons on time. You make sure that you have the money, and I'll get the weapons to you immediately." He leaned forward. "*After* the money is transferred to my account."

Abu Medien settled back in his chair and scowled at Trudoff. "I don't like those terms."

"You know that there is no double-dealing with me." Trudoff kept chewing the steak. He glanced in the window and could see his silver teeth sparkling in the light. Trudoff smiled. "That is why you come to me rather than the scumbags out there on the street. I am a businessman. You submit a list of what you need and I respond immediately. The matter is simple. You have only a few days, Yossi." Trudoff kept cutting the steak and forking slices into his mouth. "Other people want the same weapons."

Abu Medien consumed the remainder of his drink in a gulp and set the glass down on the table. "You will hear from me shortly." He got up and walked out, looking angry. Ivan kept eating.

He is lying to me, Trudoff thought. *A Moslem who drinks alcohol is a man without principle. Grishin was right. We must kill this man quickly.*

35

VERA AND CARA SAT IN A STARBUCK'S COFFEE shop near the Samson Building. There Vera drank coffee and Cara, hot chocolate, as they watched the offices on the tenth floor. Their eyes stayed on what should be Suite 1015, give or take an office or two. By seven o'clock there had not been any lights shining on that side of the building for about an hour. Trudoff and friends had to be gone.

"I've got to get back in that office and set a phone tap in place," Vera told her daughter. "It's important to hear those telephone conversations. At the very least, I need to see if I can get back in the front office. This time I don't want you to go with me."

"Oh, come on, Mom!"

Vera shook her head vigorously. "Nope! I insist that you stay right here. If I got caught bugging the phone, you wouldn't be part of the hassle. And you could call for help if I needed you to."

"Just a minute!" Cara held up her hand. "How can you legally go in there and bug the place?"

"I'm not gathering data for a trial, Cara. I just want to find out what happened to your father. Yes, I'm crawling way out on the end of the limb, and I don't want you out there with me. Under the circumstances, I don't see any way to investigate more without planting bugs."

Cara sank back in her chair and drummed on the edge of the table with her fingers. "I don't like any of this."

"I don't either, but my back is against the wall. I have to function differently than I'd like. Our time is very limited, and I've got to find out what this Trudoff guy is going to do." She squeezed Cara's hand. "That's the end of it, because I need to leave right now."

"I'll be here," Cara said sullenly.

Vera pushed her chair back and slid the pack Cara had been carrying over her shoulder, along with her purse. She then ordered Cara another hot chocolate, paid her bill, and walked out to the street. She sauntered into the Samson Building as if she worked there. The doorman sat sprawled back in a chair with his eyes closed and didn't even notice her. She quickly took the elevator up to the tenth floor. By now the regular cleaning women should be hard at work and Vera didn't want to run into them.

The elevator door opened. Vera peeked down the hall but no one was in sight. She took a deep breath and walked quickly toward the closet where she'd found the cleaning equipment. Sure enough. The door remained unlocked but the pushcart was gone. As predicted, the cleaning women were at work, but a pair of janitor's coveralls, which she hadn't noticed before, still hung in the closet. Vera quickly put them on over her clothing.

Where are those cleaning women? Vera wondered as she tiptoed back out into the hallway. *Don't want to see either of them.* She eased around the corner and peered down the long hall. No one in sight. Good news.

Vera pulled back and thought for a moment. *I'm sure Suite 1015 is still locked. I wonder if those women ever clean that set of rooms.* She heard a thud.

Vera peeked around the corner. A woman had just finished 1016 and was going up the hall. She passed 1015 and moved on to 1014, unlocking the door and letting herself in. The other woman must be working in some other hall on that floor.

Vera thought for a moment and then hurried back to the work closet where she'd seen the electrical wiring earlier. For several minutes she studied the singular long black wire running down the wall into the switch box.

Only one major wire running into this circuit-breaker box, she thought. *Maybe the Ukraine Imports Company is the only business on this floor with special sensors, and that's why the janitors don't clean there.* Vera ran her hand down the plastic-coated wire. "I may be making a huge mistake. I'll know soon enough." With careful, steady movements, Vera slowly unhooked the main wire, as well as the ones she'd disconnected that afternoon. She listened but heard nothing. No bells. No sirens. Quiet.

"Only one way to find out," she said to herself and put the tools back in her tote bag. "Let's look."

Retracing her steps, Vera inched her way back up the hall to Suite 1015. She waited a moment but hearing nothing, she grabbed her ring of lock picks and started working. She quickly stuck in the reading tool and started feeling her way around the inside of the lock. After several seconds she tried the rake and then settled on a master key that was designed to work on systems like the one she believed controlled the door.

Vera turned the key carefully and slowly, listening to hear any movement. She jiggled the brass key and felt the tumblers move in the lock. "I've got it!" she exclaimed under her breath and pushed the door open slightly.

Once inside, Vera stopped and listened intently for any hum or buzz that signaled she'd made *the* big mistake. Nothing. Vera gently edged her way into the big reception room, looking carefully in all directions. She saw no tiny red lights anywhere. Apparently, she'd cut the right circuit back in the storage room.

So far, so good, Vera thought. *Got to be careful.*

Stopping in the center of the room, Vera pulled out a pocket flashlight and slipped on a pair of rubber gloves. She quickly found the telephone again. Unscrewing the bottom of the phone, Vera attached a Leech transmitter she'd brought in her purse. She carefully worked the wires loose so that the telephone's red wire became the power source to operate the device. As fast as her fingers would move, Vera put the telephone back together and set it exactly where it had been.

With the big job done, Vera turned her attention to the files. This time she pulled from her purse a thin strip of spring steel. She carefully slipped it inside the file's lock and tried to jimmy it open. For a minute she worked the slight piece of metal in and out of the lock until it suddenly turned.

"Bingo!" Vera immediately pulled the drawers open and started through the file cabinet.

To Vera's surprise, the file drawers were mostly empty. She quickly found copies of letters that didn't seem to match anything she'd found on Sam's computer in Colorado Springs.

Spreading the correspondence out on the secretary's desk, Vera carefully read through the stack. Most of the letters seemed strangely disconnected. What was going on here?

After five minutes, Vera shook her head. It was as if the files existed to create an illusion of a business. She put the files back in place and locked the cabinets.

Vera turned to the door to Trudoff's office. She quickly found that there was no lock on the outside. Vera shook the doorknob several times. The massive oak entry had a dead bolt on the inside that felt like reinforced steel. The hinges had also been constructed to operate on the inside of the door. No one was going to break into Trudoff's personal office!

It would take a stick of dynamite to blow that door down, Vera thought. *No way. I'm not going in tonight.* She turned back to the desk and quickly checked the telephone bug one more time.

Our hotel room should be close enough to pick up phone calls from this bug, Vera thought. *Cara can help me monitor the calls tomorrow. The tap should stay hot for a long time.*

Vera looked around the office again. *I've got one more bug that will catch extraneous conversations,* she thought. *Maybe if I put it under the secretary's desk I can pick up something said out here in the reception area.* She dropped to her hands and knees and quickly attached the listening device.

Don't know what else I can find out tonight. Better check the hallway before I dart out and run into the cleaning people on the move.

Vera hurried across the office and peered out the door. No one was in sight. She slipped out in an instant and made sure the large entry door locked behind her. After reconnecting the wires in the electrical box and taking off the coveralls, Vera walked in a steady pace down the hall and quickly boarded the empty elevator.

I want to get into that inner office, she thought. *I've got to find out how the rear entry works. No telling what I might find on the other side.*

The door opened and Vera walked out. The doorman was still sleeping. She crept out the side door.

Cara sat in the coffee shop, looking more relieved than peeved. Vera smiled. Her first independent covert activity had been a success.

36

VERA AND CARA SLOAN RETURNED TO THEIR hotel around nine o'clock in the evening but didn't talk much about the day. Shortly before they turned out the lights for the night, Cara tried to break the bubble that had come to surround them.

"Mom, I know that taking me with you today was hard on you. You didn't say so, but I know that you worried about my safety."

"No one wants to put her child in a potentially dangerous situation, Cara. I shouldn't have promised you back in Colorado Springs that you could be part of ferreting out this information on what happened to your father."

"But you always keep your promises, Mom. I can't tell you how much that means to me."

"Thanks, dear." Vera rolled over in bed to face her daughter.

"You gave me confidence by being available to help me if I got into trouble. Thanks for being part of a tough situation."

For nearly a minute neither said anything. Cara finally broke the silence. "I want to find out what happened to Dad as much as you do. Not knowing is torture."

"I understand, Cara. The unknown is the worst part. The emptiness, the blankness, the unanswered questions—they haunt us."

"At least today we did everything we could."

"Yes," Vera said, "and tomorrow we start again."

"Tomorrow . . ." Cara's voice drifted away.

"There is one other thing that I want you to remember. I should have told you this fact earlier in the day."

"Okay." Cara sat up in the bed expectantly.

"On the desk you will find Ace Newton's telephone number, as well as my credit card number for long-distance phone calls. If you don't hear from me by the time I've said I'll be back, I want you to call Ace and tell him what's going on here. Okay?"

Cara didn't answer for several moments. "You think that something bad might happen?"

"I'm just leaving you instructions to follow if I'm not back in this room when I should be. Understand?"

"I understand," Cara said hesitantly, "but it makes me uneasy."

"Sure," Vera said. "Don't worry, dear. Everything is going to be fine. I guess this is as good a time as any for us to talk about the special assignment that I've got for you starting in the morning."

"Really?"

"You know the tap I put on Trudoff's phone and the bug I

planted under his receptionist's desk? I want you to be my monitor station here in this hotel room."

Cara sat up straighter. "Wow! Now we're talking a big-time operation here."

Vera nodded her head. "It's essential that we know what goes back and forth out of Trudoff's office. Probably most of it won't be anything, but I need to have some idea what he's planning. Your job is to keep an accurate record of what's said. You can't miss a thing."

"Sounds serious," Cara answered. "You bet I'll cover that phone. Don't worry, Mom. You're talking to a pro."

"And I want you to call me immediately when anything comes through."

The next morning Vera and Cara slept late. Once she awoke, Vera wandered into the bathroom to take a shower and be alone for a few moments. Her first thoughts of the day had been about Sam. She missed him enormously and knew that if she let loose, her sorrow would surge over her like an ocean tide. Tears ran down her face. She couldn't let that happen. She hurried into the shower and started getting ready to face the long day.

Five minutes later Vera called out of the bathroom, "Cara, you can go downstairs and eat breakfast. I'll stay up here and monitor the phone calls. When you come back, then I'll eat."

"Okay, Mom. I'll get ready." Cara got up and slipped on her jeans.

Vera stepped out of the bathroom and opened the closet door. She laid her clothes out on the bed. "I'm going to be leaving soon, Cara. I want you to do your schoolwork while you listen for phone calls. You keep studying and I hope to be back around eight this evening. Probably get here sooner." Vera slipped on the ponyskin skirt and long-sleeved T-shirt she'd bought last week. Then she tugged on the black knee-high boots.

"Mom, you're getting rather dressed up. Where are you going?"

"I've got some business to take care of," Vera answered. "That's all."

"Give me a hint."

Vera looked at Cara. "I need to put some more pieces into place, and I need to look sharp today."

"You're certainly doing that."

Vera tucked the blouse in. "Cara, I don't want you fretting about me. I'm going back to the Samson Building to check on the place where Ivan Trudoff parks his car. No big deal. I need to look into the parking area and see what's back there. Okay?"

"Sure," Cara said, pulling on her socks and tying her shoes.

"I'll keep the ringer on my phone turned off, but I'll periodically check to see if you've called. I don't want the noise at a sensitive moment. I'll phone you back from a safe place. Now go downstairs and eat breakfast. I'll be here when you return."

"I'll hurry back." Cara shut the room door behind her.

Vera waited until her daughter was gone before she pulled the bulletproof vest out of her luggage and slipped it into a plastic shopping bag. Vera shot a glance in the mirror. She didn't look too bad. Rather typical of a smartly dressed New York City shopper going from store to store. She hoped she wouldn't be obvious.

The time had come to set up the monitor station. She had to get the equipment wired quickly so Cara wouldn't have any trouble hearing the phone calls. Vera took a metal coat hanger out of the closet and straightened it into a long piece of wire. She sat down by the hotel's clock radio and turned the small set around. All she needed was a receiver covering between 88 and 108 MHz, and the radio would do the trick.

Using the tools from her tote bag, Vera quickly got the cardboard back off the radio and started working inside, poking here and there with her screwdriver.

"Should be in a small box in here somewhere," Vera muttered to herself. "About one and one-half inches square . . . about a quarter-inch thick." She kept fishing around through the radio's components. "Got to be here somewhere. Ah, here it is. The variable capacitor!"

Vera switched on the radio and tuned in a local station. She very slowly turned one of the screws until the station started to fade. She kept adjusting the radio's 20 MHz coverage slot so that it would pick up below the normal 88 MHz level. "Just about there." Vera adjusted the screw a tad more. She stood up and fastened the metal hanger to the aerial input to maximize the range of the radio.

"The adjustment ought to take care of bringing the phone calls in." Vera pushed the receiver back in place and set the cardboard backing in place. "All we have to do is wait for Trudoff to call or someone to ring him. Shouldn't be long." She put her tools in her purse and finished getting ready for the day.

About ten minutes later Vera heard the sound of someone dialing a phone number from the radio. She immediately sat closer to the speaker. *Click . . . click . . . click . . . click.* The phone rang.

"*Dah,*" a voice said.

"Is this Senka Volo?" a woman asked.

"Yes."

"This is the secretary at Ukraine Imports. Mr. Trudoff wishes to speak with you. Just a moment, please." The phone popped several times.

"Senka?" a gruff man's voice came on the line.

"Ah, Mr. Trudoff. Good morning."

"Senka, I've been considering what you told me about this strange woman who showed up in the reception area when you were last here."

"You should. She followed me."

"What?"

"I saw her at the subway station immediately after I completed a phone call. Couldn't have been an accident."

"I see." Trudoff's voice faded. "I don't like the sound of any of this. Not at all."

"I told you she was looking for a Bashilov." Volo's voice sounded rough and hard. "You are the only one I know."

"I want you to find her immediately," Trudoff said. "I don't know where you'll look, but find out who she is. I want to know what she is looking for and why."

"This is different from my usual jobs." Senka hesitated. "It may take much more time."

"Have I ever not paid you adequately?" Trudoff barked.

"No."

"Then I won't fail this time. Find her." The phone went dead.

Vera was sitting with her mouth open and her stomach tight. She was lightheaded. For a second she felt faint.

He saw me! Vera gasped. *No wonder I lost the man.* She rocked back in her chair, her heart pounding. *Trudoff knows about me. God help me! Ace was right about how dangerous these people are.*

Vera began pacing back and forth across the hotel room's

carpet. "Got to get control of myself," she kept muttering. "Have to get things in order before Cara comes back." Her heart kept pounding. *This is worse than I thought.*

37

WHEN CARA RETURNED TO THE HOTEL ROOM after breakfast, Vera explained how the radio receiver with its improved antenna relayed phone calls and the HWA 1100 remote microphone receiving device picked up the bug under the secretary's desk. All Cara had to do was sit tight and pay attention.

"I don't think I should have any problems, Mother," Cara insisted. "Don't worry about me. I'll be fine."

Vera nodded. "Just listen carefully and write down whatever is important. You'll do fine. I'll pick up a small tape recorder today that will make your task easier tomorrow." She waved and hurried out the door.

Once in the hall, Vera stopped and took a deep breath. She had to think for a minute. Confronting Ivan Trudoff—or Bashilov—would be terrifying. She was getting ready to walk out in the deep water. No longer was she just the hunter; now she was also the hunted. She would have to be much more careful. Pay studious attention. Watch her back.

Riding down the elevator, Vera thought about the possibilities. Senka Volo should have a hard time finding her. After all, she was nobody. Then again, who knew what the man's capacities were? He might be more clever than she imagined. Vera hurried out of the hotel to catch a ride back up the street.

Minutes later she stepped out of the cab in front of the Samson Building. She cut through the crowd and walked inside. No doorman in sight. *Must show up when he pleases*, she thought.

The directory said that the building's business manager could be found in Suite 213. Taking the stairs, Vera walked up a landing and quickly found the room. She reasoned that the office had to occupy a relatively small space that was a long way from Trudoff's elegance.

"I'm looking for the business manager," Vera said to the lady sitting at the desk.

"I'll do," the large black woman answered without emotion. "What can I get for you, honey?"

"I'm interested in a parking space in your enclosed garage. Is one available close to the back entrance? There is a rear entrance in this building, isn't there?"

"Sure." The woman stood up and scratched her head of closely cropped hair. "That parking rental book is around here somewhere." She stepped away from the desk into the small office behind her. "Just a moment," she called out. "It's in here . . . I think." The woman came back out of the office with a black book in hand. "We should keep our rentals on the computer, I guess, but this is the way we've been doing it forever." She opened the book. "Let's take a look."

Vera watched as the woman turned pages.

"We don't have many changes," the manager said. "Once people get spaces, they don't usually let go of them unless they move out of the building." She ran her finger down the page. "Don't see any openings yet."

As the woman's finger slid down the page, Vera suddenly saw what she was looking for. *Ivan Trudoff, 103.* She caught her breath. Exactly what she needed.

"Sorry, dear. I don't see any openings in our enclosed space. We've got some outside areas around at the—"

"Thank you." Vera cut her off. "I understand. Let me reconsider for a while." She started backing out of the office.

The black woman flipped the book shut. "Sorry. Come back again."

"Do you mind if I take a stroll out there and look the area over?"

"Fine with me," the manager said. "Go back to the first floor and go through the unmarked door at the back side of the entryway. Take care now."

"Thank you." Vera smiled. "Thank you very much."

Vera hurried toward the stairs and back down to the first floor. If nothing else, she'd discovered that Bashilov used the name *Trudoff* consistently. In addition, the back entrance must be what Ivan Trudoff and his partners used to come and go from his office. Vera quickly walked across the lobby and through the back door to the parking spaces. The parking lot covered several floors with ramps running down from one level to the next. Vera could see that cars jammed all the spaces; it was hard to see the assigned numbers. Walking slowly across the lot, she found what she was looking for: space 103.

A large, shiny, black Mercedes sat there. Had to be Trudoff's car. Only steps away she could see the back door that must lead to another set of elevators going up to the tenth floor. Possibly the back entrance would prove to be even more dangerous, but at least she'd found her way. Now the task was to make sure that she didn't get caught inside the building.

Vera reached into her purse and pulled out the pistol. For a moment she studied the gun, making sure that the clip was in place. She jacked the gun, slipping bullets into the chamber. The gun was ready. She pressed the safety on.

Vera wasn't sure what would come next, but possibly Trudoff's parking place would prove to be important. If nothing more, she now had a clear sense of the lay of the land. She slowly walked toward the back entrance, taking a deep breath. She didn't feel very good.

Once inside the back door Vera saw two sets of elevators and a long hallway with a door at the end. *Must be the door to the lobby.* Rest rooms lined the back wall. *The elevators must service similar hallways on the other floors,* Vera surmised. *Only way to know is to ride one up.* She pressed the button.

Vera glanced over her shoulder and took a quick look at the parking area. At that moment a man in a dark-brown trench coat came through the door from the lobby, walking down the hallway toward the elevator.

Oh, no! It's Senka Volo! The elevator door opened. Vera rushed inside and pounded the tenth-floor button, praying the door would shut quickly. As Volo approached, the elevator closed and started up. He showed no sign of seeing her.

Vera's knees felt wobbly. What was she going to do? She had to get out of there. The elevator slowed and the door opened.

Vera stepped out. Just as she had expected, the tenth floor

looked like the first floor except that the landing was smaller and more compact. She glanced up and down the hall.

The entrance to Suite 1015 has to be one of these doors, she thought. She desperately looked up and down the hall, noticing at the same time that the light had come on above the other elevator.

Vera whirled around and saw the women's room behind her. She reached inside her purse and switched the safety off on her pistol. She stepped inside the rest room and waited. Vera could hear the elevator slowing. With her fingers, she slightly cracked the door. Volo got off and turned to the right. She could hear his footsteps and then a door closed.

Vera opened the door wider and looked down the hall. From the sound of his steps, she figured Trudoff's office was the second door down. She made a mental note of the location, then dashed for the exit stairs. Without stopping, Vera rushed down the back steps of all ten floors to the ground level. She couldn't risk a meeting with that man.

At the first floor, Vera took the long hallway to the lobby door, then exited the Samson Building and crossed the street into Central Park. Only after she sequestered herself behind a clump of trees did Vera stop.

That was close, she thought, wiping the sweat off her forehead.

38

VERA PEERED OUT OF THE TREES AT THE Samson Building. She'd really done it this time: Volo would probably have recognized her if he'd reached the elevators a little sooner. He certainly would have if he'd run into her up there on the rear entrance to the tenth floor. Working around the Samson Building was now more dangerous than ever.

Need to see what Cara's found out, Vera thought. She pulled out her cell telephone and saw that there was one message. She dialed the Renaissance Hotel.

"Hello." Cara didn't sound nearly as authoritative as she did in their private conversations. She seemed a little on the edgy side.

"It's me, kid. Your mom. What's happening?"

"Not much, except that about twenty minutes after you left this Russian-sounding guy called another Russian-sounding guy named Senka and ordered him up to his offices. The first guy sounded urgent and irritated."

Vera nodded. "Must be something going on."

"That's about it. On the other bug there's been nothing except the sound of the secretary typing letters. The place is so quiet, it's boring."

"You're doing a good job, Cara. Stay with it. I'm going to watch the building for some time and see what happens. Call me immediately if you find out anything."

"You bet." Cara hung up.

Vera needed to get positioned so she could watch both the front entrance and the exit at the same time. For the moment she needed to do some basic surveillance and think about the situation as she watched.

The Starbuck's coffee shop looked like the best place to settle. At least the options on everything from different flavored coffees to cappuccino made the possibly long wait more endurable. Vera pushed out of the trees and headed for the shop.

Two hours later, Vera saw the long, black Mercedes pull out of the Samson Building's parking area exit. She thought she could see three men in the car. All she could do was keep waiting and watching.

Ivan Trudoff sat in the backseat of the car speeding down the broad boulevard. The Mercedes eventually crossed the Manhattan Bridge and onto Flatbush Avenue. After a few twists and turns Sergei Omsk, the chauffeur, drove under the Queens Expressway and turned toward the docks lining Gowanus Bay at the tip of Brooklyn. The car cruised past warehouses and short, empty alleys.

"Sergei, there's the place." Trudoff pointed with a newspaper toward a warehouse. "We are nearly there."

Omsk drove over toward the door into the large, long warehouse and stopped. "I will go in first and make sure that everything appears to be acceptable," Sergei said. "If I'm not back in a few minutes, come in shooting." He hurried away.

"There should be no problems today," Trudoff told Nikita Grishin, "except that I imagine Abu Medien will grumble about the price of these weapons. I expect him to put on a show to create the right appearance of resistance. I worry about tomorrow."

"I am prepared as always," Grishin answered. "Should there be any tension I have my guns loaded."

"I'm not sure what sort of game these Palestinians are playing with us. They need our weapons. The struggle against Israel continues and will do so for a long time, if not forever. It appears that the Moslem god is working more for our business than their success. For that reason, I think Yossi might want to kill us." Trudoff laughed but Grishin's face didn't move. "Come on, Nikita! You are always so serious unless we fill you with vodka." Trudoff laughed once more but Grishin said nothing.

Sergei Omsk came out of the warehouse and motioned for Ivan and Nikita to come in. The two men got out of the car quickly.

"I do not think there are any assassins hidden in that building," Omsk said. "I believe Abu Medien and his associate are the only people in there."

"Good, good." Trudoff patted Omsk on the back. "Sergei, you will walk in first and I will follow. Nikita will be last. I will appear to be totally relaxed and accepting of the locale but if either of you sees anything suspicious, shoot. I trust this Arab fat boy about as far as I can throw the pig."

The three men walked into the building filled with barrels, boxes, and crates. To one side, the door of a small office was open and a light shone out on the floor. Sergei Omsk nodded toward the door and the two men followed him into the trashy room with a desk at the back. A large Arab stood behind Yossi Abu Medien.

"Ah, Yossi! My old friend." Trudoff extended his arms. "Good to see you again so soon." The two men hugged but Yossi didn't smile.

"Please sit down." Yossi pointed at the chairs around the room. Trudoff sat down but the other two men remained standing.

"I trust all is well with your family," Trudoff began, as if visiting with a long-lost relative.

"Of course," Yossi snapped. "Thank you."

"Good. Good." Trudoff sat back and smiled broadly.

The somber Arab opened a file on the desk and handed a sheet of paper to the Russian. Trudoff turned to let the light fall over his shoulder. For a moment he carefully surveyed the entire list.

"Hmm. You want twenty thousand Russian AK-47s. Am I correct?"

The Arab nodded.

"And then you are ordering fifteen thousand Tokarev TT-33 pistols, which I presume you want with the 4.57-inch barrels." Trudoff watched Yossi's eyes carefully. "The muzzle velocity is approximately 1,280 feet per second."

Yossi blinked. "That is correct." His expression did not change but he moved uncomfortably in his chair.

Trudoff kept smiling. The twist was enough. Along with the blink of the eye, the nervous turning caused Trudoff to believe that he had once again gained the edge on the Arab. Yossi's nervousness betrayed an intent beyond buying weapons.

"Sounds like you are ready to start killing Jews the way we once hunted rabbits in Russia. Ready for a big war, Yossi?"

The Arab stiffened but said nothing.

"You are also wanting grenades, I believe." Trudoff looked at the paper. "The usual Soviet RGD-5 type. We should have no problem supplying these in any quantity you wish. Certainly this amount is no problem."

"Good." Yossi maintained his deadpan stare.

Trudoff smiled. "Ah, a little extra has been added here."

"Something is wrong with the figures?" Yossi leaned forward and glared.

"You didn't mention earlier that you wanted rocket launchers. Of course, the Soviet RPG-7 is standard equipment for terrorists everywhere. I assume you want the five-pound rockets that go with the launchers?"

"No." Yossi shook his head. "And we are not *terrorists.* The PLO is the rightfully elected representative of our people."

"Whatever you say, my friend." Trudoff shrugged. "You know my terms. When the money goes to my bank account, I send the weapons."

Yossi shook his head. "I am instructed to tell you that your price is too high."

"Really?" Trudoff laughed. "Then I don't need any instruction to tell you that you won't be receiving the weapons. My prices aren't negotiable."

Yossi's eyes narrowed. "We have other sources of weaponry."

"Then contact them!" Trudoff stood up. "As I told you earlier, I have more business than I need right now. After all, you did not even mention the rocket launchers earlier."

"You have tried to make us sound like American fat cats," Yossi protested. "For some crazy reason you think we have all the money in the Middle East in our pockets."

"Yossi, you are amusing. You seem to think that doing business with me is like buying cabbage in the market. If you offer half price, then I'll come down and we can end at about 60 percent of my original price. Right?"

The Arab said nothing.

Trudoff smiled again. "You think that I'm going to sell to you at a discount when I can instantly move every piece of this merchandise for full price?" Trudoff nodded to Sergei and Nikita that he was prepared to leave. "As I told you earlier, we do business on my terms or we don't do it at all." He started walking out.

"What makes you so arrogant?" Yossi shouted menacingly and cursed.

Trudoff stopped and stood motionless for a moment. He turned slowly, staring intently at the Arab. His smile was gone. "Because I have the weapons and you don't," he answered. Trudoff nodded good-bye and walked out of the warehouse.

Omsk drove out of the area much quicker than he'd come in.

"What do you think will happen now?" Grishin asked sullenly.

"We are being set up," Trudoff answered. "We must prepare to strike first. If not, the Arabs will hit us."

Trudoff watched the buildings fly past but his mind was elsewhere. *I wonder if that woman is a part of any of this Arab plot,* the Russian thought. *She could have been casing my offices for these fools when Senka saw her. This situation must be dealt with finally and at once.*

39

FORTY-FIVE MINUTES AFTER VERA WATCHED Trudoff's Mercedes disappear, she decided it was time to return to the hotel. She expected that nothing more would happen on this street for some time. She'd watched Senka Volo leave and hurry back toward the subway. Most of the last twenty minutes, she'd thought about Sam but she had already come to the edge of what was emotionally tolerable. What would Sam do under these circumstances? Vera didn't know. She needed to get her legs pumping and her mind off of the man she loved.

For a moment Vera remembered yet again what Reverend Dozier had promised: the help of God comes during our times of helplessness. Vera had never felt so helpless. The loss of the man she loved had split her like an axe emotionally. If it was true that redemption came through suffering, then she should be in the realm where God's power could be released significantly. The price she had paid for these lessons had been high indeed.

Vera left Starbuck's and started walking back up the street, thinking about her next plan of action. She certainly couldn't try to enter Trudoff's inner office while the secretary was there. Any more work around that suite would have to happen after dark. She probably ought to spend some time making sure that her use of the pistol was sharp—just in case she and Volo had an even closer encounter than the near miss they'd had earlier. A little time at a shooting range would be worthwhile.

On her walk back to the hotel, Vera bought a Sony recorder for Cara. "Cara," she said, walking into their room. "How's my professional monitor?"

"A little on the tired and bored side. Nothing has happened."

"That's okay. We simply listen and see what comes across. These things take a significant amount of time."

"I've already put hours in today and I'm hungry."

"Why don't you go down and eat? I need to rig up this recorder so you will be able to record the next bit of data that comes through." Vera glanced at her watch. "My goodness, it's already 2:30! You must be starving."

Cara nodded her head. "You bet! I'm still a growing young woman." She raised her eyebrow at her mother and hurried out the door. "Come on."

"I'll catch up with you. Go on down."

"Whatever you say." Cara shut the door behind her.

Vera sat down and started attaching the small Sony recorder so Cara would only have to release the pause button to record. After a few minutes of tinkering with the hookup, Vera decided everything was ready. She had started toward the bathroom when she heard the radio start clicking. Someone was dialing.

Vera immediately punched the pause button off and sat down next to the receiver. After several rounds of clicking, she heard the ringing, then an answer.

"Senka, you there?"

"Yes, yes. I couldn't get this phone out of my pocket."

"I don't buy those telephones for laughs. I expect you to have it ready at all times."

"Yes, sir."

"I am working on something that will demand your immediate attention. Have you found out anything on this woman that you spotted in my office?"

"No, sir."

Trudoff cursed. "I want her found! I am concerned that she may in some way be part of our current problems. You pay attention to that angle!"

"Yes, sir."

"Because this situation is moving quickly, I cannot take any chances. I see no alternative but to kill her. Understand?"

"Yes, sir."

"Therefore, I want you to act quickly when the occasion arises. Shoot her."

"I will."

"Keep the phone handy as I will be back in touch with you shortly." Trudoff hung up.

Vera stared at the radio. *Shoot her.* She was no longer just being pursued; she was being stalked. Volo now had instructions to kill her! Vera's hands started to shake.

I can't let Cara hear this conversation. She immediately rewound the tape so that the next recorded material would erase it.

Then she set the recorder back in place to catch anything else that came in.

"Oh, Lord," she prayed, "I need Your help like I never have before in my life. This man could kill me and I'm scared to death. Please, please, put a hedge of protection around me. Without Your covering, I will surely perish. I beg You for Your safekeeping."

Vera couldn't call the New York police. She'd already thought that option through, and she didn't know anyone locally who could help her . . . or at least anyone who appeared trustworthy. Ace Newton truly seemed a million miles away.

What good would it do right now to call Ace? Vera thought. *Perhaps I should but I have to face this situation by myself. I have to count on what I've learned to pull me through.*

The clock radio told Cara that it was now four o'clock. No more phone calls had occurred, and the bug under the secretary's desk relayed little more than the noise of typing. She had no alternative but to go back to her schoolwork. There was no telling when her mother would return.

Having finished her work in biology and American history, Cara picked up the assigned novel for her advanced literature class and flipped through the pages. She hoped reading would focus her mind elsewhere. She thumbed through the copy and found her place near the back.

In a few seconds her mind drifted into the world of the frozen prison camp. Outside distractions slipped away. Worrying stopped. She was back in the ice-covered forest that Alexander Solzhenitsyn described so well.

Russian prisoners had put in a hard day of working with bricks and mortar. Shukhov was resting on his bed while the prisoner named Alyosha, a Baptist, lay on the other side of their bunk, reading the Gospels again. The Baptist stopped and asked Shukhov why he didn't pray more often.

Shukhov explained caustically that his prayers were like his complaints sent to the camp higher-ups. "Either they don't get there or they come back to you marked 'Rejected.'"

Cara stopped and lowered the book. Maybe her prayers weren't getting through. What if she wasn't praying right? Up there in the heavens, God might be sitting with a great rubber stamp in His hand, marking her intercessions "Rejected."

"Oh, Lord, please don't do that to my mother," she prayed. "Please help us right now and get Mom back to this hotel room safely. We truly need Your hand to guide us through this big mess. Please don't reject our request. Amen."

Cara started reading again, recognizing that Shukhov struggled with the injustice of imprisonment and the question of whether divine justice was even possible in this world. Alyosha argued that freedom wasn't as important as keeping their faith pure. Shukhov pondered Alyosha's argument but wondered if he even wanted to be free again. Maybe his struggle really wasn't that important anymore.

Cara wondered about her own struggle. Maybe this search for information was a waste of time. Maybe there were no answers. She felt as if she and her mother had created their own prison with this crazy search. Life back in Colorado Springs was looking better all the time. At least there, people cared about them. This city was too big, too cold . . . and maybe even too dangerous.

If only Cara could talk to her father. A simple discussion always changed everything. Sure, they'd argued the last time she'd seen him, but he could tell her what was right and wrong, and then everything would make perfect sense. Of course, that was exactly why they'd come to New York City: to find out what had become of him.

Cara started reading again. After a minute she stopped to reflect on how the episode ended. The Baptist and Shukhov had argued about their purpose while in prison. Alyosha insisted that he was in prison to be a witness to the power of Jesus Christ. Shukhov's logic was that if the idea made sense to Alyosha, then the man was in the right place; but Shukhov had been imprisoned for nothing more than telling the truth. Why should he be in this terrible prison for simply speaking with veracity?

And Cara thought that was their dilemma too. The Sloan family's struggles were nothing but unjust. Reverend Dozier had told them that the issue wasn't why it had happened but how they would use the tragedy. The idea sounded acceptable but, as Shukhov reasoned about his own situation, it didn't seem to matter anymore.

Ten days ago everything was fine. Cara had gone to school, talked to her friends, and been a normal kid. When she came home in the evenings, her father always had something to argue about but life was wonderful. Today she was all alone in this huge, people-filled city. Like Shukhov, she felt imprisoned without a decent reason. It just wasn't fair!

Most of the time it took a long while to figure out what God actually had in mind, Cara remembered the minister saying. "What can't be fathomed can still be redeemed," he had promised, but she couldn't see any of it happening.

Cara closed her book and pulled her knees up under her chin. She wanted her mother to come home and the endless night to become morning again.

40

At six o'clock, inside the New York City Gun Club, Vera had finished an hour of practice shooting her pistol. Getting into the club had taken some doing, but she pulled enough strings to purchase the time to fire her gun.

Vera removed the ear protectors. The smell of gun smoke hung heavy in the air. Pulling the clip out of her weapon, she left the room and sat down on a chair in the hall.

Vera had found that firing the pistol accurately and hitting the targets was well worth her time. She felt she had the hang of it. The last several rounds had gone very well, and she felt ready for whatever had to be faced. Not that she wasn't scared—she was, deeply. But at least she could protect herself if she had to.

She remembered that learning to shoot a pistol had proved easy. She'd gone out to the Colorado Springs firing range and practiced endlessly, hitting the center of the target often, but that was exactly what she expected to do. Little did her instructor know that her father, Henri Leestma, had spent hours teaching her to shoot the family shotgun when she was a girl.

"Vera," Henri had said late one afternoon, "why don't we go out and see if you can make the old family gun work?"

Vera had thought for a moment. At thirteen years of age, she'd never fired a gun. She wasn't sure she even wanted to. On the other hand, her father didn't offer many opportunities to be alone with him, and he'd never asked her to do something as daring as shooting a big gun.

"I thought we'd go down by the pond and see what happens."

Vera nodded slowly. "Okay. But why? You've never let me shoot a gun before."

"Yes, yes." Henri nodded his head. "You weren't big enough before, but I think that you might be able to shoot the .410 now that you've turned into a teenager." He leaned over and whispered in her ear, "Don't tell your mother."

Vera grinned. "I understand. This will be just between us."

Henri had winked. "You've got it, kid!" He pointed to the shed out behind the house. "Put your coat on and go out there and wait. I'll meet you in a few minutes. And pull the stocking cap down around your ears. It's cold out."

Vera hurried through the house and out into the backyard. A blast of cold wind caught the branches in the old peach tree, gently shaking their long tips. She glanced at the sky. The clouds looked like they might bring snow. Vera jammed her hands down in the bottom of her pockets, hopping from one foot to the other, trying to keep warm.

A couple of minutes later, Henri Leestma walked around the side of the shed carrying a small shotgun. "Had to get it out of the top of the closet." He pointed toward the small cow pond. "I'll carry it until we get down there in those trees by the pond in case anyone is looking from the house."

"Like Mom, for instance?" Vera asked.

Henri grinned but only nodded.

Stumps of broken husks crunched beneath their feet as they hurried through last year's rows of cornstalks.

Henri gestured down along the banks of the pond. "There are some old oil cans on the other side of the pond where I changed the oil in the tractor last time. See them?"

"Yes," answered Vera. "And Mom certainly can't see us here."

"Some things have to be done with discretion," Henri answered. "That's the best way to start shooting a weapon."

Henri Leestma lined up the yellow cans in a row about thirty feet in front of them, then sat down on a stump. "Sit down here beside me, Vera. We need to go over a few things before you pull the trigger." Henri turned the gun over in his hands. "The most important lesson that I have to teach you deals with safety." For fifteen minutes Henri explained the dangers of such a weapon. He took the gun apart, showing Vera how to load it, clean it, and keep it properly maintained. He meticulously described how she was to oil the gun. By the time he had finished, Vera felt like she was ready to join the army.

"Can I shoot it now?" she asked impatiently.

Henri carefully lowered the shotgun into her hands. "You have to remember that this weapon hits with a fairly decent kick, so hold it as tightly as you can. You'll get less of a jolt if you do."

Vera pulled the gun against her shoulder, slipping her finger around the trigger, not thinking much about her father's warning. She took aim.

"Can you see okay?" Henri asked quietly.

"Sure," Vera whispered, carefully eyeing the target beyond the end of the barrel. "No problem," she barely whispered.

At that moment a red-necked pheasant suddenly walked out of the bushes. Vera saw the large bird and felt her father's hand on her wrist.

"Don't shoot the cans," Henri whispered. "Aim at that bird."

Vera nodded and slowly turned the shotgun's barrel toward the pheasant.

For some reason the fat pheasant seemed completely unaware of them. He pecked at the ground and scratched in the dirt, slowly edging his way up toward the pond, strutting along like he owned the field. Neither Vera nor her father moved. Vera held her breath. The bird walked a couple more feet and stopped, suddenly looking up at Vera and her dad.

"Shoot!" Henri commanded.

Boom! Vera flew backward and dropped the gun on the ground.

Henri Leestma laughed. "I think he got the worst of you, Vera." He reached down and picked up the gun. "Think you'll live?"

Vera rolled over and rubbed her shoulder. The dull ache throbbed for a moment and she thought of crying, which would have been completely unacceptable. "Certainly packs a wallop," she groaned.

Henri went dashing down the small hill and off into the bushes. "Look here!" He bent over and picked up something in the tall grass. "See what you did?" He held up the dead pheasant.

"I shot that bird?" Vera asked in disbelief.

"Sure did, kid. We can have a pheasant dinner tonight." Henri Leestma began to run to the house, beckoning her to follow. "Whoopee!"

On this cold New York afternoon, leaning against the wall, Vera could still see the astonished look on her mother's face. There had been quite an exchange between her mom and dad about his taking her to the pond for a "shoot-out," as her mother had called it. Henri kept pointing to the pheasant and insisting, "The girl's a natural! Can't be inhibited by her mom's petticoats. Got to let her grow up."

Her mother had stomped angrily around the kitchen but her father kept chuckling while he showed Vera how to clean the bird.

Vera remembered that, if anything, she'd hit that bird by pure accident. Maybe it was beginner's luck, but with time, her skill had definitely improved. She'd developed a good eye for shooting quickly and hitting the target. If it became necessary, she could shoot an assailant much easier than she'd killed that pheasant.

She glanced at a wall clock. *Time to get back to the hotel and make sure Cara is okay.*

41

THE FRIDAY MORNING SUN SLOWLY SPREAD needed warmth over Manhattan Island. Vera sat quietly in the hotel room, staring at the clock radio and waiting while Cara ate breakfast downstairs. Her electronic bug had already told her that the secretary for Ukraine Imports Company was sitting behind her desk in the lobby, typing. Ivan Trudoff seemed unusually busy this morning. His first two phone calls had not been discernible. The initial one had been in Russian and the second in English, but she couldn't get the gist of what he was talking about. She listened as he punched in more numbers, then heard the ringing.

"*Aloh*," a gruff voice answered.

"Yossi, how are you?"

"Who is this?" The Arab slurred his English.

"Your old friend. Ivan Bashilov."

"I see," Yossi said slowly. "Why are you calling me?"

"I haven't heard from you yet today and time is running out. I thought perhaps we should meet one more time to see if something can be worked out."

"I see," the Arab repeated and paused for several moments as if he were thinking. "Perhaps this afternoon."

"Fine. Shall we make our conversation at your place again? The warehouse down there on Gowanus Bay?"

"Yes," Yossi said. "Bring me a list indicating the exact price of your weapons."

"Of course. See you at, shall we say, three o'clock?"

"That is acceptable." Yossi hung up.

Vera stared at the receiver without any clear idea of what she had just heard. Something was coming down, but what? More clicks. Trudoff was dialing again. The telephone rang.

"Yes," a man's voice answered.

"Senka Volo!" Trudoff responded. "Are you paying close attention to the assignment that I gave you?"

"Ah, Mr. Trudoff. Yes, of course."

"Found out anything about who the woman is?"

"No, sir. I don't have much to go on, but I'm still looking."

"Keep trying," Trudoff grumbled. "Senka, in the meantime I have a little job for you to do this afternoon at three o'clock. If you do this right, I will pay you five thousand dollars."

"I am always at your service, sir."

"Good. You must arrive several hours early and position yourself to strike quickly. I expect several men to show. I want you to kill them all."

"Of course."

"You will need to travel over the Manhattan Bridge to Flatbush Avenue. Turn south until you come to the docks lining the Gowanus Bay. Your targets will show up at Pier 56, but you must hide your car so there will be no suspicion when they arrive."

"I see," Senka said slowly. "How will I identify the right target?"

"I'm going to fax you a picture of the man that you must kill. If you don't get him, I will not pay you one ruble. Understand?"

"I must shoot everyone who shows, but I have one prime target that I must hit or get nothing?"

"Correct."

"I believe such a difficult assignment should be worth at least ten thousand dollars. Is that not a fair price?"

"You are toying with me, Volo."

"No, I am only trying to come to an equitable price for such a dangerous assignment."

"Hmph," Trudoff grumbled. "Six thousand dollars and no more."

"Agreed. Send the fax at once."

"Spahsseebah." Trudoff hung up.

Vera rocked back in her seat, overwhelmed that she'd just heard a murder discussed. She swallowed hard and felt her heartbeat race. She couldn't just sit there and do nothing. On the other hand, calling the local police could set off a chain reaction that might backfire and explode in her face. For a moment Vera felt she was going to panic. Even though she'd heard a conversation about evil people shooting each other, the targets were still human beings.

And she was also one of Volo's targets.

Vera picked up her cell phone and dialed Ace Newton's home number. It was too early for him to be in the office but not too early for him to be awake. After he answered, Vera said, "Ace, I want you to be aware of what's happening."

"You sound frightened, Vera."

"I am concerned. I overheard a conversation about a killing that's going to occur this afternoon somewhere on the other side of the Manhattan Bridge. It sounded like the shooting will occur somewhere along the Gowanus Bay."

"Gowanus Bay." Newton sounded like he was writing it down.

"I'm not sure about calling the local police. I'm also afraid that I'm one of the man's targets."

Ace cursed. "Vera, I warned you about how serious these issues are. I want you to get out of there right now."

"I can't, Ace. I've got to follow this through. At least I know where the killer will be all afternoon." She shuddered. "I need to push my investigation to the limit. I wanted you to know what's happening and that I will be at the Samson Building today. Possibly in the garage. I'm leaving the matter of what to do in your hands."

"Vera!" Newton protested. "You need to *leave* that area."

"I can't, Ace. I came here to find out what I may discover today. Please do anything you can from there. Good-bye."

Vera switched off the phone before Ace could say any more. She knew this was her opportunity to go back to the Samson Building. She could at least roam without Volo showing up.

At that same moment in Colorado Springs, Dick Simmons walked briskly into Chief Al Harrison's office. "Sir, if I might have a minute of your time?"

The heavyset Harrison looked up in surprise. "How'd you wander in here unannounced?"

"Guess your secretary went down the hall. Nobody's out there."

Harrison leaned back in his chair and crossed his arms over his chest. "What can I do for you?"

"I just wanted to say that I don't believe Vera Sloan has a clue about what Sam did on this Alexander case," Simmons said. "At least it doesn't appear that Sloan talked to her about his job assignment."

"You talked to her?"

"Well," Simmons hedged, "not exactly, but I got this information straight from—"

"'Not exactly'?" Harrison responded. "What do you mean by 'not exactly'?"

"It appears that Vera Sloan is now working over at Ace Newton's private investigating firm. You remember Newton. Used to be one of us. Anyway, I—"

"You talked with Newton?" Harrison bore down.

"I thought maybe it would be better if I took a sort of circuitous route on this investigation. You know, leaves me a little room for a significant follow-up."

The police chief cursed. "I didn't tell you to turn this into a big game with one of our ex-employees."

Simmons shrugged. "But you didn't tell me that I had to talk directly with Vera Sloan."

Harrison groaned. "So, you brought me back Ace Newton's reading of the situation?"

"Ace is a top-drawer guy," Simmons insisted. "I'd trust his judgment under any set of circumstances."

The police chief shook his head and looked down at the piece of paper lying in front of him. "This case gets messier the further it goes." He stood up. "But I'm certainly not interested in a secondary source, a guy like Ace Newton." The telephone rang.

"Harrison here." He listened for a moment. "You're sure?"

Dick Simmons stood silently.

"Okay. I'll be there in a minute." Harrison hung up the phone. "Stay here, Simmons. I'll be back in a moment." He hurried out of the room.

Dick sat down. *I shouldn't have let that information about Newton slip out. Harrison doesn't like anybody who quit working for the police department,* he thought. *Been better if I'd sounded more like I got the stuff straight from Vera.*

The fax machine behind Harrison's desk signaled that it was receiving a transmission. Then it abruptly halted and beeped. Simmons walked around and looked at the message window. *Check paper,* it read. Simmons reached over and started jiggling the paper until a sheet caught on.

"Mr. Electronic Brain needed a little assistance from a human." Simmons chuckled to himself. "At least I'm smarter than you are," he taunted the machine.

Simmons watched the paper emerging at the bottom of the machine. The sheet caught on the edge and looked like it might bunch up. He had to guide it away from the machine. "Stupid device," Simmons mused. "Can't you do anything right?"

For a moment he stood by the machine, making sure that nothing got fouled up again. The agency heading caught his eye and caused him to look more carefully. "CIA?" Simmons's eyes widened.

Then his mouth dropped. "Oh my goodness," he sputtered. "I can't believe what I'm seeing." He quickly read the letter, straightened up, and backed away from the machine. For a moment the detective stared at the wall.

Chief Harrison walked briskly into the room. "Okay. I took care of that problem. Simmons, I don't like what you did in talking to Newton, but I want you to keep working on this case." Harrison stopped and stared. "You all right, Simmons? Your face has turned white."

"Yeah." Dick gasped more than spoke. "Just need a little air." He started backing away. "I'll be fine in a moment. Give me a few seconds in the rest room. I'll be back later."

42

MORNING TRAFFIC WAS HONKING AND BUZZING by the time Cara returned to the hotel room. "Mom, they had the best French toast that I've ever eaten in my life. Maybe my earlier judgments about New York City were a little hasty."

"That's what I like," Vera answered, "mature evaluations based on firm evidence, like syrup-covered toast."

"I am warming up to this place. The hotel really seems to be great."

"It should be, at the prices we're paying." Vera sounded cynical. "You do understand that we're living at the top of the ladder?"

Cara sobered. "I know, Mom. I'm just trying not to be so pessimistic this morning."

Vera hugged her daughter. "Thanks, dear. I appreciate your putting your best foot forward."

"Anything come in over the monitor?" Cara asked.

"Yes, and I think it may be possible for me to take another look at the back of the Samson Building this afternoon. I believe I can get back on the tenth floor without being observed."

"That's more than a little on the negative side." Cara's voice changed to a worried tone. "I don't like your wandering around down there by yourself."

"I don't have any choice, Cara. Now, I want you to stick like glue to this radio once I leave here. If you hear anything of substance, call me immediately." Vera raised her eyebrow. "I mean *quickly*."

"All right, Mom. I'll do my best."

"I'll be ready to go in a moment," Vera said, slipping into the bathroom. "Be right out."

With the door closed, Vera quickly put the black protection vest on under her blouse. The jacket she planned to wear would do more than shield her from the cold; it would hide the vest from Cara's view. Cara didn't need to catch a glimpse of what would only make her worry more. Vera slipped her leather coat over the top and whirled a scarf around her neck. She was ready.

"Remember to call me the second you hear anything," Vera said over her shoulder, closing the hotel door behind her. "Be a good kid."

Shortly after lunch, Senka Volo drove an '87 blue Ford that he had stolen an hour earlier in Manhattan. Rather than take the route Trudoff had suggested, he drove the Prospect Expressway over to the Hamilton Parkway, and then turned onto Thirty-ninth Street, driving toward the docks. He wanted to make sure

Trudoff wasn't setting him up for any surprises. Senka didn't trust his payoff man any more than Trudoff trusted him. After some time behind the wheel, he found Pier 56 but drove on past the old, weather-beaten building. Senka Volo did not plan to be caught short on any front.

After several sweeps through the area, Volo parked on the other side of Pier 40 and started walking toward the site of the rendezvous. Small ocean waves lapped against the wooden dock and seagulls flew overhead. Senka saw only a couple of men working around the grayish, worn buildings. He quickly discovered that no one was in Pier 56; it would be necessary for him to break in. Laying the small case that he'd brought with him on the ground, the Russian knocked out the glass on a back window and crawled through.

For several minutes he scouted the warehouse and was satisfied that, at the moment, nothing was going on there except that goods were being held for later delivery. The pile of crates didn't look unusual. From dust patterns he could see that the large rooms had recently been filled with cartons, boxes, and crates, but most were gone now.

Better try that small office over there, Senka thought. *Looks like it could be a place for trouble.* He slipped around several large crates, pushing the door open.

Nothing in here, he thought. *Looks like where they keep books.* Volo didn't turn on any lights but sat down at a desk chair in the dark to think out his plan of action. The office appeared to be a typical business room with a desk, a couple of chairs, and a filing cabinet.

Senka slowly and carefully considered what would be the best way to mount his attack. He realized the need to get in a position to hit his target hard and fast, then run. In the oblong case sitting at his feet, he had an M-16 military rifle that could fire at least seven hundred rounds per minute in full-auto mode, along with plenty of ammunition. All he needed was a drop on the car when it arrived, and he ought to be able to knock off all of them before they even had a chance to fire at him.

Volo walked out into the warehouse and looked around. On the open flight above him a landing walkway ran along the wall. An old, murky window looked down on the parking area in front of the pier. He could fire out of that window and nail them. Senka climbed the rickety stairs to get situated next to the window and ready his M-16.

Volo settled down to wait, smoking cigarette after cigarette. He had always been a chain-smoker. Smoke hung heavy and slowly drifted out the window while Senka waited calmly. His rifle felt warm and he itched to knock off an easy target. He reached for another cigarette.

At 2:15 a long, dark blue limousine pulled alongside Pier 56. The sound of tires crunching gravel instantly sent Senka into position. For more than a minute, no one got out of the car. Senka Volo carefully laid down his smoking cigarette and blew a puff of smoke in front of him. He inched the M-16 rifle out the window and waited.

Nothing happened.

Senka slipped his finger around the trigger. "Come on," he whispered under his breath. "Just step out."

The doors on the blue car abruptly flew open and four men leaped out, firing Glock-17 pistols and one old machine gun at the upstairs window where they'd seen smoke seeping out as they pulled in. Senka pulled the trigger quickly.

The gunfire flew fast and furious. Two of the men in the car fell immediately, but their rapid firing instantly crashed through the thin wall and hit Volo. Senka's last shot sprawled a third man over the hood of the limousine. The M-16 rifle slipped to his knees and he collapsed silently against the wall.

Only one man still stood behind the car with his pistol aimed at the window. The punctured and perforated siding looked as if a hundred bullets had hit the second floor around the broken window. The lone survivor on the ground edged into the front seat, pushing the dead men out of the way and sliding behind the wheel. He zoomed the dark blue car away from the building, squealing around the radically sharp turn at the end of the block.

Off in the distance near Second Avenue, the sound of police sirens filled the air.

43

COLD WEATHER CONTINUED TO GRIP NEW York City's busy streets and it slowly worked an icy reach around the Samson Building's parking garage. Vera tugged at the bulletproof vest, pulling it tighter around her chest, but her fingers had already started to ache and she kept cramming them into her pockets. Warming up seemed harder today.

The frigid conditions forced her to take a taxi from the hotel down Park Avenue. Vera stepped out at what had become the familiar corner, where the café and the Samson Building sat across the street from each other. She bought a cup of cappuccino and studied the rear entry into the building.

A few people began emerging from the exit and several cars drove out. Crouching next to the cement entrance, Vera didn't seem to attract the attention of the departing commuters. She slipped inside and started up the driveway.

The slightly inclined entrance quickly turned into a ramp much steeper than she had expected. Vera walked determinedly forward to give the impression she knew exactly where she was going. In a couple of minutes, she discovered space 103 was empty.

Trudoff wasn't there! She had a chance to get inside his office. Without slowing down, Vera walked straight to the back entrance and quickly boarded the elevator.

The timing seemed to be perfect. She had caught him away at exactly the right moment. Vera knew she needed to work quickly. The elevator slowed and the door opened.

Vera looked cautiously up and down the hall. Not a person in sight. Remembering her experience from the day before, she reasoned that Suite 1015 had to be two doors down. Tiptoeing through the corridor, Vera quickly rummaged through her purse, producing the set of lock picks.

The regular back door looked different from the others in the hall. It was more substantial—massive, thick, impenetrable. Vera dropped down on one knee and, assuming Ukraine Imports was open for business and the alarm would be off, started working the lock.

The lock proved to be tougher than Vera had expected. Trudoff hadn't intended anyone to break into his place easily. She'd never worked on such a complex lock. Vera pulled a safety pin out of her purse, sticking the long metal point into the lock above her tubular-cylinder lock pick. She started jimmying the pin-tumbler cylinders and could feel movement inside the lock. After a few minutes, Vera felt she had a sense of the system. Carefully pushing the safety pin up, she moved the pick slightly and heard the sliding sound she'd hoped for. The lock opened.

"Good," Vera said under her breath and stood up again. She slowly pushed Trudoff's office door open.

Vera could see a dark hallway ahead of her. She walked noiselessly up the eight-foot length. The corner turned into another hall. At the end of at least another twenty-foot hallway, she could see a desk and what appeared to be an office. Had to be Trudoff's.

Large and expensive furniture filled the office. Thick, soft drapes hung from the windows. The art on the walls looked original and high-dollar. Trudoff obviously had plenty of money. Papers and documents covered his enormous walnut desk and an executive telephone sat to one side. On the credenza behind the desk, Trudoff kept a computer with a screen saver flashing across the monitor.

Vera put her hand on the wall. The long hallway that suddenly opened up into an office didn't feel right. It seemed like the space was larger than the office. The L-shaped area from the back door into the office was simply too big and expansive. She felt the surface gently. Something had to be behind the wall, but there weren't any doors.

Abruptly the cellular telephone in her purse rang. For a moment Vera thought she'd have a heart attack. She'd forgotten to switch the buzzer off. Vera grabbed inside her purse to silence it as quickly as possible.

"Hello," she whispered in the receiver.

"Mom! Trudoff's coming back to his office!" Cara exclaimed. "I just heard him talking to his secretary. His car is pulling into the downstairs parking lot at this moment."

"Thanks." Vera hit the off button and ran toward the back door, pulling it closed behind her. It didn't lock. She tried again.

"Oh, no!" Vera slammed the door a third time. Still unlocked.

I can't leave this door open, she thought. *I'll never be able to come back here again! Got to get it to snap.*

She reached behind the door and started trying to find a knob, a handle, anything that might lock it. Nothing.

Vera glanced at the elevators and saw the light above the door come on. Trudoff had to be coming up. She grabbed the door and slammed it as hard as she could. It locked.

"Thank the Lord." Vera rushed toward the women's room. *Got to get out of here. That elevator will open any second.*

She jumped inside the rest room and leaned against the wall, her heart thumping like it would explode. She heard the elevator open and slid the bathroom door open a crack. Sure enough: the same bald head, thick neck, broad shoulders. Trudoff and two other men walked straight toward his office. Vera didn't move.

She heard the men's footsteps stop and then the jingle of keys. Trudoff said something in Russian. The three entered and the door closed behind them.

Her heart slowed but Vera's mouth was dry and her hands felt clammy. She couldn't leave until she was sure no one would come out of Trudoff's office. She had to give them some time to settle in. *Wait. Don't panic.*

Here I am, trapped in this bathroom, she thought. *Stuck! Like a car in a dead-end alley.*

Reaching in her purse again for the pistol, Vera made sure that the safety wasn't on. The gun proved primed and ready. Keeping the pistol in a posture to fire instantly wasn't the safest way to go, but she couldn't take any chances with this Russian. If worse came to worst, she needed to be ready to react instantly.

Vera walked over to the dressing table surrounding the sink and leaned against the edge. She had no choice but to wait and think about another course of action. Obviously, she wasn't going to get back into that office this afternoon. Vera knew that she must reposition herself and wait for the Russian to leave.

Drawing in a deep breath, Vera straightened up. Maybe the best she could do right now was go back downstairs and wait for Trudoff to leave after hours. She could hide behind one of the cement beams that supported the building and wait. Hopefully, Senka Volo wouldn't turn up, but if he did at least he shouldn't have an easy time finding her crouched behind a pillar against the back wall of the parking garage. She was prepared to do whatever was necessary. One more time Vera put her hand in the purse and ran her fingers down the cold steel of the gun barrel.

44

BY 5:45, MOST OF THE CARS IN THE GARAGE had cleared out. Vera edged out from behind the cement column and could see only five or six still waiting for their owners to show. Trudoff's large, black Mercedes sat immobile in the same place it had been since his return several hours ago. She watched a couple more cars come down from above and drive out of the garage. The long wait had begun to make her edgy and nervous. Vera wanted this Russian to show up so she could get back into Suite 1015.

Vera kept thinking about what Ace Newton might have done with the information she left with him. Maybe he'd called the police. She prayed no one had been killed.

A blue Porsche slowly drove up from the bottom level. The unusually slow pace of the car made Vera think the driver was looking for something. As he drove past her, Vera could see the man had a dark complexion. He hadn't noticed her. The person stopped about fifty feet from Trudoff's Mercedes. He didn't get out of the Porsche but stared in the direction of the Mercedes as if scrutinizing every detail of the car.

"Come on," Vera mumbled to herself. "Do something. Get out of the Porsche and move on with whatever business you have in this place. We're not into baby-sitting out here in this frozen garage."

But he didn't move. In fact, the driver slid lower in the seat. The whole scene bothered Vera and made her even more nervous. He should have gotten out and gone inside, but the man stayed in the front seat, nearly tucked out of sight.

After a few minutes other men appeared, walking in and out around the garage, almost moving aimlessly. They seemed to come and go through the exit door, but they weren't following the usual pattern of the commuters. Whoever they were, Vera didn't like their appearance either. Too many people were lingering. Their presence could ruin everything. She didn't want any witnesses when she slipped out of her hiding place and walked back into the building.

Where did all these characters come from today? Vera wondered. *Get on with it. We don't need you people wandering around.*

Abruptly the exit door opened and three men walked out: Ivan Trudoff and his two previous companions. Trudoff stopped and said something to the tall, thin man with a narrow face and large, dour eyes. The man took a quick look around the parking garage. The other man walking behind Trudoff had a crew cut. He was still taller than Trudoff and had a chubby face.

Vera studied the men for several moments. Trudoff and the two men were talking unhurriedly, but she couldn't catch what they were saying. *Come on,* Vera thought. *Get out of here. I'm freezing and need to get back inside.*

Out of the corner of her eye Vera noticed that the man in the Porsche was no longer in sight. She looked a second time and saw the shape of his body crouched behind the car as if he were positioning himself to attack.

Surely this guy isn't after Trudoff! Vera thought.

Vera reached in her purse and slipped her hand around the pistol. She kept her trigger finger up high on the shank of the gun barrel, lest something cause her to fire by accident. At the least, she was ready to fire in a moment's notice.

Trudoff and his two associates stopped talking and started toward the Mercedes. The tall, thin man moved in the direction of the driver's seat and Trudoff looked like he was going to sit in the back. Vera saw the man from the Porsche move around to the back of his car. *He'd have a clear shot at Trudoff's party from there!* Vera realized. She watched him rest a pistol on the back of the car for a moment. He'd have to move out in the open to hit Trudoff, but that was exactly what he appeared to be getting ready to do. No one in Trudoff's group had spotted him yet.

Good heavens, Vera thought frantically. *I'm about to watch an assassination attempt on Trudoff! This guy from the Porsche is deadly serious. I can't just sit here and let this happen.*

Suddenly the man from the Porsche leaped several feet forward into the open space. "Hey, Trudoff!" he shouted. "Tried to ambush me, didn't you?"

"Abu Medien!" Trudoff gasped. "Where'd you come from?"

"You had your gunman positioned down there at the warehouse!" Abu Medien yelled back and quickly lifted a sawed-off shotgun out of his overcoat. "You thought I was dead? Well, I'm not. Try this one on for size." He brought the gun up in Trudoff's direction.

Vera instantly recognized that if the Abu Medien character shot the Russian, he could forever end any possibilities of her finding out what Trudoff knew. She stepped out into the open. With sharp movements Vera drew her gun.

"Drop it!" Vera yelled, leveling her gun at the Arab.

Yossi Abu Medien froze in place, staring at her in disbelief. Trudoff whirled around, his mouth dropping in consternation.

Time abruptly seemed to shift gears and everything began happening in slow motion. Vera watched Trudoff's associates turn toward her with astonished looks on their faces. They obviously had no idea what had happened except that this woman had interrupted Abu Medien's assassination plot. The three men drew their guns and the sound of gunfire exploded across the parking garage.

"Drop it!" Vera screamed again and leveled her pistol at Trudoff. "Get your hands up!"

The men looked perplexed and seemed momentarily halted by her scream. Then the shooting abruptly started again.

The pinging sound of bullets ricocheting echoed around the garage. Abu Medien grabbed his chest and fell to his knees. Trudoff's men kept shooting at the Arab, blowing him backward. Vera realized she was about to have a shoot-out—with three men—that she couldn't possibly win. One of them would hit her. She hadn't even fired a shot yet.

"Trudoff! Tell them to drop those weapons or you're dead." She pointed her gun at his chest.

Trudoff only stared at her with a look of quizzical indecision. His hand moved inside his coat.

"I mean it! Drop those guns!" Vera aimed squarely at the middle of Trudoff's chest.

At that moment four men ran from the exit doors with guns drawn. Voices screamed in a harmony of demands that no one move. Idle pedestrians had abruptly turned into armed gunmen. Vera could hear them yelling, but one man's shout froze her in place.

"Everyone put their guns down!" a hauntingly familiar voice echoed from the exit door.

The man stepped out pointing a Smith and Wesson .38-caliber pistol at Trudoff and his friends. Vera stared. The man rushing toward Trudoff and company had to be an apparition, a ghost stopping in from out of the dark skies. How could she ever mistake that face? Of course Vera recognized him. She'd lived with him for all those years. Sam!

Every sense in shock, Vera seemed to be watching a phantom drifting across the parking lot, as if Sam Sloan had descended like an angel from heaven to protect her at this given moment. Her mind froze. Nothing in her body would move. Her hand held the pistol limply. Maybe she was hallucinating. Maybe she'd gone completely and totally crazy.

At that moment Ivan Trudoff drew his pistol and aimed at Vera. Gunshots went off in every direction across the garage. Men kept screaming demands. Vera felt the awful force of one, two, and then three shots ripping away at her body. The bullets sent her flying backward against the guardrail.

Her pistol fell from her hand and she tumbled over the rail in a straight drop toward the bottom. Vera had control of nothing. The sensation of falling and Sam Sloan's voice were Vera's last thoughts.

45

VERA SEEMED TO BE SWIRLING AROUND IN A sea of bizarre, disconnected scenes. Faces, bodies, places, people swished past in the never-ending flow of images. The face of Bashilov kept surfacing. The structure of the face changed slowly, stretching the skin into other hard faces like those of Stalin, Khrushchev, Yeltsin, and Mad Vlad Zhirinovsky. Sometimes hair would suddenly sprout on his head, and sometimes she knew that he was Trudoff. The sounds changed from roaring explosions to the clashing sound of metal objects bumping against each other.

Part of the time she felt like the vivid whirlpool was slinging her around. Then Vera felt as though she were perched on a high cliff looking down on this maelstrom of emotion and fury. One thing was for sure: she was a prisoner of the imagery. She couldn't move or speak.

Voices began to cut through the flow, sounding like angels standing outside and beyond her, watching, talking about what they were seeing. Only then did Vera begin to sense fully that she was unconscious.

She batted her eyes, trying to bring whatever was out there into focus. At first, the images were only strange, twisted, without form, but in a few moments they began to look like people. Vera closed her eyes tightly for several seconds, then opened them slowly. Above her was the face of Sam Sloan.

"I've died," Vera groaned. "I've died and gone to heaven."

"Vera? Are you okay?"

"Sam, we must have both made it to heaven." Vera took a deep breath. "Thank God."

"Vera, can you hear me?" Sam asked.

Vera blinked again several times. "Oh, Sam! I'm so glad we can be together."

Sam reached down and took Vera's hand. "You took a nasty fall. I've been deeply worried about you."

"A fall?" Vera felt her ribs. Pain and soreness answered her touch. "What happened to me?"

"Trudoff and his people shot you three times, but you had on that bulletproof vest. The bullets didn't get through but you took the impact, which was like being hit hard by a baseball bat. They knocked you over the railing and you fell down onto the level below the gunfight."

"They killed me?" Vera asked wonderingly.

"Killed you?" Sloan laughed. "Dear, you're in New York City General Hospital. Heavens no, they didn't do much more than give you some bad bumps and bruises. You've had a concussion."

"We're alive? Still on earth?"

"Absolutely!" Sam bent down and kissed his wife. "How does that feel?"

"Wonderful!" Vera hugged his neck like she'd never let it go. "Oh, Sam. I thought you were dead. We received a report that your airplane had crashed and—"

"Wait!" Sloan held up his hand. "Wait a minute. I know. In all this secret-assignment business, we had a couple of bad mix-ups that got everybody confused about what was really happening. You acted so fast that we didn't have time to get things straightened out. The next thing I knew, you and Cara were here in New York City."

Vera took a deep breath and studied Sam's face for a moment. "What was the airplane crash story all about, Sam?"

Sam crossed his arms over his chest. "My wife, the relentless detective!" He shook his head and laughed. "Can't believe it." He pulled up a chair next to the bed. "I guess I'd better explain everything."

Tears welled up in Vera's eyes. "Sam, I'm so glad that you're alive, I don't care if you tell me one thing or not."

"You don't?" Sam chuckled. "That's what you're saying right now, but give you a couple of days and we'll be right back in the detective business again. I think I'd better tell you the whole story."

Vera inched up painfully in bed. "Whatever you say."

"You really thought I was dead?"

"I certainly did!"

Sam grinned. "Well, the whole thing started with a death. I'd been working on the George Alexander case for some time. My job was to find out exactly what this man was doing with a lot of money flowing into Colorado Springs."

Vera abruptly stuck her hand out and grabbed Sam's arm. "That's the man you took the money from!"

"Took money from? What do you mean?"

"You had a secret account at the Peak National Bank and—"

Sam held up his hand. "Whoa, there! I think you've been letting your imagination run away with you. I intercepted a cash transaction and put the amount in a private account to make Alexander's records come up short. That's what you mean?"

"You . . . you mean the police knew about that bank account?"

"The CIA did, but the Colorado Springs Police Department didn't. It was that shortfall that got Alexander in big trouble with Ivan Trudoff. Alexander had been skimming a bit, but the loss of $200,000 pulled the plug on everything that he had been doing. I expected it to create a crisis but not get the man killed. When the police found George Alexander's body in the parking lot, I knew the roof had fallen in. We had to act fast."

"So the truth is that the money you took brought the house down on the investment bank."

"That's about it. We didn't have any idea that Ivan Trudoff was something of a homicidal maniac who believed in murder as a way of doing business. Turns out that Trudoff had a tendency to kill anyone who crossed him. A rather dangerous way to do commerce."

"But the airplane wreck! Chief Harrison said you'd been killed in a plane crash. I flew to Culpeper and no airplanes had crashed around there."

Sam nodded his head. "A very unfortunate twist in this story. Just shouldn't have happened." He shook his head. "The CIA had three similar cases going at the same time. These kinds of mixups don't happen often, but a false report was accidentally sent to Harrison. I didn't know about it until the day of the shoot-out. No one figured you'd jump in the middle of the problem and change everything."

"I can't believe what I'm hearing," Vera gasped.

"I didn't expect to be gone as long as I was, dear. The chain of events went crazy, and we had to play out this whole scenario as it unfolded. Particularly after you showed up in Trudoff's office disguised as a cleaning woman."

"How in the world did you know about that?" Vera's mouth dropped. "I don't think I told anyone that I went in there dressed up as the local cleaning lady."

"You didn't. Our inside source told us. We had one of our people working in Trudoff's business. That's how I got the photograph of you coming in as a cleaning lady. Absolutely threw me when I saw that picture. Here's my wife, who's supposed to be at home in Colorado Springs, waltzing into this Russian mafioso's office like—"

"Stop it!" Vera demanded. "I didn't see anybody in Trudoff's office when I broke in." She suddenly stopped. "Oh, no! You don't mean that . . ." Her voice trailed away.

"Sure, we've been following you ever since you hit that place. The secretary—Trudoff's receptionist—is a CIA employee."

46

ON MONDAY, TWO DAYS AFTER VERA WOKE up in the New York City hospital, the Sloan family returned to Colorado Springs. By then, the truth about Sam's incorrectly reported death had spread across the city. Enough rumors were floating on the streets that both Sam and Vera had been bestowed with celebrity status.

Ace Newton waited at the airport terminal exit gate for the Sloans to come off the airplane. "Hey, All-City Confidential's firm has done it again!" he shouted and waved at the family. "Sam, you owe me a big fee for this one. We saved your life."

Sam Sloan shook his hand. "The truth is, you nearly messed up the CIA's whole operation."

"Weren't me." Newton pointed at Vera. "I just hung on while your wife did all the driving."

"Yeah? Well, I know how that feels." Sam winked at Ace.

"I've been hanging on to the fenders and trying not to get run over since the day we got married."

"People are certainly relieved that you aren't dead, Sam. Even Dick Simmons is wearing a big grin." Newton's smile disappeared and his voice turned serious. "It's been a rough ride."

"Ace, I appreciate your kind words. Let's try to keep a good story ringing in their ears."

Newton looked awkwardly at the floor. "Sam, your wife signed on to work for my agency with some reservations. The big one was whether you'd approve of her working with me rather than down at the police department. You come to any decision yet?"

Sam looked sternly at his wife. "She started work without my permission, huh? Serious problem." He suddenly grinned. "You think I'm going to get in the way of some woman who flies off to New York City looking for criminals? Not on your life. Sure, if she's pleased with All-City, then I'm a happy man. However, I think the time has come to start paying her."

"Great!" Ace hugged Vera. "We're in business big-time now."

"I guess we are." Vera smiled at her husband. "Thanks."

Fifteen minutes later the Sloans exited the airport. As Ace drove them home, Cara sat close to Sam's side. Three hours after the shoot-out in the parking garage, when Sam had shown up at the hotel, Cara had fainted. Like her mother, she thought a ghost had floated in. Since then, the two had been virtually inseparable.

Once home, Cara pulled a chair up to the kitchen table. "Daddy, how did you discover all those things you knew about Ivan Trudoff's illegal activities?"

Sam smiled. "Even intelligent crooks, and there aren't many

of them, generally make significant mistakes when they're seeking the right place to commit a crime. They think the local cops are nothing but fools. Citizens are indifferent. Nobody will report them. Our friend Trudoff had that problem. He was bright, but his failure was in thinking that he was smarter than Interpol, the CIA, and everyone else in the crime prevention business. Turns out Trudoff didn't have any idea how many people were paying attention to his arms deals. We had a small army electronically eavesdropping on his every conversation."

Vera sat down gingerly at the kitchen table. Her ribs were still bruised from the shoot-out. The familiar smell of the kitchen settled around the family. "You had quite a fat file on Trudoff, didn't you, Sam?"

"The U.S. government wanted me to discover enough facts locally to make Trudoff prosecutable in Colorado Springs. We knew what the man was doing internationally, but we needed to get him on something that would stand up in a United States court and put his whole operation out of business. Trudoff never had a clue about how closely we were following him."

"Did you know enough to shut him down?" Vera asked.

"Yes and no." Sam sat down across from her. "The Alexander murder was a problem and identifying the murderer was tough. Then Senka Volo turned up in Trudoff's New York City office and our CIA receptionist's planted camera got his picture. Sadly, Volo died after a gunfight down at a New York City harbor. His death would have made the Colorado Springs caper much harder to complete if Trudoff hadn't been killed in the shoot-out at the parking garage. Interestingly enough, the police were down on the docks looking for Volo when the shooting started. They were simply too far south."

"Mom was in on that play!" Cara said.

"She sure was. I truly thought that I was through with any involvement in this case when I found Alexander dead in the bank parking lot. Turned out that I was far from right."

"Mom fixed that problem up good for you," Cara chimed in.

"Yes, she did indeed." Sam laughed. "The shoot-'em-up in the parking garage brought everything to an end. When your mother called Ace Newton and explained how matters were moving to an apex, Ace called Dick Simmons for help. Dick called the New York City police. Later that day, when I called the Colorado Springs Police Department, Dick told me about your mother being in the garage at the Samson Building. That's how the CIA people got there. Trudoff's getting killed, along with Omsk and Grishin being shot up fairly well, knocked the legs out from under the organization. I don't think we'll have much trouble stopping the rest of his men. Right now Trudoff's business associates are on the run across the state of New York."

"I guess your spy receptionist gathered plenty of inside information on the operation," Vera said.

"Sure." Sam rubbed his chin. "She got evidence that will put the remainder of Trudoff's European terrorist operation in deep hot water. It won't be much of a problem to convict any of those people when we catch them—and we will. Actually, the shoot-out in the parking garage probably saved the state of New York a significant amount of money."

"You got back inside Trudoff's inner office?" Vera asked.

Sam nodded his head. "Of course I went to the hospital with you, but our people raided the upstairs operation. Trudoff never allowed our CIA-planted secretary to stay inside his own office and even bolted the door shut at night, but we took the place apart. Even found a hidden room filled with weight-lifting equipment and files. The exercise stuff didn't do much for us, but I think those files had a record of everything this crook had ever done. We ended up with enough evidence to put him away forever if we'd had to."

Cara looked toward the front door. "Do you hear something? Sounds like a car stopped out there." She hurried into the living room.

"Sam, I don't *ever* want to do one of these wild roller-coaster rides again. You have no idea what a terrible time this was for Cara and me. We truly thought that you had been killed."

"Dear, I was horrified when I found out everything that had happened. For the first time since I had disappeared, I got on the phone with Dick Simmons only hours before we closed in on Trudoff. Of course, Ace had called him by then. When I found out that everyone, including you and Cara, thought I was dead, well, I nearly did die."

"So you talked with Simmons on Friday?"

"Apparently, Dick was standing in Harrison's office when the CIA sent a fax explaining that the airplane crash report was a misstatement. They didn't explain the details but said enough that Simmons had a good idea that I was still alive. Newton's phone call wrapped everything up."

"Look who's here!" Cara bounded into the kitchen. "Detective Abbas dropped by." The tall Arab walked in behind her.

"Welcome home, my good friend." Basil came through the kitchen door with a big smile. "I hope I am not disturbing your tranquility, but I wanted to welcome you back personally."

Sam stood up to shake hands. "Basil, I appreciate the good thought. Glad to see you."

"Especially since I never expected to see you again!" Abbas shook his head.

"Vera tells me that you offered her assistance and insight during this difficult period."

Abbas shrugged. His unusual long link of hair, which dropped down over his left eye, dangled. "I tried to offer a condolence that might help Vera maintain her stability in such a tenuous time."

"I'm sure you offered her good words," Sam said.

Basil frowned. "My main concern was to warn Vera that evil would attempt to use this time of confusion and chaos, distorting the truth, and making it difficult for her to sort matters out."

"You were right, Basil," Vera said. "I found it quite easy to become confused."

"We all get turned upside-down at some time or another," the Arab commented.

Vera looked Abbas in the eye. "You have no idea. I truly struggled and grieved over Sam's seeming death, but I had to keep trying to find out what happened. I realized how dangerous it was to corner Ivan Trudoff. I just wanted to get back into his office. I never expected to end up in a shoot-out in that garage. Even with the safety vest, I was little more than a sitting target for that muscle-bound gorilla and his thugs."

Sam nodded. "Vera, you crawled way out on the end of a shaky branch."

Basil Abbas shook his head. "It certainly sounded scary to me. Weren't you afraid, Vera?"

Vera nodded her head. "Every minute of the day I wrestled with fear. Terror pushed me toward the edge. My reach almost extended beyond my grasp, but I clung to the promise that the help of God comes to us in our times of helplessness."

"Reverend Dozier told us we needed not to worry about

why a tragedy had occurred as much as *what* we would do with it," explained Cara.

"I think we both worked extremely hard to do that—to keep living and trying to accomplish good in the midst of bad," Vera said.

"You did well." Sam reached over and hugged his wife. "I'm proud of you both. You did an amazing job."

"Sam, Chief Harrison seemed to think that you knew from the get-go that George Alexander hadn't died of a simple heart attack," Basil said. "Was he right?"

Sam nodded. "It was starting to snow hard that morning, but I noticed that Alexander had fallen on his knees in a direction that indicated somebody could have hit him from the area of the back door. He had tiny, thin cuts on his face, as if it had been struck by pieces of something sharp. Once his heart stopped, Alexander didn't bleed, so officers who came later wouldn't have noticed the abrasions the way I did. I started checking the area around the body as well as around the cement support beam. I found slivers of glass and surmised that the man hadn't died only of a heart attack. I knew enough to believe that Bashilov, or Trudoff, had probably ordered Alexander killed in some fairly sophisticated manner."

"Turns out that he certainly had," Basil said.

"By the way, who was that man who drove into the parking garage in the Porsche and started the shooting?" Vera said.

"The Arab who got killed in the shoot-out was Yossi Abu Medien, a terrorist and an assassin," Sam said "The early police reports indicated he and his people killed Senka Volo. Apparently, some disagreement went on between Abu Medien and Trudoff, but we haven't got the details completely sorted out yet."

"Really?" Vera said. "All that I knew was that he certainly

looked like he intended to kill Trudoff right there on the spot."

"He did," Sam agreed. "Abu Medien was the front man for some organization operating out of Kazakhstan. At least that's the preliminary report from the CIA. The agency had been working on his case since Abu Medien started coming in and out of Trudoff's offices. I think our government knew more about Abu Medien than Trudoff did. Obviously, they had some argument that made Yossi and his people angry enough to attempt to kill Trudoff and his gang."

"I couldn't let a murder happen," Vera said, "but I wasn't sure how to handle the situation. I knew I just couldn't stand by and watch a shooting."

Sam laughed. "You scared the CIA people to death. No one had any idea you were hiding in that garage."

"Very presumptuous," Basil Abbas noted.

"Now, Basil," Sam said. "Don't let any male chauvinist tendencies overpower you. My wife is only explaining how she ended up in that parking garage when she *should have been* sitting down in her office chair at the All-City Confidential Agency in Colorado Springs." He looked intensely at Vera. "The point is that we aren't going to do this again, *right?*"

Vera sighed. "I guess." She paused and looked fiercely back at Sam. "If you're not planning to go running off again for several days without telling me that you're still alive."

Sam grinned. "You quit starting your own investigations, and I'll call home more often."

"Agreed," Vera said firmly. "The bottom line is that it's certainly easier to work together than having to strike out on your own."

"I hope you remember that fact," Sam added.

"She will," Cara said. "For at least a week."

About the Author

THE AUTHOR OF TWENTY-FIVE PUBLISHED books, Reverend Robert L. Wise, Ph.D., also writes for numerous magazines and journals, including *Christianity Today, Leadership*, and *The Christian Herald*. He is a bishop in the communion of Evangelical Episcopal Churches. He collaborated on the national best-selling Millennium series, which includes *The Third Millennium, The Fourth Millennium*, and *Beyond the Millennium*, and is the author of *Be Not Afraid* and *Spiritual Abundance*.

THE FIRST BOOK IN THE SERIES, *THE EMPTY Coffin* introduces Sam and Vera Sloan, a Christian detective and his wife who live their faith in the rough and sometimes brutal world of crime solving.

The daily work of a policeman can push an officer into the most debased side of life. Sam Sloan struggles to stay faithful to his Christian ideals while solving brutal murders and heinous crimes. *The Empty Coffin* finds Sam and Vera faced with the greatest challenge of their lives. In addition to solving a difficult case, this tough cop still tries to live out his faith with honesty and conviction. The problems Sam faces at work create tension at home. As the Sloans struggle to keep their marriage together, the couple evolve into a crime-fighting force, working together on difficult cases that baffle the police. Sloan's hard-nosed detective work, coupled with his faith and humility, brings an unusual solution to a murder case in which there is no corpse!

ISBN: 0-7852-6687-9